THE BLUE STONE PEOPLE

Book Six

In
"The New Life Series"

BY
LOUISE BOUCK

PERMISSION

Scripture quotations taken from The Holy Bible, New International Version® NIV ® Copyright © 1973, 1978, 1984, 2011 by Biblica Inc.™ by International Bible Society. Used by permission. All rights reserved.

TABLE OF CONTENTS

Page

Dedication

This is for my family, those gone before me, those with me now and those to come and for all my brothers and sisters in Christ.

†

ACKNOWLEDGEMENTS

It is important to say thank you to all the people who have encouraged me. A special shout out to Mary Koestner. Thank you for your unfailing prayer support. A big thank you goes to my husband, Dale Bouck, who managed to keep my computer running in spite of the monsoons. Thank you for being a willing editor. Thank you for not complaining when meals were late and simple. Thank you to my family members that suffered through reading rough drafts. A big thank you hug to R. J. Dick who was the first to want to read "The Story of Ben Slater" and to Brenda Dick who read "The Story of Sarah" to RJ when he was ill, and thanks to Donna Shaw, who enthusiastically helped me to keep Sarah's feet on the right path.

Thank you to the people at the computer lab, for their technical help. What would any of us do without the public libraries and the wonderful people that work there?

To Ray Shaw, for his patience and kind repetition until I got it... goes a big thank you hug. He has encouraged me and has used his specialized skills to help me make this series become an available reality. He is amazing!

God bless all of you.

PROLOGUE

As the stories of "The New Life Series" have unfolded, of course God's blessings and provision are evident. As much has happened and many adventures have taken place, new people and new locations have added to the depth of the lives of our characters as both drama and joy have filled their days.

Book one, **"More Than Survival,"** introduces Ben Slater and shows us how a fifteen year old boy could survive the loss of his family and build a life from nothing in the wilderness of the new frontier.

Book two, **"Life's Many Journeys,"** takes us along the Hickory and Silver Rivers as two young men form a lifelong, brotherly bond and rescue a woman that brings love.

Book three, **"The Land's Heritage"** watches the development of homesteads; and another rescue that requires courage. A settlement and a fort, play a part as they struggle to build a lasting heritage with strong faith for the coming generations.

Book four, **"The Story of Sarah,"** at nearly nine years old she was taken from the Slater's covered wagon. Her mind, her faith, and her strength of will and courage are tested by the Winahatah Indians. She develops many skills while planting seeds of faith. Her discovery, and her ability to see and pass on its potential, saves the people she grows to love.

Book five, **"Together,"** brings Sarah to the arms of her brother and his family at last. She uses her skills to save lives and a man from the Indian village finds her. They return to the people just in time.

Now, please enjoy book six.

THE BLUE STONE PEOPLE
CHAPTER ONE
THE BLACK ROBES

After the three young adults left the village, the daily activities continued as usual, but for Moonflower, wife of Chief Dark Wolf, things felt very different. She had raised Sarah, as her own daughter since the day she had been placed in her care when her husband had returned with her after a raid on the white men's wagons. Chief Rising Eagle, Dark Wolf's father had given the little girl, the name Brave Sparrow as she stood at the naming ceremony shaking.

She had grown into a beautiful and capable woman.

That very morning she had left the village, saying she would search for her own people, her own kind. She sought people with her own skin color and beliefs. Sharp Knife and Singing Wind had left then also. Each had their own reason for going. Sharp Knife tried to convince Brave Sparrow that she should travel with them, but they parted company at the wagon trail. She headed across the prairie grass and they followed the wagon trail further west.

*****

The Jesuit priest arrived, mid-morning, riding a mule and leading two others.

Father Bob's heart beat faster with joy as he viewed the large Indian camp in the distance. What he wanted more than anything else was to find an Indian village where he could bring its people to God. He could see at least one hundred individual tents and in the far left of his view, stood an unusually large tent. He had come with a crate of books and a large ornate carved crucifix that had

7

been carried for the entire trip on the back of an old tired pack mule, named Rudy.

The young man guarding the horse herd had watched him advance slowly along the edge of the grass passing near the horse herd to avoid the huge boulders that seemed to serve as a fence on that side.

Falling Stones had been so fascinated by the odd little caravan that he had allowed it to advance without questioning its right to do so. Father Bob saw the sparkling lake and walked his thirsty animals to it. He strolled to a spot on top of a large, gentle rolling hill and knelt.

"Thank you, Jesus, I have found where I will build your church and teach your children about you." A smile spread across his face showing his white teeth against the dark brown of his suntanned skin. He was eager to start and enthusiastic in his zeal to fulfill his assignment, to build a school and church and to convert the Indians to Catholicism.

During his brief prayer, tears of joy had escaped his eyes. He walked around and gazed at the blue lake in front of him, noting his reflection. He had several days' growth of beard that matched his brown hair. He needed grooming. He pushed his hair back as he continued to watch with curiosity, the busy village on the other side of the small lake.

Only a few minutes passed before everyone in the village was aware of his presence.

Chief Dark Wolf received the news before the mules had finished drinking.

Growling Bear, his lead warrior, wanted to challenge the stranger immediately.

"How does someone dare to come here, so near our camp?" said Growling Bear.

8

"He is just one man. He is harmless. I will speak to him in a little while. He can see that we are here. Perhaps he intends to rest his animals and then move on."

"I think he is a spy for the soldiers," said Growling Bear. He was eager to do something. He thought anything was better than just waiting.

Flying Eagle, the chief's son-in-law had learned the language of the white man growing up with the Omati. It was he who set up the trading spot on the wagon trail. The chief's daughter had gone with him sometimes. Snow Star, his wife, had learned enough of the white man's words to trade but the white man's language was not spoken in camp and deliberately not taught to the children.

It was natural that they would all be curious about the stranger near the lake, but they tried not to stare and went out of their way to stay away from his camp. His ways and clothes were foreign, and the bloodied body depicted on the cross instilled fear. He had erected it on the side of the hill where it was in full view.

Within minutes of his arrival, Chief Dark Wolf held a meeting in the communal tent.

"Listen, my people. I know that you are all aware of the arrival of the black robe. He has great power. He has a book with the words of the God that Brave Sparrow told about. We must not anger his God. I ask that you not bother him. I have heard of the black robes from other Chiefs at the summer council. I feel deeply concerned for the changes that the priest will try to institute. Try to avoid him if you can but be careful not to offend him or his God. Be kind. Go about your day as usual and don't stare at him. Time will show us his intentions."

Surely I don't have to allow him to be here, he thought, but how do I drive him away without angering his

God? The Chief returned to his own tent and Moonflower, his wife, followed. They were troubled.

The words of his book were even stranger than he seemed to be, and they rang with the sound of Brave Sparrow's God. They wouldn't experience that until later when they had all learned enough of his language.

Day after day, the Jesuit worked from first light until dark; clearing a spot and building a small log building on the hill near the lake. He erected the cross in the yard surrounded with stones as large as he could drag. This was to be the school and church for now. The children were coaxed to come near by handing out beads a few at a time or trinkets of little actual value. His efforts were to first teach the English language, but since he did not speak the tongue of the people, communication was difficult. Sharp Knife could speak the white man's language, but he was away.

Moonflower knew many of the white man's words. She had learned them from Brave Sparrow, her adopted white daughter, but she didn't want to admit it. She missed her and wished that she had not left to seek her own people. The small white girl that Dark Wolf had taken during a raid brought them many challenges. The Chief had given her the name Brave Sparrow, but years later, after an absence that caused much concern; she had returned and announced at a communal fire that her name was now, "Sarah, of the Blue Stone People." She told the people they should no longer refer to themselves as the Winahatah. She spoke of the Great God of the Bible, her father's Holy Book. She told them that if they would honor Him, that the people would prosper. She was the one who discovered the turquoise in the rocks near the little pool in the woods and suggested that the people use it for trade and they did prosper by trading the turquoise for many new foods and useful items. The women enjoyed sewing clothes from the cloth brought back to camp from the trading spot.

Other tribes continued to attack the wagon trains, causing hostilities and conflicts against their villages by the soldiers.

The Blue Stone People developed skills to make jewelry and cultivated a trust at their trading spot.

The priest knew none of the history of the people. He simply stopped here and there searching for someone to direct him when possible and ended up talking to a soldier that had directed him to the general location of a large Indian camp and wished him luck.

The priest's intentions were good but his methods were fruitless. Soon the children stayed away. His superiors had sent him here alone, fresh from the seminary, with the directive to teach the Indians to read and write and to teach them the Catholic religion. He wasn't sure even how to start.

At first he thought they were stupid, but soon he found that he himself had a lot to learn from them if he was to survive the fast approaching winter.

He saw that with the exception of the meat the men brought to the camp, it was the women that provided everything else. They grew the corn, and gathered wild foods, processed hides and made the tents and its contents, all by working very hard. He worked too, and always observed, and so he learned their ways, bit by bit. His skills left a wide margin for improvement, but he tried hard.

When the women left camp to gather food, he would quickly get his water bag and leather pouch and followed along. He had tried to weave a basket but he just didn't have the knack for it. His basket soon fell apart.

Chief Dark Wolf spoke with his daughter Snow Star.

"When Flying Eagle returns from the hunt, tell him that I would speak with him."

"Yes Father." Snow Star was sure that her father looked upset, but she didn't know why. She went to her mother, Moonflower and asked.

"What is troubling Father? He carries his head down and wrinkles cover his forehead."

"It is the black robe. He will freeze or starve if we don't help him," said Moonflower.

"He should leave and go back to his own kind!" said Snow Star.

During the weeks that followed the Jesuit began to fully realize how ill prepared he was for his assignment and that he would have to learn the ways of the people before he could teach them anything.

He was able to make them understand enough to ask to go hunting with them when the men prepared to leave camp. Chief Dark Wolf decided to allow it. They never invited him, but they didn't stop him from tagging along.

Once in a while, though not the best of shots, he actually would hit something. The hunting party scoffed at the idea of the Jesuit ever being a good hunter but laughed when Growling Bear, their top hunter, suggested that perhaps they would get lucky and lose him.

By the time they returned, three days later with horses laden with big game they had more respect for the black robe and without even realizing it; the hunters had learned several words in English.

His canvas tent was thin, and dripped inside when it rained. It didn't offer the protection like the greased, waterproofed, double walled leather ones used by the Indians. It certainly would not be enough to keep out the cold of the coming winter.

The hunters had shared their meat with him and dropped a deer hide near his tent. They actually felt sorry for him. He seemed so ill equipped for being there. They wondered why he had no woman to make his life more comfortable. Why was he alone? He had used much of his time before winter to build a structure that would have been more comfortable to live in but he didn't use it. It stood empty except when he prayed to his God.

The hide was there on the grass in full sun all day. The Jesuit watched as one of the women staked out a large deer hide and began to scrape it. He tried to lay his out, but each time it curled back up. It was getting stiff. He gathered stones to put on the edges. That way it did stay flat, but he couldn't scrape the edges. She noticed his struggle. Coming over she moved the stones one by one and staked the hide as she had her own. She handed him the sharp stone she had been using and showed him how to pull the stone across the hide to remove the tissue without damaging the leather.

He saw that the knife he had tried to use had nearly cut through the hide in several places. He knelt and worked for a long while, but the rancid tissue from the stale hide was sticking to the front of his clothes. He ran to the lake and dove in, clothes and all. It sickened him.

He soon found himself surrounded by giggling children all splashing and having a good time. He couldn't help but laugh at himself, too. When he said "Yuk" and they repeated it, he saw that laughter was an easy teaching tool.

The next day when he stepped out of his tent, he found two new raw hides near his doorway. He praised God for his gift. Soon he would have enough hides to make a small leather tent. He had learned to peg the hides flat and scrape them while they were fresh, and to rub it with fat and work the fat into it, once it was clean of tissue. He processed them properly. Thanking God.

CHAPTER TWO
FIRE IN THE CHURCH

When the black robe saw the women head out on a gathering expedition, each carrying empty baskets and water bags, he got a water bag and his pouch and strolled along. The women laughed at the thought of a man wanting to do woman's work but they humored the priest and showed him how to dig the cattail roots at the lake and continued on to gather nuts in the woods, thinking it was better to show him how to gather food, than to have him come begging for food when the cold weather and snow arrived.

The women talked among themselves wondering why the black robe lived with no wife to cook and gather for him. They giggled when the priest went to the lake and washed his garments, laying them on the grass in the shadow of the church to dry.

When Father Bob heard the sound of drums coming from the communal fire, he wondered if he dared to draw nearer.

When he did, he could see the body up on the pyre being consumed by the flames. Red Fox, their holy man, was dancing. He could see him in the light of the fire. They had not brought Red Fox back with them when they had returned from the summer council. He had simply followed. He didn't like Red Fox. He could feel the evil in the man. He wondered who had died.

"Lord what soul have I lost?" he murmured. He returned to his tent and ate his meager meal and read his prayers by the light of his fire until his eyes grew tired of straining at the small print in the dim light. He knelt in the dark, bare church and wept at his own inadequacy.

During the night the rain started. It poured down hard all night and into the next day. Everything he had in his tent was soaked. The water ran in under his bedding and into his fire pit outside, forming a round pool. He sloshed to the church and sat dripping on a bundle of dry grass in the middle of the sod floor, thinking it was probably the only dry spot in his area. He looked up when he heard a scratching sound on the oiled hide that covered the doorway. Moonflower and two boys stepped into the church. Each had their arms loaded. She carried a pan of hot stew and a basket of freshly made crackers. One boy carried clothing, the other wood.

She moved the small table that served as his altar, back against the wall and had the wood placed in the center of the room.

Looking up she could see that the roof was solid. After shaking her head in consternation, she said something to the older boy and he soon had crawled onto the roof and chopped a rough edged smoke hole near the peak, directly over the spot where the wood for the fire rested.

From a fire horn she produced a coal that took the chill from the air as the fire crackled. They left as quickly as they had come. He looked at his robe, stuck to his body. Cold, wet and uncomfortable, he decided to change into the pants and shirt they had left. It felt strange on his body after years in the seminary, wearing only the dress pants and loose fitting cotton robes of the priesthood. The leather was heavy but pliable, and the surface of the clothes had a soft sheen.

He was warm and fed.

He was glad that he had thought to put his bible and books in the church so at least they were dry and safe. He looked out at the rain and gray sky and noticed the drooping ears of his poor mules.

"God forgive me," he said as he dashed out and led the three animals into the dry building.

The children had helped him gather bundles of dry grass to sit on. They now became a generous supply of feed as the mules chewed and enjoyed the comfort of the warm building. He looked at them and started to laugh.

"I came all high-minded thinking that I would save the poor savages and they end up the ones doing all the teaching. Well, Christ was born in a stable so I guess he won't mind if I give refuge to my wet and hungry mules."

The next day, when things began to dry off, Moonflower and two other women came to help him spread his bedding and clothes out in the sunshine to dry on the bushes. They showed him more with motions than words that he would have to scrape the hides that had gotten wet. The sun was hot and would shrink and harden the hides if they were not cared for properly. They had pulled everything from his little tent. What a mess he thought, as he looked at all his soggy belongings.

As soon as his clothes and bedding dried, he carried them into the little church. He suddenly knew that it would not be a few months of work to teach the Indians about God, but perhaps years. He was starting to face the fact that first he had to prove himself worthy to the people and be accepted. He couldn't know that Brave Sparrow had planted seeds of faith in the people, but one thing he was sure of, they were kind and good.

He knelt on the floor of the church and wept as he made the sign of the cross.

"I Pray, In the name of the Father, and of the Son, and of the Holy Ghost. Amen. Father, I am so unprepared for this job. Without your help I won't even survive the months ahead. Show me how to bring these children to you. Give me patience, wisdom and your grace. Forgive my ego and sin of pride. I thought that I would come here and save the world. They seem to be the ones doing the saving. I love you Jesus and want to serve you well. Help me to learn quickly. Be with me here in this wild land. Our Father who art in heaven...."

He held Mass on the grass in front of the church, singing loudly. No one came to see what he was doing. He was discouraged.

The idea came to him in the night, as he lay on the dirt floor of the church, listening to an owl in the trees.

"If I build a small room on the back, I can sleep in there and if I extend one wall and the roof I will have shelter for the mules. Thank you God! Thank you Jesus for showing me that."

In the morning he set to work in the nearby trees, using his mules to bring the wood back. He filled between the logs with a mud and grass mixture and found that even the smallest fire in the church warmed it enough to be comfortable. He continued to work on the bedroom and mule shelter; until he was finally satisfied that he had accomplished what he needed.

His next job would be to preserve food for himself and the mules. He knew that with the children helping he could gather enough grass for all winter in just a day or two. He decided to use the last of his meager sugar supply to make a batch of sugar candy, as a reward for helping. His sugar was stored in a big tin, but when he opened it, it was as hard as a rock. He chipped off pieces and put them in a pan. It was then that he decided he didn't have to make candy. The rock hard chunks of sugar would do nicely. He offered a piece to Moonflower. She hesitantly tasted it, nodding her head and smiling. He asked her to get the children to help him and he would give each of them some sugar. She wasn't sure what he wanted but knew it had to do with the children and a sweet treat. She walked about the village telling the children to follow the priest that he had a treat for them. Like the Pied Piper, he headed for the lake and the sweet grass that grew there with the youngsters following and giggling behind him.

As the job proceeded he distributed occasional nibbles. Before long the grass was stacked in bundles against the inside wall of the mule's shelter and the back wall of the church.

He gave each child a generous chunk of the sugar and a hug.

"Thank you, you did a good job. God bless you," he said over and over.

Soon I will need to tap one or two of the maples in the woods and then start gathering as much grain as I can find, he thought. A hide will make a big pouch to gather grain, but what can I collect syrup in? He wondered. He sat by his little fire and realized that winter was just around the corner. He cleverly fashioned the grain pouch from part of the canvas of his tent, in such a way that it had a loop for his shoulder. He stitched it up the sides and was happy with the results. At least I have a few little skills, he thought.

"I hope I never have to sleep in one of those again."

He used his only small pan for the tap on the biggest maple tree he found, fastening it in place with a piece of the precious rope that had held his tent in place. It was then that he realized all the possibilities that the canvas tent offered. He cut a large piece from the side of it and made another pouch. He folded it and put it in his saddlebags, feeling that he had accomplished something important. As he filled his water pouch from the lake, he promised himself that he would not eat until he had found food.

"We are going hunting," he told his animals. He was riding one mule, with the others tied behind. He headed into the woods on the backside of the lake. His ear caught an occasional note from a flute as he rode away from his camp. Several people saw him go and wondered at his decision to venture out alone, with the clouds hanging heavy over the trees in the distance. He had been so busy that he had not noticed the weather change.

Once he had reached the cover of the trees he followed the rocky bluff. Thunder announced the approaching storm and he sought a place to wait it out.

As he looked up hoping to spot a cave or overhang, he saw the mountain lion above him on a ledge. Without thinking about it, he raised his gun and fired.

The big cat fell at the feet of his mules and the ride of his life commenced. The branches of the trees hit his face and chest nearly knocking him off, as the mule plunged into the dense virgin forest leaving the trail far behind.

"Whoa boy, easy now, whoa there," he shouted while struggling to stay on. His shouts were further upsetting the mule. The sounds of the other mules tethered behind him kept him running. The poor animal thought the cat was hot on his tail. He was running for his life!

By the time the mule was finally stopped and Father Bob was able to dismount, he knew that any hope he had of marking his trail as he went along was long since lost. Both he and the animals were exhausted from the experience.

At first he tried to lead the mules back the way they had come but he wasn't sure which direction that was.

It was raining lightly when he spotted the top of the bluff through the trees. It was a long way off. He was amazed how far they had gone. By the time they reached the bluff, the rain had stopped and the sun was out. A small pool formed by a spring near the base of the rocks offered a drink for the tired mules. He wondered which way he should go to see if he could find the cat. He could hear growling and decided to leave the mules by the water and see what was causing the fight. He walked slowly back along the bluff, until there before him on the other side of a huge boulder was the dead mountain lion. Standing guard over it was a very big wolf. A second wolf, snarling and growling loudly was trying hard to convince him to leave. Just my luck, he thought. I see three animals and none of them are good to eat. Then he thought perhaps he could trade the hides for food. He shot quickly dropping the biggest wolf. The second one instantly sprang into the bushes and out of sight.

"Maybe if I wait, the greedy thing will come back. He should hunt his own food!" He sat perfectly still, waiting. Sure enough it stepped into view sniffing the air. He was ready. He shot again, and this time he felt like a hunter. He skinned all three and rolled the hides, wrapping them in a piece of the tent he had thrown over the second mule as a blanket. I still want to get a deer and gather some food before I go back he thought. He led the mules away from the scene praising God for providing the good furs.

"We need to get away from here. This will bring other predators," he said to his old mule, Rudy.

When they had walked a long way, he could see a clearing up ahead. He tied the mules to a tree and

21

proceeded quietly to check the area. There in the edge of the clearing stood a large deer.

"God I know that you are putting these animals in my path. Thank you, for watching over me." He prayed silently. He steadied his gun against a tree and one shot did the job.

Looking around he realized that he was on the edge of the woods. Just ahead through a screen of brush lay the open prairie, covered with wild grain and drying wild sunflowers. He cleaned the deer and hung it high in a tree to protect it. There it would be safe. He did the same with the beautiful hides he had rolled in the canvas. He led his mules to the edge of the field of grain and tied them where they could eat all they wanted. It wasn't until then that he felt how hungry he was.

"God you are my provider. I have before me meat and grain. I'll spend the night here and pick grain in the morning."

He set up his camp with just his bedroll and a ring of stones around a bare spot he made for his fire. He was very tired by the time he had his little fire going. He made a mental note to ask Moonflower about the fire horn she had used. He put a piece of deer meat over the fire and leaned back against a rock with his eyes closed, listening to the breeze rattle the leaves of the trees, and something else. He wasn't sure what the sound was.

He followed the sound into the trees to the left of his camp. It coaxed him away from the rocky bluff, into the dense woods where some of the tallest trees grew. He found a little stream with a miniature waterfall, not as tall as he was. That is perfect, he thought.

This is a beautiful place to come when it gets beastly hot. There are lots of animal prints but I don't see any human prints. I wonder if the Indians know this is here. I will have to bring the women here on one of the hottest days. They will love this spot.

Bringing his companions for a drink, he emptied his water bag and filled it from the waterfall. The mules stood in the cool water as they drank enjoying the stream as much as he did. He put his clothes on the bank and sat down in the water letting it pour over his head and shoulders. It was refreshing but too cold to stay in for very long.

As soon as he was dry he was grateful for the warmth of the leather clothes he pulled on. He had started his trip in one of his black cotton robes, but now he appreciated having something more substantial and was glad that he had brought them. Thank you Moonflower, he thought as he felt the soft comfort of the well worked leather.

After enjoying some of the juicy meat, he pulled it off to the side of the fire, curled up in his bedroll and fell asleep during his night prayers. He slept soundly. A fly crawling across his nose woke him to the beautiful sight of a doe and her fawn crossing the open prairie. He stayed still and watched as they stepped silently and cautiously through the tall wild grain and into the trees in the direction of the stream.

"Father God, Your creation is so beautiful, I wish I didn't have to kill anything to survive," he said, before he began to recite his morning prayers.

His fire had gone out during the night, but he covered it with dirt anyway. He rolled up his bedding and wrapped the rest of the cooked meat in big leaves and tucked it into his saddlebag to keep it clean.

The big pouch he had made was picked full of wild grain and the sun was high in the sky when he lowered the deer onto the back of Jack, his most compliant pack mule and tied it securely. The bundle of furs went on Mabel, with the grain.

"Mabel, you are getting the easiest job," he said, as she complained loudly all the while. He tied the grain pouch closed and settled it on her back in front of the furs. He rode Rudy with his bedroll behind him. He felt joy at knowing that he brought back to his camp, so many provisions.

"Rudy, I think I should go back and pick lots more grain so I have enough to share with you guys when the weather turns cold. I like the little waterfalls. I know that has to be a good hunting area."

The sun had given him his bearings and he headed back confidently walking the mules at a slow steady pace. He spotted the place where the cat had landed. Nothing was left now but a stain on the ground and many footprints. Rudy avoided it, and they continued on; coming out of the woods near the trail where he had entered it. He stopped at the edge of the lake to let the mules drink and then moved toward the little building that was the church and now his home.

As he started to unload the mules, he discovered that women and children surrounded him. None hid their curiosity as he dropped the canvas wrapped furs on the grass. They touched and felt each fur and commented in their own language. The deer was difficult to lift from Jack's back. It took the help of two of the women. The thing that amazed them the most was the big bag of grain. They nodded approval and smiled broadly.

"Thank you. You did a good job, God bless you," they said. They were repeating the phrase he had said to the children. He wondered how much, if any of it they understood.

Moonflower looked at his puzzled face and simply said, "You come," and walked to her tent, where, in front of it, stood many racks filled with drying meat surrounding her fire.

"Like this, you do for snow time." She ducked into her tent and signaled for him to follow her. "See, you put in like this." She lifted some furs that covered the lid of a cache in the floor of her tent. It was lined with woven mats and neatly corded full of dried meat. She lifted another lid on a second cache and showed him wild apples and some things he did not recognize.

"Thank you, God bless you," he said as he turned and hurried back to the waiting meat. He had a huge pile of branches behind the little church that he had cut from the logs when he had added onto the building. Now they would be put to good use. He carried some to the side of the church and worked to make them into racks. He cut strips of canvas and twisted it to form cords to fasten the racks together. He continued until he had several standing near the deer. He cleared an area, away from the building and circled it with stones to hold a larger fire. Two young girls came bringing a coal and lit his fire for him. He was grateful and even more so when they carried many armloads of wood to help keep the fire going. They sat down on the grass and began to pull the skin back on the deer and sliced thin pieces of meat, hanging them on the racks as they went. They were young and not as quick as the mature women of the camp but they worked steadily with him until the entire deer hung drying on the racks. He wondered what he could offer them in payment for their work, but they indicated that they wanted the smaller wolf fur. He let them take it but also rewarded them each with a generous chunk of the hardened sugar.

"Thank you. You did a good job. God bless you," he said as they hurried back to their mother.

The deer hide was pegged out, flanked on either side by wolf and lion furs. He knew they would provide good warm clothing for him this winter. Then the idea hit him that he should give one of the hides to Moonflower for all that she had done for him. He smiled to himself as he scraped. Trying to decide which hide to take to her. The problem solved itself when he looked at the comfortable pants and shirt he was wearing. He would give her the deer hide to replace some of the leather she had used in his clothing.

He had to use his pick and shovel to dig his cache in the floor of the small sleeping cubicle. He lined it with tightly tied bundles of grass. The lid was made from split logs.

When the meat was dry and corded into the cache, he felt very pleased with his accomplishment. He knew that God had played the major role.

"Thank you, Father, for your bountiful provision."

A few days later, he was nearly ready to declare the skins done when he saw that the women were preparing to go to the far woods, with empty baskets on each arm. He quickly put the hides inside to protect them. He had poured the grain into his only pillowcase and tied it shut, so once again he had his large canvas pouch. He tossed it over his saddle. Inside he had another big canvas bag. He brought his knife and gun, water bag and one saddlebag held a supply of the dried meat. He walked along leading the mule watching as here and there a woman would bend and dig something up and drop it in her basket. He asked what they were gathering, but no one seemed to know what to answer. They showed him the various roots and leaves they had. He still had nothing.

When they reached the woods, Moonflower immediately started to gather hickory nuts from the ground. The tree was loaded with nuts above their heads but no one climbed up to get them. He pulled himself up branch by branch until he was higher than he really wanted to be, then he began to bounce and shake the tree. One section after another gave up its crop. The nuts rained down and the women laughed and cheered, applauding. The ground beneath the tree was covered in the nuts still in their heavy brown casings. Getting down was not easy.

They hadn't forgotten him as he worked; they had filled his bags, too.

Before going back they showed him where the wild apple trees grew. Many still clung to the higher branches. He made a note to get them soon.

As they headed back he handed out pieces of the smoked dried meat. They were received gratefully with a smile. The day had gone well. Most of the women had heavy baskets to carry. He tried to ease their burden by fastening some to the mule but one basket tipped and they had to stop to pick up the nuts. He had repeated the word "nuts" often enough that they had all learned it.

The casings had stained his hands and the tree bark had scratched and soiled the leather of his pants and shirt. He was a sorry sight when he walked up to the little church building to see another priest standing outside waiting for him.

As the women filed past heading for the village they repeated the much used phrase.

"Thank you, good job. God bless you," they had heard it often. The new priest was favorably impressed until Father Bob explained.

"They haven't any idea what they are saying. They think it is a parting good bye of some sort, I think." The visitor introduced himself as Father Peter O'Reilly.

Next he wanted to know where he could put his things. Father Bob looked at the three sturdy horses patiently standing in the shade waiting to be unloaded.

"Father this is the only facility we have. It is church, school, and home. I built it by myself this summer. You are welcome here and may put your things wherever you feel is appropriate. He pulled the bags of nuts from Jack's back and led him to the lake to drink and eat the grass.

"I am going to take a bath," said Father Bob, flipping his clean robe and only towel, over his shoulder, he headed for the lake. The new priest stood there sputtering.

After pulling all the bundles, boxes and bags from his horses, Father Peter set up the canvas tent that had been provided for him by the church. Father Bob had a kettle of deer stew cooking and ready by the time Father Pete was finished.

"If you have any things that need to stay dry, you should put them in the church."

"You can't use the church as a storage shed! What would the Bishop say?"

"He would probably be glad that we had the sense to come in out of the rain. How long will you be staying?"

"I am supposed to see how well the school and church are doing and then report back to the Bishop."

"I see. Well I can certainly use the help. Are you a good carpenter?"

"I really don't know. I have never tried."

"We will need to add to the lean-to for the animals, and gather more hay and grain. We will also need to go hunting and dry the meat and if we are lucky there will be some apples left on the trees in the woods that we can collect. I saw some sunflowers when I picked the grain. We should get those. They would be fun to nibble on by the fire this winter."

"Do you mean to tell me that you have no supplies? Where are all the people you have trained to help? Can't they gather food?"

"Father Pete, we have only what we are clever enough to build, kill or gather. The Indians tolerate us. They don't understand us and I don't understand them. They certainly are not a people that can be expected to serve us. So with that, I think we should eat, say our prayers and then rest. Tomorrow we have a lot of work to do."

Chief Dark Wolf had observed the arrival of the second black robe with displeasure. He laughed when he saw the same type of small cloth tent go up.

"Each one must learn the same lesson. Do they not talk to each other?" He walked beside Red Fox, the shaman, to the top of his favorite knoll to sit and observe the activities of his people.

As the weeks passed and the weather grew steadily colder, Father O'Reilly had agreed that it would be best to add on to the sleeping area so that he could have his bed inside. The shelter for the animals had already been extended. Father Bob made a batch of sugar candy from the supplies Father Peter had brought. It paid for the children's labor of gathering more bundles of grass to stack as insulation and feed for the three additional horses during the cold months ahead.

Father Bob held Mass each morning at daybreak and Father Pete assisted. No one else was in the church.

"It's a sad thing that you haven't made one convert in all the time you have been here."

As they said the prayers of the Mass, a woman knelt and raised her arms facing the rising sun. The song to the sun god echoed across the lake.

·

CHAPTER THREE
THE GREENHORN

"Father we must learn their ways and their language. We must gain their trust and respect before we can teach them something so new and different."

"Tomorrow I need to go hunting and gather more food before it snows. I'll be leaving at first light. Will you come with me?"

"Yes of course I'll come but I don't know that I'll be of much use. I have never shot a gun in my life."

"How did you make it all the way here without hunting?"

"I traveled with the wagon train all the way to the settlement on the Silver River."

"I told them that I know a little doctoring and so they let me ride along and they shared their meals and fires."

"Are you a doctor?"

"No, but I know how to fix a bad stomach or a broken arm."

"Somehow we have got to get you a rifle and teach you to use it."

"I have a gun, but I have never loaded it. It is in one of the crates that we put in the back of church. There are some boxes of bullets there, too, somewhere." Father Bob located the rifle and shells and loaded it.

"Your first lesson in shooting is tomorrow," he said.

*****

Chief Dark Wolf had sent scouts to locate the buffalo. The hunters were getting ready to leave when Father Bob noticed the activity. He hurried to ask one of the young boys that had begun to understand fairly well.

"They will hunt buffalo," he reported.

31

"Let's go along with them," said Father Pete.

"Surely they will get enough to share."

"No, Father Pete, we can't do that. You aren't ready. Maybe next year," said Father Bob.

"I hope not to be in this dreadful, uncivilized place by next year. If I hadn't upset the Bishop, I wouldn't have been sent here in the first place. He can't stand to have anyone disagree with him."

"The hunters headed out through the big rocks to the prairie, while the priests went in the direction that Father Bob had taken the last time when he had shot the deer. "Would you have gone with them if I hadn't come?"

"Yes, if they had allowed it."

"You would have had lots of meat for winter if you had just one buffalo."

"There is no need to worry about it; God will send what we need."

They stopped at the beautiful little stream and watered the animals and continued on the short distance to the edge of the clearing.

After setting up their minimal camp, Father Bob said he was going scouting. Father Pete said he was tired and thought he would rest for a bit. He was soon asleep on his bedroll with the sun warming his backside.

As evening came, the chill in the air woke him. Father Bob had not come back.

"He went off and left me in the middle of nowhere, with no fire and no food, what am I supposed to do?" he asked the trees.

He walked around the immediate area for a few minutes grumbling and then decided that he would build a fire. It can't be that hard. I saw women on the trail do it, he muttered. The alternative of soon sitting in the dark was frightening.

He plopped his more than ample bottom down near the ring of stones and looked left and right for kindling and wood.

"What is the matter with me? Do I expect them to be right here? Of course I have to gather them," he said out loud. He knew he was talking out loud, but didn't want to admit that he was frightened. He had never been alone in the wilderness before. He pulled his rifle near his side as he settled again near the fire pit. This time he had the kindling and wood. He had even gathered some dry leaves.

"Sticks," he said, "I need two sticks to make friction." He got up again wandering the area for what he thought would work. He was sweating from the exertion.

Finally he sat down near the fire pit for the third time. It was nearly dark. He pulled the rifle against his leg for security. He still hadn't shot it. He fumbled clumsily with the sticks as he began to rub one of them back and forth on the other. He heard a twig snap behind him and dropped the sticks grabbing his rifle. He swung it around in the direction that the sound had come. He sat rigid, holding the gun awkwardly in front of him.

Father Bob stepped out of the trees.

"Why didn't you light a fire?" he asked. "I had trouble finding you."

"You left me alone," said Father Pete. "I could have shot you!" He blurted the first things that came to his mind.

"I'm sorry if you were worried," apologized Father Bob. "I was gone longer than I had intended, but it was worth it. Look what I have on the travois."

"What is it? It's too dark," mumbled Father Pete, unwilling to get up again to get near enough to see.

"If you would light the fire," said Father Pete, "it would help a lot." Father Bob stooped and found a comfortable position, pulled his fire sticks from his belt and began to twirl. Before long, a bright fire illuminated the area.

"Now, let me see what you have on that skid," said Father Pete. "Well, it looks like a bear!"

"It is a bear, a fat one," said Father Bob. "It will make a warm bedcover and give us rich meat for the coldest part of winter."

"But how did you know where to find it?" asked the newcomer. "In the morning I will show you."

"That is very extraordinary!"

"Not really," said Father Bob, "not for this area."

"Now, I think we should have something to eat," said Father Pete.

"And thank God for the bear," said Father Bob. They munched some of the dried meat that Father Bob had thought to bring in his saddlebag and talked late into the night. By morning Father Pete appreciated the skills needed to survive and had set a resolve to learn them. Father Bob had told him about the beautiful doe and fawn that had walked through the clearing the last time he camped there. They said their evening prayers together and thanked God for the bear. Father Bob slept in his bedroll, and felt at home, while Father Peter had dozed but woke at every night sound. He was awake most of the night.

As the false dawn, lightened the sky, Father Pete nudged Father Bob at the same time shushing him with a finger to his lips. A huge buck with a trophy rack was munching on the grass on the other side of some small bushes. The buck raised his head, just as the shot rang out. He dropped in the grass without taking a step.

"The fire needs to be built up and we will need to clean him there," said Father Bob. Once again he used the same tall oak. As it hung above them swaying even he was amazed at the size of the animal and its beautiful rack of antlers.

Father Bob took a canvas sack and told Father Pete to follow. They walked along the little stream and he showed him the bear tracks and the spot where he had rousted the bear.

Next he showed him how to identify the wild onions growing along the stream. He didn't tell him that he had only learned to identify and pick them a few weeks earlier, from the women of the tribe.

"Do you like liver and onions?" Father Bob asked.

"I love them, but let me fix it," said Father Pete. "That's one thing I can do. I like to cook. Oh and when there is no one else around, can we drop the "Father" stuff and just use first names?"

"Sure that's fine with me, Pete." They both laughed when he said it.

After their delicious meal they worked hard and fast at gathering grain that grew generously in the area where they had camped. Father Bob knew they should process the meat back in camp before the day warmed. With Mabel complaining and pulling the skid with the heavy bear and the buck tied on a skid pulled by Barney, one of Pete's pack horses, the men tied the bags of grain and bed rolls on their other animals and headed back.

"That buck would have been too heavy for a horse to carry on its back, but making another skid with branches and rope worked really well," commented Pete as if the contraption was a new invention.

"Let's keep both of them behind the lean-to in case we want to use them again," he said.

Father Bob stopped the strange caravan near the edge of the wood and explained to Pete that they needed to cut branches that were strong and about five feet long to make additional drying racks. They put bundles of branches on their mounts, one on each side and a huge one on top and tied the cumbersome loads securely.

The horses and mules were led to the spot where Father Bob had made his fire pit. He released first one travois and then the other. With the bundles of branches and sacks of grain removed and bed rolls off, he handed the reins of the animals to Pete.

"These guys have worked hard. Please take them down and fasten them where they can eat and drink."

Father Pete had been picturing himself sitting down with a cup of tea, thinking that he could rest once he got back. His duties as assistant to the Bishop had allowed him to develop a taste for some of the niceties of life.

Father Bob smiled to himself as Pete moved away with the animals. They sure sent a greenhorn. I thought I was bad, but this guy is older than me and hasn't done anything! Father Bob made the racks as fast as he could. He was running out of things to tie them together. I need to ask one of the women how they make cord, he thought.

Once the racks seemed ample he prepared the wood for the fire, bringing more from the stack behind the church.

Father Pete came back in time to see Father Bob walk to the nearest campfire in the village, to get a burning branch.

Once the fire was going Bob immediately set to work on slicing the bear.

Father Bob had wondered at the absence of many of the women in the village, until he realized that if the hunters were successful, they would need the women to process the buffalo meat before bringing it back.

Father Pete wandered around as if lost. Finally coming out of the building, he set a pan of water near the fire to heat. He carefully measured tea into the water and sat down.

"Real English tea," he said.

"That's nice, said Father Bob, handing him a sharp knife. The meat must be sliced thin, like this so that it will dry all the way through."

"But can't we rest first? I am tired after that long trip and I didn't sleep very well."

"If we wait, the meat will spoil." Father Bob continued slicing.

Father Pete looked around and said, "Where are the cups? I couldn't find them."

"They are on the wall hanging on a set of antlers from the first deer I shot where we camped." He returned and poured the tea through a strainer smiling broadly until he noticed that Father Bob's hands were covered with blood from the meat.

"Oh I am sorry. Would you like me to get you a pan of water?"

"No Pete. This isn't a tea party! If you want to eat this winter you will need to help!"

"Well I just wanted a cup of tea first that's all," said Pete, feeling ruffled. He took a sip of his tea as if he had all the time in the world and set it down on the grass beside the fire.

"Now if I may make a suggestion, if we cover the grass in front of us with a piece of canvas, it will be easier to slice the meat laying down on the canvas instead of holding it in the air the way you are." He went into the church returning with the last section of Father Bob's tent. He cut it in half and carefully laid each piece down on the grass as if it were a linen tablecloth.

"Now to work," he said. He pulled his robe off over his head and sat down on it in his underwear.

"What on earth are you doing?"

"They are all too far away to see what I am wearing. Besides I am covered and I don't want to ruin my robe."

Pete worked hard until he decided that he had done enough. His back ached. His shoulders were stiff and he knew that his body was badly sunburned.

"Bob I am going to rinse off in the lake and then fix us something to eat. Would you like me to make a roast with greens or a stew?"

"It will have to be a roast; the stew pan is full of fat from the bear."

"Yes of course." Father Pete realized that he had not been helpful in the way that Bob had wanted, but he hoped that in time the few talents that he had developed would be appreciated.

The tender roast, rubbed with dried garlic and accompanied with greens, was eaten as the sun dipped behind the trees. It was late when the last of the meat had been sliced and put on the racks. Father Bob rolled both hides and placed them against the church wall where he knew they would be in the shade in the morning, until he could peg them out and start to process them.

After cleaning up the area they sat quietly sipping the tea that had steeped for many hours before either of them had thought to pull it away from the heat. They had added water to it and now, reheated; it was a pleasant and refreshing drink.

"One of us can get some rest now while the other keeps the fire going. We can switch during the night. Which shift would you prefer?" asked Father Bob.

"Just keep the fire going?" asked Father Pete, "I can do that."

"Keep your gun nearby. Animals may try to steal a free meal," said Father Bob. "Take the safety off like I showed you. It won't fire unless you do."

"Oh dear, it is so dark, I won't know they are here until they are near me," said Pete.

"Just stay alert." Father Bob went in to rest. He was very tired. He slept soundly until the songs of the birds in the trees woke him.

Rushing out he was greeted by Father Pete's voice beginning the prayers of the Mass. He had set up an altar outside and had sat vigil all night. Grain was cooked and covered, ready to be eaten for breakfast. Father Bob was astounded. He joined the prayers and assisted in the Mass, thanking God for the provision of enough meat for the winter, the grain and warm hides, and at the last moment Father Bob added, "And the fellowship during the coming cold months." Father Pete had proven that he was willing to do his share. He just had to learn how.

After breakfast, Father Pete went in to sleep, and didn't come back out until evening. When he stepped out he found Father Bob in a hole near the animal shelter, as deep as a grave and six feet square.

"Hello, said Bob, did you sleep well? I tried to be quiet. I figured this was far enough away that you wouldn't hear me digging."

"I slept like a baby. What are you doing?"

"I am making a storage room for the meat and anything else that we want to keep cold, like the grease."

"That's a good idea. Have you eaten?"

"Not since this morning with you," answered Bob.

"Let's have something together and then I will take over on the shovel. It will stay light enough to work for a while yet."

"Thanks again for last night. I appreciate you letting me sleep." They checked the meat that was now getting stiff, and ate a bit of the leftover roast and greens. By dark, Father Pete had increased the hole to seven by seven and it was getting deep enough that it was difficult to climb out.

"I think the roof should set at a slant, higher at the back so the rain will run off the overlapping boards like a wood shingled roof on a house."

"Yes, I was thinking the same thing, Pete. Here I think this ladder is sturdy enough to help you out of there now. Maybe we should leave it standing in there so if we need to climb in, it won't be quite as difficult." As they stitched huge canvas bags from Father Pete's tent to use for storing the meat, Pete got an idea.

"After layering branches in the bottom to keep the bags up in case the bottom of the pit gets wet, we should put in a layer of dried grass bundles on top of them."

They built the dirt up around the sides of the hole and made it higher in the back. They had created a frame with logs.

"We will soon be ready to lower the bags of dried meat when every piece is dry and smoked enough," said Bob. They used that time to make the top and fashioned a strong latch so that no animal could get in the top. "This looks a lot like the door to go to my uncle's basement," he said with a chuckle. "My Aunt canned peaches and other good things and they were down there on shelves."

"Do you have a big family, Bob?"

"Yes, our house was always busy."

"You must miss them a lot. I was an only child and my parents are both gone to be with the Lord. There is no one back home to miss, but I must say I still think about the nice Christmases we had." Bob was glad that Father Peter had not waited for a reply. He had gotten used to not having contact with his family, but he admitted to himself that the mention of Christmas as a child caused a feeling of loss.

In the morning, the people returned, leading heavily burdened horses. Their hunt had been very successful. The people would be warm under many new buffalo robes this winter. Their bellies would not go empty.

The camp was quiet the next few days as the hunters and women rested. The children of the village came to investigate the strange music coming from the camp of the black robes. Father Pete sat on a log near the fire, where he had made a large batch of sugar candy. It sat on a plate cooling. He strummed a guitar and sang softly. "Jesus, Jesus, let all the children come to know you." The children came nearer. He motioned for them to sit. Each dropped where they were, having noted the sweet treat on the plate.

He started again with the simplest hymn that he knew, "The Alleluia, Holy, Holy," playing softly and singing along. Father Bob joined in, motioning for the children to sing, too. One by one they repeated the unfamiliar sounding words and before long most of the young voices were singing God's praises. They didn't understand the meaning, but they liked the sound. They would learn what it all meant one day.

He changed to a lively round of "Old McDonald," asking Father Bob to make the animal sounds. The children giggled and smiled broadly. They laughed with the sound of a horse and a mule, but having never seen one; they giggled and looked puzzled by the sounds of a chicken and a cow. Father Pete hugged each child and handed out the candy. They ran back to their mothers to tell of the fun. Father Pete stood smiling.

"It's not much, but it's a beginning," he said. "Children always seem to love music."

Days stretched into weeks.

"Have you noticed the men returning from the woods on a regular routine? One with heavy saddlebags goes directly to the chief's tent. When he leaves he has empty bags."

"Yes, surely their source for the blue stone is somewhere in that woods. That must be why the Chief told us we could not hunt there anymore, that we had to go to the far woods away from the lake." Father Bob had noticed that someone now guarded the far side of the lake where it was most likely that anyone would enter the woods from this area.

Flying Eagle, Snow Star's husband, had developed a trade with the white men. His people would wait at a set spot beside the wagon trail. They wore no paint and carried only enough rifles in sight so they did not appear vulnerable. He had taken women with him and even his own son, Watching Owl, so that the white men would know that he meant them no harm. That fall the people took corn and pumpkins to trade, as well as furs, but the special thing they had that the white people wanted most was the blue stones with the yellow metal in it.

Their wares were spread on colorful woven blankets or beautiful soft furs beside the trail. At first the wagon masters and scouts were wary. The hostilities with the Indians continued in many areas along the route. It was difficult to draw near and believe that they intended no harm. Yet the people in the wagons were eager for any break in the sameness of their days. The Blue Stone People had coated a large boulder with a paste of grease and white chalk stone. It was easy to see from far away and it marked their trading spot.

After several wagon trains had passed their way and no harm had befallen them, from The Blue Stone People, the scouts had spread the news.

"They have nice things to trade, along the trail by the big rock territory and they are peaceful." One of the scouts had traded his knife for a chunk of stone the size of a small egg. He wore it on a leather rope on his neck. Later he was able to trade it at the post for a new rifle. Word spread and people came long distances to trade.

As a result of the interaction the people of the village learned more of the white men's language. This was a great help to the priests. They could now communicate on a simple level. The people listened as they told the stories from the Bible and were awed by the miracles they related.

Being a truthful people, it never occurred to them that the priest's stories could be made up. They had stories of their own, handed down from one generation to the next. Each was memorized and repeated word for word. The stories told of a time when the people traveled from place to place, or of successful hunts. They told of great battles where many warriors died to protect the people or their hunting grounds. In times gone by, Talking Mountain had told stories of the spirits, now Red Fox was their shaman but none could compare with the stories that the priests told.

More people came to the church to hear the stories and learn about the God of the black robes. Red Fox was angry and jealous. He could feel his power slipping as the people learned more about the great power of the Almighty God. He hated the priests and held secret ceremonies asking the dark spirits to kill the black robes.

One morning as Moonflower and Snow Star gathered grass for making new mats, Red Fox heard them talking in English.

"Brave Sparrow was wise beyond her years," said Moonflower. "She knew about the God of the black robes. She said that he is the Greatest Spirit. Brave Sparrow said that he heals and protects and that he made the blue stones for the people so that they would prosper. I would like to ask the black robes about it but your father said we are not to talk to the black robes about the blue stones."

"For now we must be happy to make our mats and baskets for trade and be glad that our people do well," said Snow Star.

"I wish she would come back," said Moonflower, "I miss her."

CHAPTER FOUR
ADVENTURE AND LEARNING

Sharp Knife and Singing Wind left the village the same morning that Brave Sparrow had. They followed the wagon trail west and crossed the Silver River. They saw the crumpled, burned cabin there but didn't stop. Instead they headed north along the tree line until finally the trees became dense and difficult to ride through. Little streams along the way had joined the Silver River. None of them were big enough to cause them difficulty. They were able to splash across and continue without a problem.

Weeks had passed before they met an old trapper. His pack mule was loaded with furs and his rough exterior appeared unfriendly. He said that he had come down from the mountains to avoid the deepest snows. He was headed to Silverville to the trading post to trade for winter supplies he told them. Then he was going to follow the Hickory southwest until spring.

"You boys are heading the wrong direction for this time of year. When the snow comes you will be up to your waist in it. You can't just ramble around in those mountains in the wintertime. Come with me and we can share a fire tonight and talk."

Both young men realized that the old trapper was confused, but they appreciated his experience.

"Perhaps he hit his head," said Sharp Knife. They knew that it was summer. Yet they did ride with him until they again reached the spot on the Silver where the wagons crossed and then they parted with him and skirted the town and headed further down the Hickory. He had warned them that they would probably be shot at if they rode into the settlement wearing Indian clothes.

At first they stayed clear of the loggers too. They had circled Tom's camp near Silverville and managed to pass unnoticed. They had drawn the conclusion that all white men were untrustworthy and a little crazy. The trapper had done nothing to change their minds.

The rafts being poled down the Silver River with loads of boxes and barrels and even livestock, amazed them. Families were on the move, looking for something better than what they had. They saw men cutting trees and building cabins, miles from anyone else. This puzzled them. They were used to a community that worked together and played together. Why would the white man choose to live alone?

They continued on south and west, avoiding contact with the white man, until one day they stopped their horses on the crest of a hill overlooking another river that joined the Hickory. The trees ahead had been cut knee high and lay stripped of their branches, waiting their turn to be dragged to the river to join the logs already on the surface bumping along.

Teams of shirtless men pulled crosscut saws as tree after tree fell to the ground quivering on broken branches. The cook rang a large bell and all work stopped. The breeze carried the scent of the food. After a short discussion, they dismounted and led their horses slowly into the logging camp. The foreman sprang to his feet when he saw them.

"What do you Indians want? What are you doing here?"

"We are peaceful," said Sharp Knife, as he looked into the barrels of several guns. "We are from the Blue Stone People." He lifted the large chunk of stone on his chest, which hung from a leather cord. "We want to eat, and then work. I would like to learn about the cutting of the trees and what you will make out of them."

"We don't make anything from them here. We just cut them here. They float down river to the saw mill. There, they pull them up, let them dry and then they are cut into lumber. People buy the lumber to build houses, barns and stores. I'm Jim London, foreman, this here is Brute, that's Smoky, he makes the meals and over there, well, you will meet them in time if you stay, I guess. What are your names?"

"I am Sharp Knife of the Blue Stone People and this is Singing Wind. He does not speak your words but will work. We are strong. We will work hard."

"Ok you're hired, but here, you are Sharp, and he is Windy. Got it?" "Yes, thank you, got it."

"Go get yourself a belly full of beans, and then we will put you two on an axe cleaning logs."

The rifles had disappeared while they had talked. Men nodded and continued to stuff their mouths as Sharp Knife and Singing Wind walked toward the fire. Smoky handed them each a tin plate of beans and a large slab of bread. Singing Wind commented that if these are all white men they are a strange people. What he was observing was whites, Mexicans, men of even darker skin, and the Chinese cook. Each different from the next and every one of them looked tough and strong.

Sharp Knife and Singing Wind gobbled their food noting that others were already finished. As they pulled the gear from their horses they saw that no other riding horses were up in the work area. They had all been tied to trees or staked in a safe area where they could reach the grass and water below.

Sharp Knife motioned to Jim that he was taking the horses down and Jim nodded. By the time he had climbed back up, work was in full swing. Jim had handed Singing Wind a large axe and he had started him cleaning logs without having a communication problem. Sharp Knife looked around but couldn't see Jim to get an axe. When he did spot him he started through the trees just as someone yelled.

"Timber!" The huge tree missed Singing Wind by only a few feet. It made a thunderous sound as it crashed to the ground behind him, producing a cloud of dust and debris.

Jim came running. He explained that everyone in the area must constantly be alert for falling trees and that "Timber" was called as it started to tip. Sharp Knife explained to Singing Wind who wasn't sure this was an environment that he wanted to be in. He had only been chopping branches a few minutes and he was already covered in sweat and dust was sticking to it. He had pulled his shirt off and it lay on a trunk nearby. It was now coated in dirt raised by the fallen tree. He was used to watching the herd and playing his flute or hunting. He wanted adventure, but not hard work. Sharp Knife detected his attitude and warned him that this was only one of many jobs the white men do that they were going to learn and that the Blue Stone People would be judged by the way they performed.

Jim handed him an axe and Sharp Knife walked to the newly fallen tree to remove the branches starting at the tip. When he had finished he immediately went to another and then another.

When he looked up he saw Singing Wind sitting on the tree that he had started that afternoon. He still hadn't finished removing all the branches. He had several men around him as he played his flute. Sharp Knife thought that Jim would be angry. He jogged over.

"Singing Wind put the flute away and work. Clean the branches from the tree. They will make us leave."

"That is not a bad idea. I do not like this work," said Singing Wind.

Smoky rang the bell again and all the men turned toward the fire and their evening meal. All the saws and axes were placed inside a small shed until morning. Each man was handed a plate piled with fried potatoes and a generous chunk of fire grilled meat. Their cups were filled with strong black coffee.

Jim sat with a group of men near the fire talking and laughing. When the meal was over he strolled over to Sharp Knife and Singing Wind.

"Would your friend be willing to play us some music now that the work is over and everyone can listen?" He had spoken to Sharp Knife, knowing that Singing Wind would not understand. Sharp Knife repeated it in the language of the Winahatah. Singing Wind quickly got his flute and began to play. Another brought out a banjo and strummed an accompaniment. A guitar appeared and soon the sounds of the night were mingled with an unusual concert of improvisation. It was beautiful.

When the music stopped, Jim said,

"Tell him that we work hard all day. We play music at the end of the day." He smiled at the crew and crawled into his bedroll. Singing Wind huffed at the translation of Jim's last remark. Then tucked his flute into its sleeve by his bedroll and strolled down to the river to check their horses and take a bath.

After one more day, Singing Wind insisted that they move on. They followed the logs down river to the saw mill. After observing the process for a few minutes, Singing Wind shuddered as he watched the huge noisy blade removing the bark of a giant, straight pine. He didn't want to work there either.

Further on when Sharp Knife saw two men unloading a wagon of lumber in a clearing, he inquired what they were doing. They were friendly and explained that they were building a trading post.

As they talked, Sharp Knife and Singing Wind helped remove the lumber and carefully stacked it, respecting the hard work that went into its creation. Sharp Knife wanted to see how a building was put together. They stayed there and helped until the last nail was in place. Proudly they stood in front of the new store, feeling that they had learned a lot and had helped in building something special. The men parted company as friends. Singing Wind was learning to understand the white men's language and to speak it.

They followed the Hickory River further south, where they met a father with two small sons. He was building a cabin near the river. They visited with him for an evening learning his story. They had been with another family, each on its own raft, until his wife had died along the way with a high fever. He had buried her there beside the river and so he had chosen to stay. The others had continued on down the Hickory River, heading west.

The next morning Sharp Knife and Singing Wind went hunting, returning with a deer. They helped the man prepare the meat for drying and then spent the next six days rolling logs up a ramp to finish the walls of a small cabin he had begun. They carried rocks, from the river for a fireplace.

When they left, he had hugged them and patted their backs. He had decided that Indians were just like everyone else but perhaps a little kinder.

"I hope that you will stop and visit us if you come back this way. I have enjoyed talking and working with you both. Singing Wind, I wish I could play the flute the way you do. Thank you both for all the help. This cabin would not have been finished before cold weather set in, if you hadn't stopped to help. It would have been extremely hard on my little sons.

Soon after, as they rode along; a man watching a large flock of sheep, shot at them. They decided they wanted to see the herd closer. They dismounted and approached the man slowly on foot. His hair and beard were as curly and unkempt as the wool on his sheep. His black and white dog growled and looked as fierce as he was. He placed himself between his flock and the two intruders, showing his teeth and continuing to make a low rumble.

"Hello, I am Sharp Knife. This man is Singing Wind. We have never seen such animals before and would like to know all about them. We will do no harm to you or your animals."

"Dog, quiet, good boy," he said. He looked at them for a long silent moment and then decided that they were telling the truth. "Come, have a cup of coffee. We will talk." At the man's campfire they were able to learn about the use and care of the sheep. Sharp Knife traded two large blue stones for two pair of mature sheep, which they took with them when they started their slow journey home the following day.

"These are strange animals," said Singing Wind. "I think the women of the village will love them. They can raise many and use the wool to make blankets. The man said they are good to eat, but if we eat them, then they can't multiply."

Sharp knife laughed.

"How clever you are to figure that out." He loved teasing Singing Wind. "It is going to be a difficult journey until they get used to us. Your flute will help, I think. He said they get used to a sound and follow it. The Chief will be pleased that we return with such an unusual gift for the people."

Singing Wind had been busy braiding strong straps to fasten to the sheep while Sharp Knife built two crates and a large travois so his horse could pull the sheep in the crates if necessary.

"I want Brave Sparrow to see them," said Sharp Knife, as they headed home.

"Maybe she did when she was on her journey."

"I hope not. I want to surprise her. Let's stop in the shade ahead and rest the sheep. They are small compared to our horses. They are probably tired."

"They should be. They have been fighting the straps every step of the way."

"Singing Wind, do you think you could play the little song that the shepherd was humming as he walked along and they followed?"

"I'll try. See if this sounds like it."

"That's good. That seems to be relaxing them. Look, they are walking toward you."

"I am going to sit down against the tree and play and they can rest here in the shade."

After that, the sheep were easier to move. They followed the sound of the flute, playing their song. At times they were still a challenge. The sheep were put into the crates when they crossed even the smallest streams.

"I think they are smart enough to know that if they get all that wool wet, they would go to the bottom. I don't think they can swim," said Singing Wind.

*****

As the people of the village gathered in the communal tent, they each greeted the men that had been gone as if they had just that moment returned. They knew that it was proper protocol.

Chief Dark Wolf had called the meeting so the people could hear the stories that Sharp Knife and Singing Wind had to tell. Each man in his heart wished that he too was young again and without wife and children so that he could go on a journey. Each had taken his journey of three days alone when they were boys turning men. Each had planned to journey again, but for most it didn't happen. Responsibilities got in the way. Children need to be provided for. Families need protection. These young men were bringing the outside world of the white men to them. The voices in the tent were raised in excitement.

CHAPTER FIVE
A GIFT FOR THE PEOPLE

Sharp Knife and Singing Wind had returned as they had promised, but Sharp Knife was disappointed and restless. He had a longing for Brave Sparrow. He wanted to leave again, this time to find her. He had hoped that when he returned he would find her there but she had not come back to the village. No one had any news of her.

The Chief stood and greeted Sharp Knife and Singing Wind, telling them that everyone had missed them, especially the young women of the village. The people laughed. Red Fox stood and chanted and danced a thank you to the Spirits of the four directions. Thanking them for bringing the young warriors back safely.

Platters of food creating a feast had been prepared. This was reason for a celebration.

After everyone had their fill, Sharp Knife stood and told of their adventures. He embellished the story with humor and increased the dangers they had come across for the sake of entertainment as was expected. He related several encounters with the white men, and of things they had seen and done.

They presented one sheep to Chief Dark Wolf as a gift for the people. It represented the four animals they had brought

Everyone was impressed. Sharp Knife explained about the sheep, their care and what they were used for. Some of the women touched the wool and commented that it was very soft.

The Chief had given two young men, the job of guarding the sheep. This gift was regarded as very special. A fenced in area with a shelter was immediately built for them. Singing Wind insisted that the guardians learn to hum the song of the sheep.

"It is very important," he expressed with concern. "Without their song, they become nervous, or feel lost. They will die. You must hum the song for them." After the presentation, Singing Wind took the fourth sheep to the pen. He played the song and it followed him. The people were impressed.

Next Singing Wind spoke to tell his story.

"I don't have much to add to what Sharp Knife said, except that I have found that the white men like music just as we do. He works hard and angers easily. He drinks firewater that makes him crazy and then he sleeps far into the next day. I have learned some of their words, but they don't all speak the same tongue. Some of them want all of us dead. Others want to change us so we are like them, but what that would be I'm not sure since each one is very different. Their women are beautiful and their food is delicious but I found that I like to be here with the people the best."

The people applauded and laughed as Singing Wind sat back down.

Sharp Knife hesitated and then decided he would share his heart's desire now. There was no point in waiting.

"I will leave again soon. I wish to look for Brave Sparrow."

"If you find her, will you bring her back?" asked the Chief.

"It is my wish to bring her back to be my wife."

"It is good," said Chief Dark Wolf. He stepped out of the doorway and walked to his own tent.

The next day, Moonflower and Morning Dove, her best friend, were singing as they pulled weeds and checked the corn. Her thoughts were on the news that Sharp Knife would go find Brave Sparrow and bring her back. She had never allowed herself to consider that something bad could have happened to her, or that she couldn't be found by Sharp Knife.

Moonflower missed her adopted daughter. All the people missed her. Dancing Willow's daughter, Blue Stone, had returned to live in the village expecting to see Brave Sparrow. They had been the best of friends. She and Running Deer had a pretty baby girl named, Happy Song, that was getting spoiled by the extra attention of her grandmother, Dancing Willow. The people were happy.

When Brave Sparrow comes back it will be like it was; only better, thought Moonflower. I must remember to call her Sarah, as she told us, but that is difficult for me. I think of her as the little girl that Rising Eagle named.

"The corn ripens. It will be ready to pick soon. Our garden by the lake is doing well, too. Already I can see the color change on the squash. The potatoes have big bushy tops. With them I can't tell what they are producing until we dig them up just before the frost," said Moonflower.

"I am glad that we have new foods to eat in the winter," said Morning Dove. "Trading the blue stones with the white people has improved our lives just as Brave Sparrow said it would." Morning Dove stood up bending back to ease her muscles. "I am getting old. Work seems harder every year," she said. Moonflower suggested that they make a journey to the woods to see what was growing.

"That nice rain we had may have gotten some mushrooms started. Let's go in the morning."

"We could use a day of rest," said Morning Dove with a chuckle.

*****

The women did not go to the woods the next morning. During the night the sky had completely covered with dark clouds and rain fell as day came slowly. No wind stirred the trees. The birds were silent. The rain continued. Both priests were glad to stay inside.

"This rain is pounding down. It will be a good test to see if our outside storage is as sealed as we think it is."

"Don't worry Bob; it will all be dry inside. We did a good job. It is nice to sit and read for a day. We have been working very hard ever since I got here. This is pleasant by the little fire. I think I am going to make us some English tea."

As Red Fox looked out the door of his tent he saw a huge gray wolf walk through the center of the camp. It went directly to the fire pit in front of his tent, pulled down the roast that he had carelessly left out, unattended. It snarled at him baring its teeth aggressively. Then it trotted back through the rain, the way it had come carrying the meat.

Red Fox cursed the wolf and then cursed the weather. He pulled down a string of herbs and crumbled some from each of them into the tea he was making to drink.

"I will perform a ceremony and the rain will stop. No more rain! No more animals! No more people in black robes. I am more powerful than any man or spirit, in this camp or anywhere else," He shouted, shaking his fist at the sky. He thought that he could control even the weather with his evil conjuring. He drank his potion and began to chant and dance and his head became dizzy and his thoughts disjointed and unclear. "No more trees! No more grass! No more people always wanting me to do something."

A loud clap of thunder over the camp kept everyone inside, huddled near their fires, as an ominous turning wind formed above the tent of Red Fox. Its black center lowered its mouth to the ground surrounding his tent causing a growling, roaring sound. Still he danced and chanted. Intoxicated by his potion and exaggerated self-worth he thought that he was creating the strange sound that filled his head with a loud ringing.

As suddenly as it came, the whirling wind left, taking Red Fox, his tent and all his belongings with it. The space where his tent had been was washed clean by the rain and yet... it appeared to be undisturbed to the people in the village.

He was transported by the turning wind, faraway and his tent was set down deep in an area where the woods on the mountainsides were burned by the fire, spewed by a volcanic eruption. Nothing was alive in the area, not a tree, bush or animal. It was a terrifying and barren land. He was now in another dimension, an existence parallel to the world of the Blue Stone People. This was a hell he had made and he would never escape.

When he opened the flap of his tent, Red Fox, found himself, hoping to find another easy meal. The women had always provided well for the shaman, not because they respected him but because they feared him. There was no food, no camp fire, and no village. Beneath his feet he felt a rumble that came from the depths of the far mountains.

As Red Fox leapt back with a gasp, he instantly realized that somehow he was no longer in the territory of the Blue Stone People. He knew that this time he had gone way too far.

"Where am I? What have you spirits done to me?" he wailed. "Do you know who I am? How dare you play such a trick on me?"

A thunderous voice reverberated, shaking the walls of his tent as it spoke to him.

"You are where you should be, Red Fox. You will never see The Blue Stone People again. You are dead to them. Your ways will fade. A new life is coming to my children."

As Red Fox cautiously peeked out of his tent, he saw the huge lion that had spoken. Their eyes met for just a moment, as it turned and walked slowly away, swaying its tail back and forth, leaving no prints on the ash covered ground.

*****

After two days of rain and dark skies, the people were glad to see the sky lighten and the rain stop. Tent flaps were tied open and children ran out giggling to play and splash in the big shiny puddles, squishing mud between their bare toes. The routine of the camp could now resume. All seemed normal, until someone noticed that Red Fox had not been out.

Growling Bear and some of the others wanted to leave camp to hunt and preferred not to go without Red Fox holding the usual ceremony. He scratched near the flap and waited. When he got no response, he spoke as he pushed the flap to one side.

Even he, with all his experience as a hunter and warrior, had never beheld a scene such as was before him.

Turning to his men he instructed them to guard the tent and not let anyone enter or even look inside. He walked quickly to tell Chief Dark Wolf. Moonflower slid to the very back of the tent cringing and at the same time making room for Growling Bear if he wanted to sit down. This news frightened her.

"I'm telling you, that he was killed by a wolf. No other animal kills like that," said Growling Bear.

"It's hard to believe that a wolf would come into the village right into his tent, but what else can we think?" Growling Bear paced the short width of the tent leaving muddy prints everywhere he stepped.

"It had to be one of his spirits! He made them angry or something. He was always holding secret ceremonies and drinking potions that made his eyes glazed and his step falter," said Growling Bear.

"What you say is true. He was not like Talking Mountain. Red Fox seemed like he was always surrounded by something dark and sinister," said the Chief.

"It's also true that he didn't make friends here. He was strange and different, but we still need to do the proper things," said Chief Dark Wolf. He assigned men to prepare the funeral fire, no easy job after days of rain, and some to build the pyre. Since Red Fox had no wife, Moonflower and Morning Dove were asked to prepare the body for its spirit journey.

"This is horrible. I don't want to touch him. Let's hurry and get it over with," said Moonflower.

"What are we going to do about that ugly wound on his throat?" asked Morning Dove. "We have to cover it with something. We don't want the children to see it."

Moonflower nodded as she continued to groan and moan loudly. Others outside the tent wailed not in sorrow but in respect for the position that he had held.

Once the red ochre was applied they dressed him in the best of his clothes and wrapped his neck first with leather and then a bandana, adding a string of beads and breastplate of bones and blue stones. His hair was oiled and it too was coated in the sacred red paste, and then braided with feathers at the ends of each braid. They placed a gourd rattle in one of his hands and a pouch of herbs in the other, knowing that once the fingers grew stiffer the items would stay in place, when he was moved to the pyre.

In a basket they gathered other herbs and things he had used. Hunters lifted his body onto a buffalo hide that Red Fox had painted with designs no one in the village could recognize or interpret. His body was as ready as the two women could make it.

Father Pete noticed the strange wailing coming from the village and the men piling wood for a communal fire.

"They are preparing for a funeral," he said. "I wonder who has died."

Moonflower and Morning Dove walked down the path to the lake. They wanted to scrub the red ochre from their hands and arms before the ceremony started. It resisted their efforts until the third lathering of harsh lye soap. Moonflower patted her hands dry and rubbed them with scented oil she had brought. This was not the first time she and Morning Dove had performed this function.

"Who will hold the ceremony? Do you think that Chief Dark Wolf will do it?"

"He will have to," said Moonflower with a frown as she shared the oil with her loving friend.

"Things in this village have been strange ever since Chief Rising Eagle was killed by that snake in his tent. At least that was a snake that we could all see."

"Do you think this was a spirit wolf?" asked Morning Dove.

"I wish you wouldn't say things like that," said Moonflower. "I probably won't sleep for a week as it is." Her face looked as if she had just tasted something dreadful.

Chief Dark Wolf waited only long enough for everyone to be seated on the logs and bundles of dry grass brought from the communal tent. The entire area was still muddy. The body of Red Fox was carried out and placed on the pyre and after some difficulty with the wet wood the fire was lit using some wood from the stack inside the communal tent. The fire snapped and smoked from the moisture and sent sparks into the air. The people were already edgy from the circumstances. They jumped at every sound the fire made.

The Chief stood to speak just as the sparks hungrily caught the dry bindings of the pyre feeding the path of the flames to the oiled hide that Red Fox's body lie on. A huge blaze engulfed the top of the pyre. The men had left the bindings unusually long and as they burned, they weakened and the pyre leaned more and more until it collapsed on the very top of the fire, sending a burst of sparks into the air. This had never happened before! The people thought it was a terrible omen. The women screamed and ran to their tents gathering their families inside and tying the flaps shut tight. The Chief's family was the last to leave. Growling Bear and a few of the older hunters were asked to keep the fire going. There was no ceremony. It had been a relief to Chief Dark Wolf. He had no idea what he would have said or how he could have held an appropriate ceremony. He too, felt that the air was filled with evil.

The dawn found Chief Dark Wolf, wrapped comfortably in an oiled hide and sitting on the small knoll overlooking the village. The funeral fire created dark smoke as the men continued to feed it with the damp wood. He had not slept. Father Peter saw the Chief silhouetted there against the gray morning sky. He strolled to the hill and stood beside him, but said nothing. The Chief finally turned his head to look at the seasoned priest. Without a word he adjusted the hide so that both could appreciate its protection from the wet ground. He longed for someone to talk with. Perhaps this old priest could offer words of wisdom.

"You do not sleep this night either. Evil walks among my people. I fear that more will die."

"What has happened?"

"Red Fox was killed by a wolf, in his tent!"

"The Great Spirit, Our God is angry. He allows this to happen. Chief Dark Wolf, may I suggest that you hold another meeting at the fire tonight and ask God to forgive the people. Ask Him to bless your people. It might be wise also to send your hunters around the village to look for the tracks of a wolf. Once the beast is killed, the people will feel much better. I will speak to the people and pray with them."

Before the Chief could say no, he rose and walked away. Entering the tiny church, he knelt and prayed that the Chief would allow him this opportunity.

Growling Bear had decided on his own that a good hunter could find the fearless wolf that had entered their village. Leaving others to tend the funeral fire, he headed out at daybreak. He circled the village. It is so muddy that surely any living animal would leave a trail, he thought. He entered the woods looking for any sign. As he walked inside the trees circling the backside of the village, he sensed that he was being followed. He turned just in time to see movement in the brush as it disappeared. So, the hunter is being hunted, he thought.

You know where I am wolf, I will make you come to me, he thought. He sat down on a large root and leaned against the huge old tree. The sun rose high. Still he waited. His muscles grew stiff and his eyes grew heavy as the day warmed. Like the Chief and many others, he had not slept. Slowly his eyes closed.

An awareness of his surroundings came to him before he eased open his eye lids, just enough to see through his lashes. A huge wolf stood ten feet away, directly in front of him. His right hand rested on the trigger of the rifle that lay beside him. His left hand held his knife. He opened his eyes wide and just that movement activated the deepest growl he had ever heard. He brought the knife straight up in front of his chest just in time to defend his throat. The animal fell beside him.

"You are magnificent, but you are no spirit," he said.

Growling Bear carried the dead wolf back to camp and laid it in the grass behind the Chief's tent and asked him to step out to see it. The Chief was pleased and knew that once the people heard Growling Bear's story they would realize that it was just a wolf gone bad.

Immediately he announced another meeting for sundown. The fire was fed and would be kept burning for three days. It still burned brightly. Red Fox's tent was now just a ring of gray ashes. It had been burned as soon as the communal fire had been started. Several burning branches had been tossed inside and the flap tied shut. It had swiftly burned to the ground.

When Father Pete saw the people once again gathering at the communal fire, he took it as a sign that he was to attend and speak even though no word had come to confirm it. Father Bob walked with him, expressing his doubts.

"The Chief is not a Christian. He will not let you speak before the people."

Father Peter carried his guitar a blanket and a jar of lake water that he had blessed. Father Bob had tucked his Bible and a tambourine under his arm at the last minute. Even that was a musical challenge for him. He couldn't stay on key when he sang, and it was not the most pleasant of sounds. He had no sense of rhythm.

When the two priests neared the fire, heads turned in their direction. Father Peter walked boldly to the area near the Chief and spread his blanket on a mound of dry grass on the ground, behind and to the Chief's right. Father Pete made sure that he could see and be seen by the Chief. Father Bob was uncomfortable. It was not his way to be bold. He sat down on the blanket, hoping that the pile of dry grass was a sign that they had been anticipated.

The Chief rose slowly and stood before the people. It was not necessary to signal for silence. No one made a sound. No one dared move. They were held by fear. He tried to sound casual, as he explained that they need not fear the wolf any longer; that their most experienced hunter had tracked and killed it. Growling Bear entered the circle of light, created by the large funeral fire. In his arms he held the dead wolf. He placed it on a pile of dry grass that had been positioned in front of the logs his people sat on.

"As I entered the woods behind Red Fox's tent searching for tracks, I could feel his eyes watching me. He followed me. I sat down with my rifle and knife ready. He attacked me! He will bother us no more."

The people murmured and applauded Growling Bear. Many of the younger hunters were jealous of the attention that Growling Bear was receiving. One shouted out.

"How do you know that is the same wolf that killed Red Fox?"

"I just know." Growling Bear was angry, that one of his hunters would dare to challenge his word. The Chief was shocked.

Father Bob had noticed the yellow smudges on the side of the wolf's fur. He hesitantly stood and walked near it.

"How is it that this wolf's fur has yellow ochre on its side?"

Chief Dark Wolf smiled and walked to the young hunter that had spoken out.

"Do you know where in our camp there was yellow ochre made into a paste with grease?"

"Yes my Chief," he answered humbly.

"Tell the people so they will all know."

"Red Fox kept his doorway and flap of his tent coated with it. He said that it was to honor the spirits, so they could come and go freely from his tent."

"This wolf had to enter Red Fox's tent to rub his fur on the yellow ochre. He is the wolf that killed Red Fox," said Growling Bear.

Once again the people murmured and nodded their heads in agreement and relief.

Father Pete stood and asked the Chief for permission to speak. The Chief gave permission with a simple nod.

"This night has been a time of revelation. We have seen how something can be misunderstood. We have also seen how it is possible to doubt the truth put before us. We do not know for sure why the wolf killed Red Fox, but we do know that he has taught us all a lesson. We must believe the truth when it is before us."

He picked up his guitar and strummed the strings. He watched for visible signs that the people were starting to relax. Quietly he breathed the Alleluia, Holy, Holy as the children and Father Bob hesitantly and quietly joined in. Father Pete continued to softly strum as he prayed loudly, so that all could hear.

"We praise you Holy Spirit, Our Counselor, Father of truth. We praise you and thank You, Creator Father, for this night of revelation." Under his breath he prayed that the blood of the wolf before them could somehow help him lead these people to the blood of Christ.

"Holy, Holy God, I praise you. Alleluia." He paused asking God to give him the right words. "This wolf, big and fierce, has killed one of your own," began Father Pete. "He has paid with his life. He was killed so that you could walk this camp with freedom and peace without fear of death. Another gave His life for you that you might know life. His name was Jesus. He is the son of the living and One True God. He was killed, fastened to a cross like that."

He pointed at the white cross standing beside the tiny log church. It was barely visible in the evening light.

"His dead body was placed in a cave with a huge stone in the opening, a stone so large that it took many men to roll it there. He came back to life. He rolled the stone away. He rose from death to life so that you and I may have eternal life. Faith in Jesus is the only way that we can live forever and go to heaven. His father is the one true God. He is the Great Spirit. There is no other God but Him. Believe in Jesus and you will live forever. He has granted life and prosperity to the Blue Stone People! While other tribes are at war and grow weak, you grow stronger.

Honor Him and thank Him for his gift to The Blue Stone People. He has given blessings and favor. Please stand and raise your hands and sing with me. Thank Him for His gift."

He played the "Alleluia, Holy, Holy," again and again until the voices of the people drifted across the lake, over the meadow and into the forest. The younger ones especially loved that song. All the people had heard it in their camp many times.

He thanked the Chief for allowing him to bring a special blessing to the people and as he spoke, he sprinkled holy water on them all, walking completely around the area. He made sure he had sprinkled water on every person.

He and Father Bob left the meeting then and strolled back to the church. They sat at their own small campfire sipping coffee and praying long into the night, asking that the seed they had planted would grow in the hearts of the people. They wanted so very much to have someone come to them with questions about Jesus.

Moonflower staked out the hide of the huge wolf and worked carefully to preserve it. She hoped that Dark Wolf would think it a good idea to wear it often before the people to remind them. She left the fur whole, with head, feet and tail. She couldn't bring herself to cut it.

I think that perhaps I should hang it on the wall inside the communal tent where it can be seen daily. The sacred white hide of Talking Mountain is gone, and special symbols are important. No one in camp is worthy to prepare such a special white hide, and we have no honored holy man to wear it anyway.

Even the priests have their cross for a symbol. It is gruesome but it reminds me of the priest's words. That is what a symbol does. It reminds us of something important.

She rubbed the leather side of the wolf fur with rendered bear fat. It isn't ready yet but when it is, I will ask Dark Wolf if I may hang it high in the big tent.

*****

"Mother?"

"Oh, what is it Snow Star? I didn't hear you approach."

"I asked if you and Morning Dove have finished all the mats you were making for the trading spot."

"Yes I think so."

"What were you thinking about when I walked up?"

"I was thinking about Talking Mountain and Singing Lark and wishing that things were like they were when they were with us."

"Mother they tell me that Singing Wind has expressed a desire to study with Standing Lizard. If he does, he could become our holy man and healer. Standing Lizard is respected."

"Yes Snow Star, but Standing Lizard is also feared by his people. He will not teach him to be like Talking Mountain. Times are changing. The black robes bring ideas that lead the people away from the old ways. They must not be allowed to change our people. They mean well but they bring a feeling of discontent to the young people."

CHAPTER SIX
TIMES ARE CHANGING

"Father Peter, your hands shake slightly as you set the broken bone back in place in my hunter's arm. Do you know the importance of it being set correctly so that he can hunt again?"

"Yes Growling Bear, I know. That is why my hands are not steady. I feel that I have set the bone correctly, but had I not spoken and alerted the deer earlier, the hunting party would not have ventured so far from camp to find fresh meat. I am so sorry that my first experience of hunting with you has shown my inexperience and caused this hunter to be hurt. He would have waited until he got back to have it treated. But we are too far for that. Please accept my apology and assurance that Quick Snake's arm will mend and be strong again."

"It is a matter of necessity and perhaps respect too, but you are not to take the responsibility for his injury. He was careless."

Father Pete wrapped the arm loosely in raw leather cut from the deer Growling Bear had shot.

"That will shrink some and harden." He said a prayer that it heal correctly and become strong and straight again, while wrapping a piece of cloth around it to hold it in place and another piece tied into a sling. The hunter, Quick Snake, offered a slight smile of gratitude as the pain subsided. Father Pete had given him a brew with pain relieving herbs in it. He was soon asleep.

Growling Bear tied the two large bundles of meat to the horses as they prepared to break camp. It was as he looked up at the ridge in the distance that he saw a column of soldiers slowly riding in their direction.

"We will stay in the trees and out of sight. We are not here to engage in battle with soldiers."

"Perhaps you grow soft Growling Bear. Why do the men of the Winahatah hide?"

"Flying Eagle, you speak foolishly. They are in the open. We have the cover of the trees. If they draw near to attack, we have the advantage here. You have put much effort into creating a trust at the trading spot with the Blue Stones. Why do you now want to attack a column of soldiers? I think you do not say what you mean. I think that it is me you want to challenge!"

"Growling Bear, should we make a travois for Quick Snake while we wait for the soldiers to pass?" Father Bob was trying to defuse the tension before it became a worse situation.

"Father Peter, how long will he sleep like that? We need to take the meat back before it spoils."

"I'm not sure. He may sleep several hours. I think a travois is a good idea. He can rest that way while we return to camp."

*****

"We will stay away from the trees and head for the tall grass. I saw movement in the trees. We are being watched."

"Sargent, do you think they will attack?"

"No, it's probably a small hunting party. If it were a war party they would have attacked by now. Let's just stay out of range and hold our pace. The Major said not to engage unless we were forced to defend ourselves."

"I can feel their eyes. It gives me the creeps!" said one of the soldiers.

"If they had more men with them you would probably feel more than that," said the Sargent. "This is the hunting grounds of the Blue Stone People. They have been peaceful since they set up that trading spot. I hope it continues."

*****

Moonflower sat outside her tent holding Watching Owl, Snow Star's first child.

"He is a strong boy. He will be a fine hunter," she said. Snow Star smiled proudly.

"Yes I have been given a fine husband, and a beautiful son." Chief Dark Wolf sat beside them.

"Flying Eagle is ambitious. He will not rest until he is Chief of this village. It is good that you were able to convince him to come here after your marriage. He has the knowledge of the Omati ways. He will help our people to continue to prosper but he has much to learn."

"Father, will you allow the black robes, to start a school as they say?"

"Yes Snow Star. They and others like them. They will teach our young people the white man's ways. We must be sure that they do not forget the old ways, as they learn the new."

"Why do you allow them to stay?" Snow Star asked. "Can't you just threaten the black robes and make them go away?"

"Snow Star, it is necessary that our people learn about the white men and their ways so we can understand them. It is good to know your enemy."

"I don't want my son to go to their school. I want him to be like you and Flying Eagle. They will change him."

"I wonder where Sarah is and if she will ever return?" murmured Moonflower, almost to herself.

"I would like to see her. I miss her," said Snow Star. "We all miss her. I would like her to see my baby."

Chief Dark Wolf rose to greet the returning hunters. They all were gathering in front of the communal tent. Quick Snake was taken inside to Sweet Grass immediately. He woke as he was transferred to a pallet in the tent. His wife was sent a message and she came to sit near him. Both Moonflower and Snow Star stepped in to offer help.

"I think that the priest has done well. I don't want to disturb the wrapping. His arm is swollen a little but not so much that I need to loosen the bindings. That is a good sign that he has set the bone correctly. It is times like this that I wish that Brave Sparrow would move back here to live," said Sweet Grass. She filled a pan with water and added a generous supply of willow bark to it.

"I think perhaps she will come one day, when we do not look for her," said Chief Dark Wolf as he stepped out to speak with Growling Bear.

"He is right," said Moonflower. "She will come one day when we least expect it, just as she left."

"Do you think she is with the white men?"

"I don't know Snow Star. I can only hope that she is safe and well."

"Mother, I think it is time for Watching Owl's rest. I will put him down in our tent. The breeze is getting stronger. I left the basket I was working on under the trees." She walked to her tent and ducked inside long enough to tuck the baby boy in for a nap and then hurried to collect her weaving. When she got back she found that he had wiggled his way near the flap and had dragged his small rabbit fur that Moonflower had given him. She scooped him up and tucked him back inside settling herself on a mat just inside the doorway, to work on her project. This is nice she thought. With the flap tied up, I have the sunshine and the tent blocks the breeze.

Flying Eagle was the second son of the Chief of the Omati. It had taken much convincing for his father, Chief Black Thorn, to agree that he could take Snow Star as his wife and live with her people. Flying Eagle had the disposition of a fierce fighter and was a natural leader. Had he not had an older brother that was capable of leading the Omati one day, he would not have been allowed to leave.

Now, Flying Eagle stood with the hunters of the Blue Stone People, thinking that he was more than their equal.

Growling Bear knew that it was only a matter of time before Flying Eagle, the young son-in-law of the Chief, would replace him as leader of the hunters and warriors. Eventually he would become Chief.

Now, as Growling Bear grew older, he had more concern for his personal safety because he had taken Big Flower as his wife and she had given him a son and was pregnant again. He resented the young man and the inevitable future.

Growling Bear realized that the Chief had been speaking to him and he had been lost in thought.

"I am sorry my Chief. I was thinking of something and did not hear you."

"Perhaps Flying Eagle heard me. Perhaps he would like to lead the next buffalo hunt," the Chief chided him.

"I will lead the hunt as always," said Growling Bear decisively.

"Very well then; we will allow the herd to move closer. In two days' time we will ride out with the women. Sleeping Bear and Jumping Bird have found the buffalo faraway and moving slowly. They have just crossed into our hunting grounds and are heading for the river that the white men call the Silver. They will travel the route of the

Hickory for the water supply. Grass is good there for a long ways.

Growling Bear was as angry as he could be. How could the Chief humiliate me like that in front of my hunters? His son-in-law pushes already for more authority! He will not gain it easily from me! He was still fuming when he swung up on his hunting horse and rode swiftly out of camp alone.

Big Flower saw him go. He said nothing to her before he left. She could tell that he was angry. She carried Little Cub to the shade where Sweet Grass, their young healer, sat.

Sweet Grass saw the frown on Big Flower's forehead.

"What troubles you? Are you not well?"

"I feel fine but I am worried. Growling Bear rode off angry. He has been agitated a lot lately. I don't know why."

"He has the same problem that all men have. Their step slows. He wants to stay young. None of us can change the flow of life."

"What do you know of growing old? You are young and not yet married!" Now she was angry, too.

Big Flower hurried back to her tent. How dare she say my husband grows old! The worst thing about what Sweet Grass had said was that Big Flower wasn't sure that Sweet Grass had been wrong. Growling Bear was not young. He had lost a wife and child many years back. She didn't care what others said, she could take special care of him. She would keep him young! She loved him.

*****

Until Flying Eagle took charge of it, no one had organized a work detail that brought some of the rough mined blue stones back to camp on a regular schedule. The men experimented to find the best way to polish and drill the stones. They found that the more it was rubbed with fine bone dust, or ash, the more it shone. The yellow streaks sparkled in the firelight and soon the people competed to wear the pieces with the most yellow metal.

They traded with the Omati for silver and learned from Bezalel, a marvelously skilled craftsman, how to make rings and bracelets that held pieces of the polished stone on fingers and arms. Their necklaces were heavy. Each one thought theirs the most beautiful.

Everyone knew that Flying Eagle, Snow Star's husband, had been responsible for developing the trade with the white men.

That fall the people took corn and pumpkins to trade, as well as furs, but the special thing that the white people wanted most was the blue stones with the yellow metal in it.

Their wares were spread on colorful woven blankets or beautiful soft furs beside the trail. At first the wagon masters and scouts were mistrustful. The hostilities with other Indians continued. It was difficult to draw near and believe that the Indians intended no harm. Yet people cautiously came.

The Major from Fort Connors, came to the trading spot, with a small group of soldiers. The Blue Stone people saw them coming and took cover. They were concerned that they would be attacked, but the Major stepped from his horse more than a bow's shot away, and walked slowly up to the blankets covered with wares, leading his horse and waving.

"I need a special gift for my wife," he told them. "It is our anniversary. We have been married twenty years next week." Major Bennet chose a ring and several large loose stones. For trade he had brought a wagon loaded with goods from the trading post, bolts of cloth, cast iron kettles, and coffee pots and bags of coffee, flour, sugar and salt. He allowed Flying Eagle and Snow Star to choose what they felt was fair barter, and then slyly said that he felt for the goods they had chosen he should receive another piece of the blue stone. They laughed and allowed him to pick one more.

After the soldiers left, Snow Star saw that one of the soldiers had left his gloves lying on the blanket.

Spotted Feather jumped on his horse and rode quickly after the soldiers to return them. The soldier riding rear guard saw him approaching swiftly and yelled an alarm. A shot was fired and Spotted Feather fell from his horse. It all happened so quickly that the Major didn't have time to stop it.

The soldiers gathered around the injured boy. The bullet had grazed his ribs and gone out the flesh on his back. He had fallen from his horse, landing against rocks, hitting his head. He was unconscious.

Flying Eagle rode up frantically, disregarding his own safety. The lad was an orphan of the Omati. He was under Flying Eagle's protection.

"Who is responsible for this?" the Major demanded just as Flying Eagle arrived. A young soldier stepped forward making apologies. He appeared to be nearly as young as the boy on the ground.

The lost gloves slipped from Spotted Feather's hand as they lifted him to a travois for the trip home. Flying Eagle handed them to Major Bennet.

"Flying Eagle, we are very sad that this has happened. Can we do anything to help? The boy approached so swiftly and my young soldier is inexperienced. I will come to your village and speak with your Chief, so that he will know that this has been a mistake."

"No it is not good. I will carry your words to the Chief. He will know what has happened here today. Chief Dark Wolf will not welcome the white soldiers in our village, for any reason."

"I see, well then, again, allow me to say how much we hope that the boy gets better, and that we did not intend that he should be harmed."

"I will take your words to the ears of my Chief."

The small caravan of traders trudged slowly back toward their camp without a rest. Snow Star had wisely brought a few herbs with her but could only ease the boy's pain. She had nothing to fight off infection. The boy's head had a large knot on the back and he continued to drift in and out of consciousness. The bullet wound was bandaged with a strip of the printed cloth from the bolt she had chosen as part of the trade.

Spotted Feather had been living with Flying Eagle and Snow Star but now he was taken directly to the communal tent where Sweet Grass waited. Flying Eagle carried him in and placed him on the pallet where she could care for him.

Although she had been trained well, this was the first bullet wound she had seen. The amount of swelling and bruising on entry and its exit was far more than she imagined. She pulled his shirt off and plunged it in a pan of cold water. The water turned blood red. After she had applied all her knowledge and gentle care, she looked at the young man and knew there was nothing more that she could do. She felt helpless.

Then a small seed that Sarah had planted began to grow. She raised her arms to the Healing Spirit of The Great God. She asked his powerful help.

"Sarah said, all I needed to do is to believe in you and ask and you will help. Great Healing Spirit, please, help Spotted Feather. I do believe because she said you are real!"

Later, seated by the fire in the center of the large tent, she wrapped her arms around her knees and rocked and hummed waiting for God to finish the job that she had begun. All night she kept her vigil, lifting Spotted Feather's head, placing cool pieces of wet leather on the large bump. She continued to wake him and offered a medicated tea repeatedly. She worked at cooling his fever. With a wet piece of cloth she wiped his face and bare chest over and over.

It was mid-morning, the next day, when Spotted Feather opened his eyes and smiled at her. He was fully awake. He was going to live! She ran from the tent yelling to anyone and everyone that could hear her. She ran back in touching his cheek and forehead.

"You got shot by the soldiers but you are going to be fine! I did what I could and Brave Sparrow's God did the rest!"

Chief Dark Wolf had refused to act on the incident until he knew if the young man would live. He stepped up and into the tent to greet Spotted Feather.

"How do you feel? The Chief asked.

"I am sore and I have a huge headache, but I know that I will get well with Sweet Grass taking such good care of me."

"That is good. I am glad to hear that you are getting better."

Now he called a select few to council in his own tent. Moonflower was asked to sit with Spotted Feather. He didn't want any woman around to interrupt him with tea or food.

Sitting in the small group at the meeting, with the Chief were Flying Eagle, Growling Bear, Sleeping Bear and Snapping Turtle. Although not large in build, Snapping Turtle had a reputation for wisdom and an accurate shot with a rifle. He had come to The Blue Stone People after the last summer council and felt honored to be included in what he perceived to be an important meeting.

Without the usual ceremony, the Chief got right to the subject at hand.

"Flying Eagle will tell us all again, what happened at the trading spot, when Spotted Feather was shot. He will tell just what happened and not give his opinion on what he thinks should be done." Flying Eagle stood up feeling his face turn red as the chastisement in the Chief's words hit home.

"My Chief I know that I said that I was eager to engage the white men in battle. I know that at times I have spoken from a lack of wisdom and experience. I will tell what has happened." That was as close as he would ever come to apologizing to the Chief for his behavior while out hunting.

As he spoke, he glowered at Growling Bear. When he had finished relating the incident, those present were satisfied that it had been an accident.

"I do not feel the need to retaliate for the brash actions of the young," said the Chief, looking straight at Flying Eagle. I do feel that we should give the Major an opportunity to show our people how much he regrets the injury of Spotted Feather. I will think on this."

Later that week Spotted Feather was out sitting under a tree in the shade with Sweet Grass. The Chief sent only for Snapping Turtle and Growling Bear, having decided that the two men would represent the people well without a chance of the guards at the fort misinterpreting their intentions as they approached.

"I would ask that you use your wisdom to carry a message to Major Bennet." Tell him that I will accept a gift of his choosing to show the people that he is not our enemy. Tell him that the quality of the gift will show what regard he holds the lives of our people."

"It is good. You are a wise Chief. We leave at daybreak," said Growling Bear. Both men were smiling as they left the Chief's tent. Proudly they prepared their bundles and gear so they could leave at first light. Big Flower and Butterfly prepared generous supplies of food for their men's journey, making sure each had more than he might need.

In the morning the camp was buzzing. Two of their men were actually going to ride to the soldier's fort to talk to the Major. Big Flower and Butterfly sat together discussing it. They felt proud that their husbands had been chosen. Young Walking Tall walked by.

"You know don't you that they will probably never come back? I heard one person say that they were sent to be killed so that the Chief would have a reason to start a big war!"

"Who said such a thing?" said Butterfly standing up and placing her hands on her hips. She was instantly furious and worried at the same time.

Big Flower and Butterfly were outraged and upset. "I'm sorry. I should not have repeated what Corn Silk said. She probably doesn't know any more about it than we do." He walked away quickly not wanting to deal with Butterfly.

"Don't be upset," said Big Flower, "You know that Corn Silk has always had a tongue for causing trouble. I don't blame Walking Tall, as much, but he shouldn't be spreading hurtful gossip." The two wives watched the talebearer make his way toward the lake, stopping for a moment to talk at each opportunity.

"He is worse than an old woman," said Butterfly. "That boy needs someone to take a firm hand with him. Pine Stick, doesn't discipline him the way she should."

"That's true but Growling Bear says that her husband, Jumping Bird, is a good hunter and warrior. He should start disciplining the boy before he gets hard to live with."

"Big Flower, don't you think it is strange that so many young people are allowed to join us."

"Yes, but it is even stranger that they behave so distinctly."

"I don't like things that are different. It makes me uncomfortable," said Butterfly,

"When Snapping Turtle and I came; we tried hard to blend in right away. We didn't want to be different."

*****

"Father Peter, I need your help."

"What is it Sweet Grass?"

"I think we need to change the leather that is on Quick Snake's arm. I don't want to do it alone, but I think we should take it off and wrap his arm with clean soft leather and smooth branches. His wife, Soft Meadow, is complaining that it has a bad smell."

"Yes, I can see that it might. We used raw hide from the deer the men had shot. I will go with you and we will change it for him."

Sweet Grass had all they needed to do the job efficiently. She had also warmed a pan of water and had soap there to clean his arm before they wrapped it again.

"Quick Snake, you must sit very still. We do not want to disturb the bone at all. It may hurt a little when we unwrap it but don't move." Soft Meadow sat near them watching every move.

"First we should pray," Father Pete said softly. "God is the one who made us and I am sure that he is the one that fixes us when we get broken." He asked the Great Holy Spirit to come and heal Quick Snake's arm and continued to pray as they removed the sling and cotton support. Then he did a curious thing. He pulled the pan of warm water close to the hunter and placed his hand and lower arm in the water, splashing the water onto the hide until it slowly became soft. He pressed the deerskin slowly opening it until he could reach inside to support Quick Snakes arm with his fingers and gently lifted the broken arm out of the pan of water. Sweet Grass lathered the arm and Father Peter's hand several times pouring clean water over them. She patted the arm dry and it was again protected with leather and wood splints and a cotton wrapping. He wanted the old sling back on but Soft Meadow insisted that he have a clean one.

"There you are clean and healing just fine," Sweet Grass said with a smile. "Father I felt the bone as I was drying his arm. It is straight and will be strong again soon." Father Pete nodded and asked how Spotted Feather was doing.

"He has no fever and no infection from the bullet holes but I worry a little about that bump on the back of his head. He says he still feels a bit dizzy when he sits up to eat or walks around." Spotted Feather grinned when the attention had finally shifted to him.

"I am getting better every day. She just likes fussing over me."

"I am glad that you are both doing so well," said the priest as he stepped out. He turned back just long enough to tell Sweet Grass that she could call on him anytime.

As he walked back to the church he saw Father Bob sitting outside near their fire pit.

"Did you get rid of Quick Snake's stink?" He asked laughing.

"Yes we did and Spotted Feather is doing well also."

"That's good but I wasn't worried about them. I am more concerned about the men that have gone to the fort. I hope that Growling Bear has a control over his quick temper. It won't serve us well there and Snapping Turtle is new enough that I don't know him well. His name doesn't help me picture a diplomat. I think one of us should have gone with them."

"I don't think the Chief would choose unwisely. He must have a good reason for the two he sent.

"I am sure you are right. I don't think I told you that I had a chance to speak to Walking Tall. He seemed to be listening. That young man loves to spread the word. He would make a good missionary." They laughed together easily.

CHAPTER SEVEN
A TRIP TO THE FORT

The two riders had no trouble finding the fort, but getting in was something more difficult. The soldier at the gate refused to allow them entry without permission from the Major. The Major was in a meeting. They waited impatiently for nearly an hour before the guard finally swung the heavy door open and allowed them to enter.

As soon as they heard the gate close behind them, they found they had a mounted soldier on either side.

"What is this? You act as if we are prisoners! Does the Major know that we come from the Blue Stone People? We have come to talk to him," said Snapping Turtle. Neither soldier answered.

The porch in front of the Major's office was filled with uniformed men. They had no use for Indians and would prefer to fight them, rather than allow them to enter this office without an order. The Major completely aware of the attitude of his men, stepped through the outer office and opened the door himself.

"Please come in," the Major said and then he turned to a soldier giving an order, "Private, take their horses to the water trough and give them some feed, too."

"Yes Sir," he replied. Under his breath he continued, "At least I am not serving food and water to Indians." He circled the horses and couldn't help but admire them. He especially liked the brown and white paint, ridden by Snapping Turtle.

"Gentlemen, I am Major Bennett. Please be seated." Both men remained standing. "I am Growling Bear of the Blue Stone People. This is Snapping Turtle, also of the Blue Stone People and the Omati. We have a message from

85

Chief Dark Wolf." It was easy for the Major to discern that Growling Bear was a leader among the people.

Snapping Turtle looked at the eyes of Major Bennet as he delivered the message. The Major could recognize strength of character and will in these men. He was good at quickly sizing up a man.

"So your Chief says if I send him a gift he will forget the whole thing?"

"He will not forget, but the people will know that you did not intend for your soldier to harm Spotted Feather. It will show your true regret." Snapping Turtle turned to leave and then remembered there was more to the message.

"The Chief said that the quality of the gift would show the regard you have for the lives of our people." The Major rubbed his chin for a moment and then laughed out loud.

"Your Chief is good at bartering too," he said.

"Come Growling Bear and Snapping Turtle, I have a gift of friendship for your Chief." He led them to a corral where a brown mare with beautiful lines stood next to a pair of half-grown foals. They were identical and lovely.

"The mare is mine." Then he pointed to a big stallion in a separate stall. "He is the father. He belongs to the Army. He is good at jumping fences. You may take the stallion, or the twin foals."

It wasn't by chance that Chief Dark Wolf had chosen these two men for this assignment. The Chief had guessed correctly that the gift the Major would select would be a horse, and he knew that Snapping Turtle appreciated good horses. He entered the corral and coaxed the mare to come to him.

Growling Bear and the Major watched with interest. Snapping Turtle spoke softly in the language of the Winahatah.

"If they grow to be like her, they will be fast and strong. She is beautiful." Growling Bear eased over to the stall where the stallion stood pawing the ground.

"He is strong but not young."

"Let's take the young ones."

"I agree," said Snapping Turtle. He turned to the Major and said,

"We accept the foals."

The Major was pleased with their selection. He even suggested that the foals be placed on the edge of the people's herd but tethered with long ropes.

"They may be difficult to keep while they long for their mother," he said. Growling Bear helped Snapping Turtle to slip ropes on the foals and they carefully removed them from the pen without releasing the mare.

The Major smiled as he entered his office, feeling that he had avoided what could have been serious trouble with the Blue Stone People. He could hear his mare calling to her foals.

Another reason that he smiled was that the army would be paying him top dollar for the two foals. They would require time and work as they grew in order to turn them into good mounts for a soldier. This way he felt he had gained favor with the Indians and could even receive a commendation for avoiding trouble. Yes, he thought. This has been a good day.

Gently, the foals were led away from the fort and their mother. Snapping Turtle urged them forward as Growling Bear rode behind them. The foals jerked the leads and tried numerous times to turn back.

"There is no need to hurry them. We want the Chief to see them in prime condition when we get back," said Snapping Turtle.

Growling Bear suggested that they take them across the Silver on shorter leads.

"That way we can keep them between us and they will be less afraid with our horses beside them."

"That should work and they will be tired after we cross. I think we should stop for the night in the cover of the trees there."

"Did Butterfly pack you enough to eat? I have lots left and even a big piece of sweet berry leather."

"I think I want to give a bit of that to each of the foals. If we make friends with them, it will be easier traveling."

"Growling Bear, don't give them that. It could make them sick. Remember, they are just now able to eat grass and were still getting their mother's milk. Poor babies, they are lonely and scared." Snapping Turtle stroked the foals and whispered to them softly.

"I know they belong to the people but I would like to keep them for my own. For some reason they feel very special to me."

"You are talking like a woman! They are like any other horse, Turtle. They will kick you the first chance they get!"

Growling Bear rode horses from the herd and as long they were big, strong, responsive, and fast, he didn't care which one. He was never cruel to them, but he had never formed an attachment to one.

When the foals were led past the lake and into the village, they caused quite a stir. Chief Dark Wolf came out and circled them, sliding his hands over their backs. He liked horses and was pleased that his men were back. He was eager to hear about their visit to the fort.

Two aspiring hunters were assigned the job of leading the foals to the edge of the lake and being sure they were tied securely where they had both grass and water. They would be kept tied until the foals were no longer apprehensive and skittish around the people and willingly would stay with the herd.

*****

The people missed the flute music of Singing Wind. He had gone to be an apprentice with Standing Lizard. The time he was gone was uneventful. Snow and cold came as usual. The people enjoyed the music of the Jesuits. Gray Cloud played his flute but it was at a distance for the horse herd. The priests had managed to maneuver their occasional attendance in the communal tent, telling stories and singing. They had become accepted as risk-free entertainment.

It wasn't until Singing Wind returned early, nearly a moon and a half, before he was expected, that the people knew that he had changed. He held his head high and had a confident arrogance that caused some of the other young men to look at him with resentment. He requested that the Chief have a new tent made for him. He wanted it to be set on the space that had been held by Red Fox and Talking Mountain before him. Chief Dark Wolf was troubled. He wondered if Singing Wind had learned enough from Standing Lizard in such a short time.

In a few days the women had fastened spare hides into a very nice tent with a good lining. They had woven mats for the floor and big boys not yet old enough to be considered hunters, but eager to show their strength had carried large stones from the lake to ring the fires both inside and out. It was placed near the communal tent, but not on the spot that Singing Wind had wanted.

Dancing Willow never questioned whether her son was ready to be a shaman. She was simply a mother filled with joy that her son was once again in camp. Blue Stone shook her head as she watched her brother swagger into the communal tent for a meeting.

"Mother, no good can come from this. My gentle, quiet brother has turned into someone I do not know or like. He is too proud."

Chief Dark Wolf had called a meeting of all the men in camp. Singing Wind had waited until he was sure that all the rest of the men were in the tent before he entered. He could hear the voices of many before he neared the flap. As he stepped up and in, the tent instantly became quiet. The Chief noted the reaction of the men, but he wasn't sure how to interpret it. Were they showing respect? His mind slid back to a time on the hill when he told Brave Sparrow that he had a people of followers. He had said that he had no young men in camp that aspired to be Chief and that they had no holy man. He worried about the future of his people.

Now he glanced at Flying Eagle knowing that it was only a matter of a few years, before he would yield to the young man's desire to lead the people. He looked at Singing Wind, seated beside him. He wondered again what guidance this young man could offer. The Chief held his hand up and asked that all present also raise theirs.

"Today we have a new shaman," he said. "He has let his music speak for him in the past. Now he will speak to the spirits for all of us. Welcome our holy man, Singing Wind."

The men stood as one, still holding their hands in front of them. Each stepped forward in turn, lowering their hand to drop a small gift into Singing Wind's hands. One had an eagle feather, another several beads made from bone. Each token would be fastened together to embellish a breastplate to be worn at ceremonies. It would be a symbol of the unity and strength of the people.

Since Singing Wind was not married, Blue Stone and his mother would make the breast plate for him. Having beaded her wedding dress, Blue Stone was able to work swiftly. She added beads of color here and there where she felt they were needed while Dancing Willow strung enough bone beads on a thick strong leather cord, to reach around Singing Wind's neck and allow the heavy necklace to hang and sway when he danced. An array of feathers was added, on the sides and bottom. It would be impressive.

When they had finished they were proud of their work. They were still sitting in the shade on a blanket when Running Deer, Blue Stones husband, placed a bundle of dried hollow reeds and pieces of gourd that had been dyed, and drilled, onto their blanket.

"Singing Wind will need these to tie onto his arms and legs. He asked me to bring them to you so that you could string them. He also wants lots of bone beads and feathers braided in his hair before the communal fire tonight." Running Deer was frowning as he walked away.

"I don't think he is at all happy about any of this. Singing Wind will have to work hard to gain the respect and confidence of the people," said Blue Stone.

"It will be even harder for him, with so many of our people starting to believe what the black robes say," offered Dancing Willow.

"Mother, I am not sure that they do. I think they just like to listen to the stories," said Blue Stone.

Later, Blue Stone walked to the new tent of Singing Wind, with the bone beads and some feathers she had gotten from Moonflower. She scratched at the flap and stepped in, to find her brother kneeling in the center of the tent. His knees rested on sharp rocks that he had placed there. His head tipped back and his eyes were wide open but seemed not to see. He held his arms straight out like the wings of a soaring bird. It frightened her. She hurried out of the tent and stumbled into the chest of Chief Dark Wolf. He caught her and kept her from falling.

"What is the matter, Blue Stone? You look upset," he said.

"I am," she exclaimed. "It's Singing Wind. I went in there to braid his hair but he is in some kind of a trance and didn't even know that I was there!" Chief Dark Wolf entered. Singing Wind stood in the center of his tent holding a cup containing a dark liquid. He gulped it down and dropped the cup quickly covering his mouth. He grabbed a water bag and drank from it. After a moment he seemed to slowly become aware that he was not alone.

"Are you alright?" asked the Chief. "You seem to have injured yourself." Both of Singing Wind's knees were bleeding.

"I..., it is nothing," he said seeming uncomfortable that the Chief had noticed.

"If you are alright, I will tell Blue Stone to return. She was here earlier but you were busy."

"She was here?" asked Singing Wind.

"Yes," said Chief Dark Wolf. "I'll tell her to come back." He walked away feeling deep concern.

The women of the camp had prepared the usual celebration feast, although some of them wondered whether accepting this particular young man as their holy man was cause to celebrate.

The Jesuits watched from a distance. They were puzzled at the apparent increase in activity in the camp. They had not noticed the single rider enter the camp a few days earlier. They did not know that one of the people had been apprenticing to become their new shaman.

Once again Father Pete noticed the Chief sitting in his favorite place on the hill overlooking the camp. Father Pete joined him.

"How are you my friend?" he asked, as he sat down heavily beside the Chief.

"I wait to see what the evening brings," was the Chief's reply.

"You are having a communal fire tonight. What is the reason?" asked Father Pete.

"We celebrate. We have a new shaman," said Chief Dark Wolf as he stood. He was annoyed. He felt that his place of quiet thought had been invaded.

"May I come?" The priest asked boldly. "You may both come. You may learn something tonight." He said, as he turned and walked away.

When he thought about it, Chief Dark Wolf had no idea why he had responded to the priest the way he had. Maybe it was just that the priest was always trying to teach the people about his God and he resented it.

Singing Wind was nervous as he continued to prepare for the ceremony that would make it official. He would be their holy man. After tonight, they would accept what he said as from the spirit world. He wasn't sure he believed it himself, but he certainly wanted them to believe.

His head was beginning to feel peculiar. His scalp was pricking and stinging all over and he was finding it difficult to focus his eyes. Maybe I made the drink to strong, he thought. That is good! I will need all the help I can get. Standing Lizard told me to be different and not to be afraid to shock them or scare them.

He picked up the bundle containing the things that Standing Lizard had given him to bring back. Inside was the gourd with the black powder in it. He had mixed some with water and drunk it down but it had been very bitter. It had stained the inside of his mouth and lips black. Standing Lizard said that it would help me to see the spirits of the other world, but right now it is difficult to see anything clearly. His heart was beating wildly, partly from the drug but also from anxiety. He looked at his knees and noticed the blood still red and fresh. He smeared it down the front of his legs and then wiped his fingers on his forehead.

"For you spirits, for all you spirits, a sacrifice of my blood to bring me power." Tears of fear slid down his cheeks as he picked up the bundle again. It held a small-decorated pouch. He carefully placed a pinch of it in his palm. "Blue, blue like the skies, spirits of the sky, blue like the water, spirits of the waters, I offer this to you," he called out. He mixed the powder with his spit and smeared it on his cheeks and chin.

He took a drink from the water bag and spit the water over his hands and then carefully he shook a measure of the red earth from the last pouch onto his wet hands.

"Blood of mother earth, give me power." His hands were coated red. He wished he could see himself. I could look at my reflection in the lake but then others would see me. I don't want that.

He knew that his hair and breastplate had been worked with care. His arm and leg rattles were in place and had been made exactly as he had requested. He waited.

At that very moment both priests were on their knees in the church, asking God to give them another opportunity to witness to the people about Jesus Christ. They prayed that Jesus would help them dispel the superstitions of the people. They asked that the Holy Spirit would give them the right words. They recited a prayer of contrition asking forgiveness for any sin they may have committed and then together they finished with the sign of the cross.

"In the Name of the Father, and of the Son and of the Holy Ghost, Amen," they said, as they rose. They headed for the gathering at the fire but before heading down the path in the evening twilight; at the last minute Father Peter picked up his guitar and Father Bob tucked his Bible under his arm. They had heavy hearts seeing that once again the people had chosen to have a shaman and turned from the true God.

CHAPTER EIGHT
FROM THE SPIRIT WORLD

Sarah and David could hear the voices of the people gathering at the communal fire as they circled the back of the lake. They were excited to see their friends and families. Sarah took note of the little church. David explained as they walked their horses closer, that a black robe had come and built it.

Before revealing their presence, Sarah and David stopped their horses in the dark near the church. It was then that they realized that they had actually approached the village without seeing a guard.

Although both young people were eager to enter the village, for some reason, they held back dismounting in the dark and listening to the strange cadence coming from the drums. Things had changed. The sound was new and strange.

Suddenly Sarah felt that she had been led back here for a reason. She asked David to approach quietly and to speak to one of the young men to find out what was happening.

When he returned, to her side he found that she had changed into her white clothes made from the sacred robe of Talking Mountain. She had removed the saddle from Moon Boy. His back was covered with a white cloth. Her hair and skin was dusted with chalk and he felt a chill as he approached her.

"You look a little scary, like you are from the spirit world," he said.

"What is going on in the village?" She asked.

"The people have gathered to accept Singing Wind as their new shaman. He has been studying with Standing

Lizard all winter. Before him, they had Red Fox but he was killed in his tent by a big wolf. The people have not had anyone to talk to the spirits for them since last summer," said David.

"I see," said Sarah. He could not see the smile that crossed her face as she realized that this was why the Holy Spirit had urged her to return now.

This was an opportunity to once again tell the people about the one true God. Then she remembered the little church that was here and she wondered if the people were already learning about God from the black robe.

She and David watched from the darkness as Singing Wind staggered out of his tent. He entered the bright ring of light from the large fire and stood before the people gathered there. They could see Chief Dark Wolf and Moonflower sitting together, and slightly back, but beside the Chief on his left sat two priests in black robes.

"It seems strange to me that the black robes would be at the fire. This celebration is to accept a new shaman for the people," said David.

"I agree. This whole thing doesn't feel right and David; look at the way Singing Wind is dancing. He seems unsteady as if he has been drugged." Sarah felt concern. "Something is very wrong here," she said.

They continued to watch as the drummers increased the speed of the beat and Singing Wind whirled around faster and faster. When he could turn no more, he tried to stop but the world spun passed him and his feet were out of control. He staggered, tripped and fell, landing with his arm in the flames! Women screamed covering the eyes of their children and men shouted, but none ran to pull him away. They froze in fear. Father Bob was the first to grab him and pull him away from the fire. Father Peter had taken action, raising his heavy body from the blanket, in record time. With presence of mind he had brought the blanket and smothered the flames attacking the oil on the young man's arm and hair.

Immediately, Sweet Grass directed that he be carried to the communal tent.

The celebration was over. Singing Wind would never be their holy man now! People stood near their seats murmuring. Chief Dark wolf stood, hoping to comfort the people.

It was then that Sarah rode slowly into the light of the fire. She and Moon Boy stopped. It looked like a spirit from another world had just appeared. All conversation ceased. It was silent.

"Once again the People of the Blue Stones need to be reminded that they are children of the Great Spirit," she began. The people quickly found their seats, looking on in awe as the beautiful woman in white spoke to them from the back of a large, pure white stallion. Even Chief Dark Wolf sat back down allowing Sarah to calm the people.

"Today God has spoken to you in an undeniable way. He is a jealous God. He wants no other Gods to be honored by his children. I am Sarah of the Blue Stone People, but I am also one of God's children. God has provided much for you. The village prospers. Young people come to join the village, bringing new skills and new blood to a once old and tired people. You have not seen war here. You have not been plagued with disease for many years. Since God has blessed you, life here has been good. Your crops have grown. Your children are fat. There has been no season of hunger in the village of our people. Why now do you want to anger God by choosing another shaman to honor other spirits? Did not God send a wolf to kill Red Fox? Did He not already show you that He commands the sky and the earth, the rain and the animals? They all do His bidding. He is the creator. His Son Jesus Christ came to earth as a man, to save us from being thrown into a fire that lasts forever!" Sarah pointed at the fire as she continued.

"Singing Wind felt the bite of these flames but he lives and will once more guard the horses and play his flute if God wills it. The Blue Stone People need no one to honor the spirits. They need to honor God through His Son, Jesus Christ.

If you believe that God loves you and that His Son Jesus came to earth to save you, stand and follow me."

The priests were the first to their feet. They had never seen anything like this woman, but they liked her message. She rode Moon Boy slowly out of the ring of people around the fire and slid off his back.

Sarah raised her hands high into the air walking slowly on the path toward the lake. Moon Boy followed her and the priests followed him. David stepped in line behind them. Chief Dark Wolf and Moonflower stood and after a moment of indecision followed the others. One by one it seemed that the entire gathering formed a slow procession.

"We love you Father. Forgive our offenses. We did not trust you. Help us to trust. Teach us about Your Son and bless us. Jesus died for us. We accept Jesus as Your Son. He came to save us from the fire, and to lead us to heaven. We know because He is your son, He still lives. He will live forever. We want to live forever with You God. Live with us Father God. Live here in our hearts. Make us strong. Give us faith. Make us one." Sarah's voice was loud and clear as her words crossed the lake. She stopped before the cross, beside the little church, turning to face the people. Moon Boy walked beside the cross and then suddenly lifted his gorgeous head and gave a loud, long whinny. It seemed that all of nature was agreeing with her words.

"If you want Jesus to come into your life and into your heart with His forgiveness, power, and blessings, come and kneel here by the cross." The priests chose to lead by example. They knelt. The entire village surged forward. They gathered around Sarah, touching her and touching the cross. Dancing Willow knelt and smiled up at Sarah.

"I know. I have known since Blue Stone was bitten by that snake. Thank you Sarah."

Tears slid down Sarah's cheeks as she realized that she was seeing the harvest from the seeds she had planted during the years that she had lived in the village. She glanced around to see David standing beside her. Slowly he lowered to his knees.

"Now I understand a little. Will you teach me more?" he asked.

"We both have much to learn," she answered joyfully, as she brushed away the tears of joy that continued to spill onto her cheeks.

Father Bob stepped near her.

"You are an angel. You have done in one evening what I have been trying to do ever since I arrived!"

"No. I have just brought them to the cross, now you must teach them what it means," she said. Father Pete hugged her and began to play his guitar loudly. Soon the "Alleluia, Holy, Holy," rang across the lake, as the people sang the song they had learned from him.

Chief Dark Wolf and Moonflower stepped close and each greeted her with affection. Moonflower was crying with joy that her daughter had returned but also she had a new stirring of joy in her heart that had never been there before. The darkness had been lifted.

The men of the tribe gathered around Sharp Knife and welcomed him back. Each one was eager to hear of his journey and how he had found her. They assumed that he and Sarah were back to stay. David knew that he would not be staying long.

As people talked and sang, Sarah eased her way back to camp. She told Moonflower that she wanted to quickly change her clothes and then see if she could help Sweet Grass.

Sharp Knife had brought her saddle and bundles and placed them inside the communal tent. Moon Boy was standing near the back wall where someone had tied him and given him a basket of water. She hugged his neck gently whispering in his ear.

"Thank you, Moon Boy, for that big "amen" at just the right moment." She slid her hand down his back and patted his rump as she left. Pretty Mother proudly stood beside her beautiful son. Bending Grass had gladly performed the chore again that he had been given by Brave Sparrow long ago. Thunder was also there, tethered away from the fire and people. He had been given water and grass was plentiful.

When she slipped into the warm comfort of the big tent she could see the instant relief in Sweet Grass's face.

"Oh Sarah, Thank you for coming. I was hoping you would come soon. Singing Wind slipped into a deep sleep as soon as I put the poultice on his burns. He hasn't moved at all. I didn't give him anything for pain except the willow bark in the poultice and nothing to make him sleep. I don't understand," she said.

Sarah nodded as she examined the burns and the color inside his lips.

"He sleeps now from the potion he drank before the ceremony. I don't know what he drank, but it must have been very strong. Let's not give him anything else until that wears off completely. In the meantime we should clean him up and get the paint off his face and hands. His knees are cut. It won't hurt to put some of that bear grease and clover on them after his legs are washed."

The two healers removed his ceremonial costume carefully, appreciating the work that went into its making. They replaced them with simple clean leather trousers. From his bare chest to his bare feet, he was covered with a blanket when Blue Stone, and Dancing Willow, entered the tent.

"Will he be alright?" asked his mother. Sarah waited allowing Sweet Grass to answer.

"He is sleeping now. That is good, because when he wakes he will have much pain. His arm is badly burned, but he will live and he will use his hand again to play the flute when it is healed. Do not worry," she said reassuringly. His hair is a mess, but it will grow out again.

"Thank you," said Dancing Willow as they started to leave the tent. Blue Stone turned back to Sarah.

"Come to my tent tomorrow. I want you to see my baby."

"I will," said Sarah. "We want to see everyone before we leave."

"Are you leaving again? Why," asked Blue Stone?

"We will talk tomorrow," said Sarah.

Sharp Knife was having similar conversations with his friends. They all wanted him to stay, to marry Sarah and live with the people.

"I would, but I love her enough that I will go wherever she wants to go," said Sharp Knife.

"You are the man. She must do what you say!" said Jumping Bird. He laughed as he said it.

"Jumping Bird, my friend, you saw her tonight. There is such power in her spirit. Do you think you could tell her what to do?" The other men laughed, too.

"I can't even tell my wife, Spotted Fawn, what to do and she is shy and gentle. I certainly would not try to control Sarah!" said Night Hawk. The men laughed again.

CHAPTER NINE
OUR GOD IS A MIGHTY SPIRIT

Chief Dark Wolf found consolation in his usual spot on the hill overlooking the camp. The large communal fire had burned down to a soft glow and after the initial excitement, the people had drifted back, enjoying the food that had been prepared and then visiting, sharing the wonderful feeling of reassurance they felt inside.

Later the people returned to their own campfires to rest. He was thinking how strange it was that Sarah, after being gone so long, had appeared just at the right moment to take over the meeting after Singing Wind was injured. He wondered if it was possible that she had caused him to fall. No, I saw him drink that strong potion that Standing Lizard gave him. That is what caused it. He wasn't used to it. But it is amazing that she always seems to take advantage of a situation to convince the people that there is wellbeing in believing in her God.

"Well God, we all said that we believe in you and your son Jesus. Now what do we do? How do we know that you are really out there? How do we know that any spirits are out there? I think I will go talk to the Priests tomorrow. Maybe they can answer some of my questions. He rose stiffly and walked slowly back into camp. He could hear a baby crying somewhere in one of the tents and a woman laughing in another. The camp has returned to normal, at least for now, he thought.

The two Jesuit Priests knelt in the little church thanking God that they had witnessed the saving of an entire village.

"Perhaps in some small way we helped to water the seed that was harvested into faith tonight," said Father Bob.

Later, he poured two cups of strong coffee and made two sandwiches of crusty bread and venison roast. They had been so invested in the happenings of the evening that they had not eaten at the feast.

"I will remember this night for as long as I live," said Father Pete, "nevertheless I have the sin of jealousy. I wish we had been blessed with being the vessels that brought them all to the cross."

"Yes," said Father Bob, "That was a powerful experience. We should start immediately in the morning, encouraging the people to come to classes, so they can be instructed about Jesus and be baptized. They must get baptized as soon as they are ready."

The next day Sarah and David spent visiting here and there with people that were special to them.

Snow Star carried Watching Owl out of her tent and placed him in Sarah's arms, Moonflower began to weep.

"Sarah, you can't leave again. If you do I won't be there when you marry or when you have your babies. I won't hear them laugh, or see them walk. You must not go away again. Please stay with us. We have all missed you so much." Sarah felt a tear escape her own eyes as she held the beautiful baby boy in her arms. Sarah didn't reply to Moonflower.

"Snow Star, he is wonderful and heavy, too! What is his name?"

"He is Watching Owl, and I agree with mother. There is no reason for you to leave again. You went away to find your people but instead you found Sharp Knife. Can't you see you are one of us? No one thinks of you as different, but you are special. Everyone knows that. We all love you and want you to stay."

"Snow Star; mother; I did find my people. I have a white brother named Ben. He loves me and has waited all the years I grew up here, hoping to one day find me. I have a whole family there. Now that I have found them, I can't give them up again! Please try to understand."

"Sarah, we do understand, but we love you, too," said Snow Star. She took Watching Owl and walked to her tent. She tucked him in for his nap and lay down beside him already feeling a sense of loss.

"I wanted her to see you. At least she did get to see you," she said to the baby as she closed her eyes and tried to calm her emotions.

David came close and whispered.

"Would you like to go to the woods and look for weird rocks?"

"No silly," she said laughing and feeling embarrassed as she allowed him to wrap her in a lasting hug.

"Are you having a nice visit?" she asked.

"Yes, but I have spoken to everyone here that I really missed. When do you want to leave?"

"I would like to head out in the morning if that is alright with you," she answered. It was sooner than he expected, but he didn't say so.

"That's fine with me, as long as we are together." He smiled his brightest smile and moved away with a bit of pride, feeling the envy of several young men that had observed them.

Bending Grass hurried to Sarah's side delivering a message.

"Chief Dark Wolf is on the hill outside of camp and he wants to talk to you."

"Thank you, Bending Grass," she said. "Do you know that you have grown so much that I wasn't sure it was you when I saw you. Thank you for taking care of my horses last night." Her comment on his size gave him pleasure and he stretched to his tallest as he walked away smiling.

Sarah glanced in the direction of the hill and saw Chief Dark Wolf sitting in the grass there.

As she approached she gathered her arms full of grass and after sitting beside him, she began to weave a simple mat.

"Yes father? Bending Grass delivered your message."

"Brave Sparrow, do you remember when we sat here and talked so long ago? I told you that I was troubled about the future of the people?"

"Yes father, I remember. Are you still troubled?"

"Yes, but for a different reason. I am sure that the village will have a good leader in Flying Eagle one day. He would have it be today if I would step aside," he said with a little chuckle. "We have many young, strong hunters to provide meat for the camp. The woman plant and harvest many new foods. We all eat well. We prosper just as you said we would. Brave Sparrow, you are wise far beyond your years. You were a little girl when I brought you here. How is it that you know so much about your God?"

Sarah wasn't sure how to answer, until she remembered another time long ago, when Chief Rising Eagle, Dark Wolf's father, had questioned her. He had asked her about God, too.

"Our God is a mighty spirit. He is strong and loving and wise. He gave the words to me that I spoke to the people. He knew that I needed His help. I needed Him to teach me how to tell the people about Him and so He gave me the words. He will always give us what we need, as long as we honor Him. He feeds and cares for the smallest animal, why would He not care for His children?" He nodded but didn't ask anything more about God. Instead he asked her if she loved Sharp Knife.

"Yes, I think I do."

"Will you marry him?" he asked.

"Perhaps, one day, when we are ready."

"When will you come back again to visit us? We will look to the day." Sarah was surprised that he would ask.

"I will come when the spirit moves me Father." With that, she finished the mat and handed it to him with a flourish. "Here, a gift to keep your backside clean," she laughed. "Let's put a stone on each corner so that the wind cannot steal it." Chief Dark Wolf stood and looked down at the mat and then at the beautiful woman beside him.

"Thank you," he said, "Not just for the useful mat, but for coming to visit us. It will be good, on long nights when we think of you, and know that you are safe and well." They walked slowly together to the front of the communal tent.

"I will say good bye to everyone in the morning," she said to him, as she ducked into the big tent to check on Singing Wind. Finding him resting comfortably, Sarah hugged Sweet Grass.

"You have done well for him. You remember all that I taught you. Also, remember to ask help from God, The Great Spirit. Learn more about Him from the priests. Now I need to go peek in Blue Stone's tent to visit and see her baby daughter. I may not have time in the morning. I will be leaving. Is there any question you have that I can help with?"

"No Sarah, but I wish you were not leaving again. There is so much more that I could learn from you."

Sarah smiled and stepped out into the cool evening air. As she crossed the center of camp many people greeted her. They all would have liked her to spend time with them.

When she scratched at the flap on Blue Stone's tent, Running Deer opened it wide.

"Come in Sarah. Sharp Knife just left a few minutes ago. Were you looking for him?"

"No, I came to see this precious little one," she said, as she gently picked the baby girl up from the furs. She is beautiful. Tell me her name."

"She is Happy Song. I named her that because when she was born, Singing Wind and Gray Cloud played a joyous song on their flutes. She makes me smile. I always have a happy song in my heart, since she was born. When Running Deer comes in and picks her up, she laughs and we laugh with her."

Sarah stayed for a little while longer sipping tea and enjoying the company of her best friend until Happy Song was asleep.

"It is late, I must go back to visit with Moonflower and Chief Dark Wolf. We will be leaving after the morning prayers tomorrow." Blue Stone clung to her as if she could change her resolve, by not letting go.

"I will miss you. I love you Blue Stone," said Sarah as she stepped out into the dark night. The camp was quiet. Many tents were shut tight and people slept. She knew that Moonflower and Chief Dark Wolf were not sleeping.

Sarah enjoyed her time with them and shared pieces of her new life with her family; just little things, beautiful things that they would think about, when she was gone.

She told them about her home and the carved pictures on her bed. She told about Dart Away following her and that he had sired a handsome foal. She never gave specifics of the location, and didn't tell stories that would include information about where her home was located. Sarah thanked Moonflower for always taking good care of her and teaching her many things. They talked about Singing Lark, and Talking Mountain, but not Rising Eagle or Yellow Bird. That would have stirred emotions that she didn't want to examine again. It was very late and heavy clouds filled the sky when Sarah left their tent and slipped quietly into the communal tent where her sleeping furs were arranged next to David's. He was sleeping soundly.

It rained during the night and the dawn brought a cool crisp morning. Sarah opened the tent as she had so many times before and sang praises to God and said prayers of thanksgiving and asked blessings on the new Christians within the village. To her surprise others drifted in quietly sitting down near the banked fire or standing just inside the door. As she peeked outside she discovered that many were gathering outside. She stepped outside and was embraced first by one and then another.

Moonflower and Chief Dark Wolf waited at the edge of the gathering until Sarah and Sharp Knife were almost ready to leave. Their horses had been readied and bundles secured when he and Moonflower stepped close. She wrapped her arms around her daughter.

"I love you Sarah. Wherever you go my heart goes with you. I have a gift for you. Many of our young people have learned to work with silver and the blue stone. This cross was made by one of them and given to me. I want you to have it." Moonflower slipped the cord over Sarah's head. On her chest lay a silver cross three inches long with a polished piece of the blue stone in its center.

"This is beautiful, Mother. Thank you. And thank you for raising me as if I had been born to you. You are a good mother. I am glad that you have Snow Star and Watching Owl to keep you company when I am away. You are in my heart. I will visit again one day." Sarah did not want anyone to see her tears as she swung up on Moon Boy. Her smile was a bit too bright as the tears threatened to spill onto her cheeks.

"Come back soon," Chief Dark Wolf said, holding her hand for just an instant. Quickly she turned Moon Boy and headed toward the little church leading Pretty Mother. The priests were standing outside it, near the path. David and Sarah stopped just long enough to shake hands and to ask them when they would begin to teach the people about Jesus. Father Bob replied that they were going right away to ask Chief Dark Wolf if he would talk with them about classes they wanted to hold in the church or the big tent.

"Good," she said. "We will pray for you," the priest said at the same time.

"And we will pray for you," said Sarah as she eased Moon Boy onto the path that led to the trees at the backside of the lake. They intended to take back enough of the turquoise to give as gifts for everyone at the ranch.

The priests watched them ride into the trees and then Father Pete, with guitar in hand, suggested they get started.

"Let's go talk to the Chief and plan some classes and story times." Father Pete strummed his guitar as he strolled along the well-worn path to the village. Soon he had children skipping along in front and behind him. He had caused enough of a stir that most of the village knew that the priests were in camp.

Chief Dark Wolf didn't really want to talk to them so soon. Sarah had just left. Moonflower was in their tent crying and his own heart felt heavy as he approached the group around the priests. Father Bob and Father Pete stood up in respect to the Chief. They had settled on a log that rested near the ashes of the communal fire.

"We came to talk to you, if you have the time," said Father Peter.

"Yes I will talk with you. Come to the communal tent." He looked down at the giggling, energetic children and told them to all go back to their mothers. They scampered away still giggling.

The large tent was cool and dark after the bright sunshine outside. Singing Wind was sitting up and eating soup. The fire felt warm and inviting as they sat down near it. Sweet Grass was uncomfortable near the black robes, and immediately asked if she was needed or if it would be all right if she stepped out. Chief Dark Wolf nodded and she ducked out quickly before he could change his mind. He smiled thinking that he felt the same way. He didn't want to be in there with them right now either.

Moonflower wiped her eyes and stopped crying. She knew that Chief Dark Wolf would expect her to offer food and drink to the priests. It was her responsibility. Snow Star had started a large kettle of water heating and had added several herbs. She was filling a large wooden platter with crackers, as they turned brown on the sizzling rocks. She had placed a bowl of honey in the center. Another platter was ready to receive slices of the cold roast venison. Moonflower began to slice and place the pieces on the platter in a pleasing fan shape. At the base of the meat she put a generous scoop of the cooked wild apples she had taken to the communal fire. They were tangy and sweet.

Sweet Grass was feeling guilty for ducking out of the tent. She knew that she should have offered them food or something to drink. It was the polite thing to do. She scratched on the tent flap just as Moonflower was ready to transfer the tea and trays of food to the big tent.

"Hello Sweet Grass. Did Chief Dark Wolf send you to get me?"

"No Moonflower, but I came to see if I could help you. I thought you might want to bring food and tea for the priests." She lied.

"Oh Moonflower, I am sorry, that is not the truth. I just didn't want to be in there with the priests so I asked Chief Dark Wolf if I could leave." Moonflower looked at the young face of the girl and suddenly realized that she had neglected the girl. Sweet Grass lived in their village with only an older brother and Slow Foot, his wife. She had no mentor to talk to or teach her the things a young woman should know. Moonflower had heard rumors that Slow Foot, did as little as possible in her own tent and wasn't about to help Sweet Grass with the communal tent. She had listened and learned well from Sarah, but they had worked on the healing arts. Sarah had not had time to teach her everything. Moonflower made a personal resolve to spend more time with Sweet Grass. There are many things that she could learn. She will probably never do all the things that Sarah did, but she could enjoy doing some of them, she thought as she stepped up into the tent.

Moonflower and Sweet Grass carried the tea and trays to the Chief and his visitors. They set the trays in front of the men and quietly handed each a cup of tea. The men were deep in conversation. When the women stepped back out, they wondered if they had been noticed at all.

Sweet Grass followed Moonflower back to her tent and sat down on the furs.

"You look tired Moonflower. As healer, I think we both need a short nap." Both women laughed as they made themselves comfortable on the furs. They knew they wouldn't be needed for a while. Moonflower closed her eyes. Sweet Grass studied Moonflower's face and knew that many of the lines she saw there had been caused by worry. I wonder what she worries about. She is wife to the Chief. She doesn't need to worry about anything. I wish she would tell me all about Sarah. Where she came from and where she goes. Where did she learn so much? Everyone in the village loves and respects her? I wish I could be like her, she thought as she drifted off to sleep.

Snow Star was free from the responsibilities of watching her baby for a while. Morning Dove had volunteered to take him to her tent to entertain him so that Snow Star could go to the lake with other young women and catch fish for their evening meal. She peeked in the open doorway of Moonflower's tent and saw her asleep and Sweet Grass there asleep on the furs as well. That is odd, she thought, as she moved quietly away.

"It is good," said Chief Dark Wolf as he watched the priests walking back toward the little church.

"What is good?" asked Growling Bear as he approached.

"The priests will come to a communal fire tonight to tell their stories."

"I was going in the morning, but if they are going to be here tonight, I think I will ask the men to leave for hunting this afternoon," snapped Growling Bear. "I like our old stories better."

"Yes, so you have said before. You will leave in the morning. I have promised the priests that we would all be here." Growling Bear mumbled under his breath and kicked up a cloud of dust as he scuffed his moccasin, heading back to his tent and a meal that Big Flower had prepared.

*****

Snapping Turtle stopped by the herd and watched as the pair of young horses, he and Growling Bear had selected, frisked and played in the grass by the lake.

Soon Singing Wind will be back playing his music and watching the herd, he thought. I hope that he can forget all that Standing Lizard taught him. He was a nice young man before he went to study with him.

He strolled over to the pen where the boys were doing their best to sing for the sheep. He smiled to himself. He had been around a huge herd of sheep in his youth. That was before his father and their family had traveled because he had been forced to leave their village after a fight with one of the other men in the tribe.

I can't remember anyone having to sing all the time to the sheep, he thought. Well it's nice. The horses like their flute music. Why shouldn't the sheep like their special song? He chuckled as he approached Growling Bear's tent.

As usual, Big Flower was spoiling him with loads of attention and more food than he wanted or needed.

"Big Flower, would you mind terribly if I borrowed Growling Bear for a few minutes?"

"No of course not, but I would like him to rest this afternoon. The Chief wants us all in the communal tent for the Priest's stories tonight, and you are both leaving in the morning to hunt."

"Yes, thank you Big Flower. I know you are looking out for his best interest. You take very good care of him. I wish my Butterfly did less flitting about and more pampering like you do," he was smiling broadly. She wasn't sure if he was sincere, but hoped that it was a compliment.

As they walked away from the tent, Snapping Turtle steered his friend into the woods behind the tents. He didn't want to be overheard by anyone.

"I have been thinking about something for a long time now. Ever since that meeting we had before the last buffalo hunt. First I want you to know that I am saying this as a friend. You and I both know that it is inevitable that you and Flying Eagle will eventually end up fighting. I want to help you to get ready. I want you to get stronger and I can show you some tricks that will help you fight smarter."

Growling Bear didn't know what to say. He felt offended and yet glad that he had a friend that was openly willing to support him; someone who understood what he was going through.

"Why do you think I need to be stronger? I am the top warrior of our people? The hunters still step aside when I come," he said proudly.

"You are and I want it to stay that way for a long time. Here is what I had in mind," said Snapping Turtle, as he led Growling Bear, deeper into the trees. "Look. I have cut trees in different lengths. If you roll them, it will strengthen your arms and legs and back, too."

"This was a lot of work and took a long time to prepare. Turtle, I really appreciate this."

"Also see, I have brought rocks of different sizes, two of each size. I think that if you work hard, you will be even stronger. If you accept a challenge from him at the summer games, a win there in front of everyone should hold your position for many years to come."

"If I do this, I don't want anyone to know what we are planning and I think it would help to practice all the games we play there, but how can I do that here in the woods?"

"Well my friend, I am not talking about just playing games. Hawk is not here because we thought it unwise for three of us to leave camp together, but he helped me prepare all of this and said to tell you that Flying Eagle intends to challenge you in every game. He thinks that you will get tired because you are older. I think if he loses in several of the games he will challenge you to fight. You must be ready to accept his challenge with any weapon."

"He cannot justify challenging someone from his own people!"

"I feel that he will find a reason. His pride will not allow him to fail at the games without retaliation. I know what I am saying is true. I have heard what he says when you and the Chief are not around. He too is forming a plan. He will oppose you at every game you enter. You must get ready."

"Turtle, you and Hawk are true friends. How do I begin?"

"Hawk and I thought you should start with the smallest rocks and throw them as far as you can, first right and then left, one with each hand. I will mark where they land. Next you should throw the ones that are a little larger and try to hit the same mark. Each time I will mark where they land. You will see that as the days go by, you will throw the heaviest as far as you can the lightest ones today."

"Did you try this yourself, Turtle?" Yes when we thought of it, but I am not as strong as you are. I am embarrassed to say how far they went." They laughed together easily, as the exercise began. One after another, Growling Bear threw the rocks as far as he could, first with one hand and then the other. Finally, Turtle suggested that they should take a break and he produced a water bag that had been conveniently stashed in the nearby bushes.

"You thought of everything. How can I thank you and Hawk?"

"We want you to humble Flying Eagle; that will be thanks enough for us. We know that it is inevitable that he will one day be made Chief, but he is in too much of a hurry for everything. He hasn't learned that respect has to be earned. We think you are the right person to teach him. If you are rested, maybe we should head back. Big Flower will surely have a scolding fit, if I keep you any longer.

Growling Bear chuckled as he walked out of the trees alone and Turtle strolled through the trees, over to the sheep pen.

"You know, I was wondering when you boys planned to shear those sheep. It will be hot soon. They will be glad to take off their winter coats."

As he walked away, both boys appeared very puzzled by what he had said. I am guessing that I am the only one in this whole camp that ever saw a sheep get sheared. I guess I should go talk to Chief Dark Wolf about it. The women will have fun using wool they didn't have to gather from the prairie after the buffalo go through.

Snapping Turtle was right. No one knew about it. The shearing of the sheep, without the proper equipment became a tedious job and a spectacle that brought most of the village near to watch. It took several big boys, to hold one sheep, while Snapping Turtle gathered a handful of wool and carefully cut it off with the sharp blade of his hunting knife. It took two days and a lot of gentle patient handling to complete the job. I am glad we haven't more, he thought.

"Next year, I think you boys will be able to do this without my help," he suggested. They were not eager for the honor of being guardians of the sheep and this chore added to their concern that the people would see them as sheep boys and not strong young hunters.

Each day when Snapping Turtle finished, he walked into the lake and swam with his clothes on until he felt clean. The only good thing about this was that it was a diversion so that Growling Bear could go to the woods both days without anyone noticing or wondering where he was.

At the edge of the lake, Growling Bear watched as Turtle came out of the water.

"Thank you, Turtle. I am doing well, but I find that my muscles are very sore."

"That is a good thing. Perhaps soon we will try the logs." Growling Bear moaned and then laughed as he walked to his tent.

Snapping Turtle knew how much work it would take to get Growling Bear in condition to return after the summer council, with the high status he held now. It was the goal of Hawk and Turtle to have him return with much more.

As the mid-summer meeting approached, Night Hawk went with the other hunters for a large hunting expedition. They hoped to replace the supplies used during the harsh winter months.

"It would be nice to return to a camp with full caches and ripening corn," said Chief Dark Wolf.

"Yes, you can't count on the buffalo meeting you on the trail as you head home," said Flying Eagle. He pulled his horse up close to the Chief on his left. On his right, in his accepted position rode Growling Bear.

Immediately the air grew tense. Everyone felt it.

"What do you suggest we do?" The Chief asked.

"We should go where the herds are. They go near the water, this time of year," said Flying Eagle without much thought.

"I haven't seen any herds circling our lake," said Growling Bear with a laugh. He loved to provoke the young man.

Now that he was confident that he could take him in a fight, he treated him with less respect.

"Let's go past the big rocks toward the Silver River. Many animals enjoy the cool of the trees there. It would be necessary to bring the meat back swiftly, but if we are successful it will be worth the effort," said Chief Dark Wolf.

When they entered the big rocks, The Chief deliberately crowded his horse left, forcing Flying Eagle to rein in his horse and wait while the passageway was used by the Chief and then Growling Bear. Flying Eagle's face grew dark red with rage.

"Your time is coming old men. It is coming sooner than either of you thinks!" He said it under his breath but his lips moved enough that Night Hawk decided to take advantage of the moment and sympathize at the first opportunity, to gain his confidence. He rode his horse up beside him, as soon as possible.

"You are the Chief's son-in-law. You should be riding beside him. After all, you will be Chief of our people one day. It is difficult for your hunters to watch you being treated with less than you deserve," said Night Hawk.

"Oh, you saw that, did you? I am sure that Growling Bear is not the man he once was, but it is difficult for the Chief to see it. He is old, too."

"Yes, I am getting older, too," said Night Hawk. I don't think I will enter many of the games at the meeting this year. My back has been bothering me."

"Well I intend to enter plenty. I have been working with a new bow and it shoots farther and more accurately than any I have ever had."

"Did you make it yourself?"

"No, I traded a large blue rock for it."

"I would love to see it. That isn't it. You have carried that one ever since you came to us from the Omati. I remember it because it is handsome, with its silver tips.

"I have been practicing with the new one but I keep it in my tent. You will have to wait to see it until we leave for the summer council. I will carry it then."

"It will be fun to watch you compete with it."

"I will do more than compete. I will win with it!"

"I used to be good at the log roll, but I don't think I will try that this year."

"Night Hawk, you should enter. You are still very strong. Just don't pick the red log."

"Why do you say that?"

"I have a way of knowing that anyone that rolls the red log will lose!"

"Flying Eagle, that is for a shaman to say. You can't know that."

"I know because I have a friend who prepares the logs. He is the one that measures, and cuts them. He also is going to color them this year, but before the people see it painted, he has been soaking the red one in water, all spring. It will be a lot heavier than the rest!"

"Flying Eagle, that is not honest. That will ruin the game. If the council hears what you are doing, they will drive you and your friend from the summer meeting. You might have to leave our village, too. Even though you are married to Snow Star, the Chief's daughter, he will have to send you away. Why would you take a chance like that for a silly game? It's not worth it!"

"Lower your voice. Someone could hear you. I shouldn't have told you. You are the only one that knows, so if others find out, I will know who to come to. Won't I?"

"I am sorry Flying Eagle. I wish you had not told me." He rode along silently for a long time until they stopped inside the edge of the trees. The Silver River sparkled before them and they were able to water their horses without being seen at a place where the trees grew to the water's edge.

Sleeping Bear had been riding ahead, watching for animals. He hurried back to the Chief to tell him what he had seen.

"The white men are moving many cattle down from the north. They are on the other side of the River and they are coming slowly. If we wait until they are at the wagon crossing, we can stampede them across. They will run far and we will be able to keep them moving until they are near our camp. There it will be easy to take the meat we need."

"It is a good plan. How many men are with them?"

"They are many, but we are more."

"We will be able to remove the men that guard them and bring the cattle through the water ourselves."

As Chief Dark Wolf and the hunters watched from the trees near the Silver; they discovered that their plan was not a good one. The army had sent a column of soldiers to help.

In the morning, one hundred would be taken to a field behind Fort Connor. The remaining one hundred were on their way to Mary Parker's land. They would have been easy prey for the Indians, had they stayed to watch the activity in the early light, but as the soldiers and cowboys, bedded the herd down for the night, they came to the wrong conclusion that the soldiers would escort all the cattle to the fort and guard them there. Chief Dark Wolf headed his hunters back toward the village.

CHAPTER TEN
PREPARE AND GROW STRONG

Night Hawk struggled with the knowledge that he was supposed to keep secret. He wanted to tell Snapping Turtle and Growling Bear. I can't let Growling Bear enter the log roll, knowing what I do. It could change everything!

Finally he decided that he would ask Chief Dark Wolf.

"Chief, do you know how the hosting village makes sure the games are honest?"

"Your question surprises me. How could anyone cheat? We stand in a row and everyone has a turn to shoot at the target. Each man chooses his own bow and arrow. If he is closest to the mark more times, than anyone else, he wins. It has never been something to think about. Why do you ask?"

"I was just wondering if an old man like me would still have a chance at the log roll. That was always my best game. I would like to win a game and make Spotted Fawn proud of me."

"She is proud of you, Night Hawk and you know it. We all know that you have an advantage because you have very strong arms and short legs!" Both men laughed at that and Night Hawk felt better. He had decided what he would do.

The days of summer grew hotter, and the people began to mention the summer council more often. Each tent always prepared a bundle of food to take to the hosting village. It was at least as big as the bundle of supplies they brought for their family to use while they were away from the home camp. This was done as a token of appreciation for the time and effort that was used in preparation, to receive so many people into their area and hunting grounds. It was always held in the same location on the nights of the new moon, four moons after the first spring grass turned green. No one minded if a village arrived a day early or a day late. The games waited until all the camps were represented. This year they would be the village that provided the prizes for the games. Much effort, time and hard work had gone into the planning and preparations. They would provide many exceptional prizes and unusual meals for special events like the weddings. Each took planning and time.

Growling Bear became more irritable as the morning neared that they would all leave. He disappeared from camp sometimes on foot other times on horseback. He varied the direction of his exit and Big Flower worried more than ever. She feared that his absence was caused by displeasure he felt toward her.

The day before they were to leave, Big Flower walked to the lake to wash herself and their son, Little Cub. Tears came to her eyes and she couldn't stop them. She sobbed as she darted into the church with Little Cub. She felt she could hide there. No one came here except when it was time for stories, or lessons. She sat on a large bundle of grass and began to weep uncontrollably. Father Bob heard her. He wasn't sure what he could do for her, but he wanted to comfort and console her. He sat down on the dirt floor beside her and handed her his hankie. He gently picked up her son.

"This is a fine boy. You must be very proud of him. What is his name?"

"He is Little Cub. I should go." She stood quickly, regretting her actions."

"Please don't rush away. You just got here."

"I must go. I have much to do. Growling Bear will be angrier. We leave early tomorrow for the summer council. I haven't finished my preparations. Thank you," She said softly as she left.

Father Bob was totally puzzled. What a strange visit that was. But now I know that they are all leaving in the morning. I wonder why she was so upset. He knelt and prayed for her and her son. Hoping that the Holy Spirit would reveal to her an answer to her problem, whatever it was. Father Pete entered the church soon after and joined in the prayers.

Just as they walked out of the church, they felt a slight vibration under their feet. Then a very loud rumble shook the ground.

The water of the lake danced and splashed slipping far to the other side, as the side nearest the church rose, sending its water crashing through the village. The hill, with the church on it, lifted straight up. The cross, the church and the two priests were pushed upward and then slammed back down in place! The cross fell sideways and landed in the edge of the lake which was now more mud than water. The church creaked and made snapping sounds but stood strong. The priests fell on the grass where they had been standing.

All the tents near the lake were flooded with water. It ran into the many food caches, soaking the dried food stored there. As the water rushed through the village, it tipped over tents and cooking pots, quenching fires, causing women and men to scream and yell, as they struggled and fell, trying to gather their family.

The ground beneath their feet rumbled and moved cracking open to gulp and swallow the water in the immediate area, before closing again to open somewhere else. The water that had once filled the lake was tipped back and forth in damaging waves among the tents and common area. Trees in the woods tumbled to the ground showing their roots.

The poles of the communal tent began to sway under the added pressure of the water, pushing on the leather sides. The earth beneath them trembled and grumbled. They tipped and dropped, pulling the entire huge tent to the ground.

Large fountains of water sprung up on the bed of the lake, covering the few flopping fish and creatures that were left there. The water bubbled and sprayed.

The young man guarding the herd of horses had not been able to do anything to stop the horses from stampeding. They rushed this way and that, panicked, by the motion and sound beneath their feet. They scattered, some to the far woods, while others ran into the boulders, frightened and confused. They disappeared. Only the sheep stayed where they had been. The fences of their pen were shaken loose and fell, but they crowded close to the young men that had bravely continued to sing their song, through it all. Their pen was near the back side of the lake, between the church and the woods. They had been badly frightened but remained dry.

Growling Bear ran from the woods and didn't stop until he had searched the area and found Big Flower and Little Cub. He wrapped his strong arms around them protectively and held them tight.

"It will be alright. You are alright. Look at me," Growling Bear commanded. "Do not fear. The priests told us that the people would be baptized, and that all wrong would be washed away and all would be made new. He just didn't tell us that God would do it all at once and in such a frightening manner!"

"What? You can't be serious. How can you make fun of the priest's beliefs at a terrible time like this, Oh, Growling Bear, I am sorry that I have displeased you. I know you have been staying away because I have not been good enough. Please forgive me, I will try harder," she wailed.

"What are you talking about? You have done nothing to forgive. You are a good wife. My only fear when the ground shook was that you or Cub might be injured."

Just then the rumbling began again. The ground lifted and a wave of water pushed Big Flower down, forcing Little Cub from her arms. Growling Bear grabbed him, just as he bobbed under the water. The water covered Big Flower and then receded, rushing away in the opposite direction.

Water poured into the ground where it had split open just in front of the little knoll where Chief Dark Wolf had been sitting. The fissure opened directly in front of him. It was too wide for him to cross. He clung to the sod where he had been thrown and found himself peering down into the vast opening. The walls of the huge fissure were coated with stripes of blue stone as far down as he could see. He stared in amazement as just as quickly as it had opened; it closed, leaving only a ragged line in the grass. Hesitantly he jumped over it and ran to find Moonflower and Snow Star. Their tents were lying flat in the displaced water. Snow Star held Watching Owl tightly and stood with her feet firmly planted, bracing herself for another tremor, when he spotted her. The small boy was screaming loudly. She struggled to walk away from the lake water and called Flying Eagle's name, over and over.

"Snow Star, where is your mother?" She seemed not to hear him.

"Snow Star, where is your mother?" She looked at him and slowly pointed.

"Over there, in the communal tent with Sweet Grass. She was over there!"

Chief Dark Wolf slogged through the water and mud trying to comprehend what was happening.

"She can't be in the big tent. The big tent is down!" He shouted.

Both women were pressed flat by the heavy wet leather of the tent. They could not see what had happened. They were in total darkness. Sweet Grass screamed and started crying. Moonflower lay beside her. She knew that something was holding her down, something even heavier than the many hides of the tent.

"Sweet Grass, stop that crying," she ordered sternly.

"Listen to me carefully. The girl tried to contain her sobs. "You are near the door. We were knocked back by the water, but only a few feet. Try to slide toward the door."

"Moonflower, I can't. I am scared. What if the water comes again? We will drown."

"Can you move your legs?"

"Yes, but my arm hurts really bad."

"Sweet Grass, you must be brave and strong or we will both die here. Slide toward the door. I would if I could but I am held down by one of the big poles. It is on my leg. I need help. Sweet Grass, you have to slide out and get help."

"I will try, but I am not sure which way the door is. Wait, I can feel the rocks by the fire pit but the water may have moved them too. Now I know how far back we are. Oh, Moonflower. I don't think I can do it!"

Sweet Grass began sobbing again loudly.

Chief Dark Wolf stood near the door flap to the big tent. He could hear the muffled sound of her crying.

"Men, come over here! We have people trapped inside the big tent." His heart was filled with fear at what they might find.

Night Hawk released his tight embrace on Spotted Fawn and their daughter, Nightingale. He ran to the Chief.

As soon as Night Hawk released them, his wife headed for the woods, away from the water taking their daughter with her.

Growling Bear placed Little Cub, back in Big Flower's arms.

"Walk away from the lake," he instructed her, before he ran in the direction of the Chief. He didn't see the dazed expression on her face as she pushed through the water and mud moving toward the trees.

Night Hawk dove into the space between the layers of leather, pulling out anything he could feel. Wet hides soggy grass and soaked furs were shoved beside his legs as he made slow progress. Growling Bear and Dark Wolf worked as a team removing the obstacles as they appeared. He continued moving forward until the weight of the tent, prevented his progress. He slid backwards and out.

"I think we need to shove something in to hold the leather of the tent up. It is too heavy to crawl further."

"You are not strong enough. Let me try," said Growling Bear. He followed the path made by Night Hawk and when he felt a foot move, he grabbed it.

"I have someone's foot," he yelled. "Bring me a big branch to shove ahead of me."

"No. You could hurt her. Is it Moonflower?"

He pulled on the foot and Sweet Grass howled.

"It is Sweet Grass. Can you bring me a short piece of log?"

Night Hawk brought a short log from the communal fire area. It had been used for a stool. Growling Bear rolled it ahead of him and continued to pull out debris.

"Can you get something to hold the tent open enough so I can see?"

Night Hawk looked around to see what would work. Another piece of log was not far away. He dragged it near and then, he and Chief Dark Wolf managed to stand it up, just inside the opening. Growling Bear could see Sweet Grass.

He reached for her feet and began to pull as he inched back. She screamed in fear. She was on wet furs and soggy grass. He realized then if he pulled hard enough to free her, he would cause her injury. He let go and slid out.

"We cannot pull them out without hurting them. We must cut the hides that cover them."

"I have my hunting knife," said Chief Dark Wolf. "We must do this carefully. We know there are two layers of leather and grass stuffed between them. If we cut carelessly we may cut one of them, also we must do it in a way that will be repairable, follow the seams." He handed the knife to Growling Bear who seemed eager to do it. He cut a small triangle and removed it, so that they could see inside. Night Hawk had located another knife and was opening an adjacent seam. Chief Dark Wolf spoke to them, instructing them. "Be cautious!"

"Moonflower, are you in there?"

131

"Yes, Dark Wolf, I am here but I can't move. The pole is on my leg. Please hurry, get me out of here. My leg is trapped. It hurts so much. I think it is broken. You will need many men to pull it off."

When they heard that, they began to call for help in every direction. Quickly the seams of the tent side were opened and Sweet Grass was gently lifted up and out by Growling Bear. Dark Wolf lay down beside Moonflower and took her hand.

"I am not sure how they will do it yet, but we will get that pole off of your leg."

The tremors had stopped and the priests hurried into the camp to help wherever they could. As they passed the slowly filling lake, they were amazed by the two forceful springs bubbling up in the middle of it.

A crowd was gathering around the flattened big tent and they walked in that direction. Gently and sympathetically they helped Sweet Grass to sit on a log. Father Pete examined her scraped arm and shoulder and said he would be right back. He swiftly started a fire in the fire pit outside the church and started a large batch of willow bark simmering. He prayed that they would be able to help Moonflower. Armed with a pan of hot willow bark tea and salve made of bear fat and clover, he headed back to doctor Sweet Grass. She was shaking. He wrapped her in the blanket he had intended to use to cover the wet log. He handed her a cup of the tea and began to gently cover her scrapes with the salve.

"What made these nasty marks on you Sweet Grass?"

"The pole's bark did it as it fell. It is on Moonflowers leg. She can't move her leg."

The priest bowed his head and prayed that Moonflower would not be seriously injured and that the men would work with wisdom in removing the pole so that no one else would be harmed.

As he looked around, he thought it odd that he saw few women.

"Where are all the women?"

"I don't know. They were here when the rumbling started."

Father Bob brought bandages and dry wood from behind the church, but he soon realized that all the fire pits were wet and some had puddles in them. He dumped his wood near one of them.

"It will take a day or two before things here dry up. Meanwhile, let's try to put one of the tents back up."

The men at the big tent felt helpless. They knew the pole was too heavy to lift, and hold up while others pulled her out. Moonflower suggested that they should find a stone that was a little bigger than her leg. Before long they had one there and it took six men to lift the pole up onto the rock and hold it there while two others got her out. Just as her ankle was about to clear it, the rock shifted in the soft ground and they couldn't keep the pole steady. It rolled off the rock and across her ankle. She cried out in pain!

As soon as she was free, they lifted her up and out of the big tent, through the opened seams, carrying her to sit on the log beside Sweet Grass. The soggy, newly-erected Chief's tent still held all the wet grass lining and belongings. Chief Dark Wolf flung everything in the tent out the door and onto the wet grass beside it, including the sacks of raw blue stones. He wanted everything out.

"Thank you," the Chief said to the two priests. "Can you help her? Her leg is badly injured. The big pole was on it here and then when we were getting it off, it rolled on her ankle."

"I will do what I can," said Father Peter. "Moonflower, you are calm. That helps a lot. Can you tell me where it hurts?"

"Here," she indicated the area that was red, purple and swelling rapidly. "Also here on my ankle."

Father Peter firmly grasped her leg and felt the bone as if she was a hunter. She gritted her teeth but didn't cry out.

"It is broken but I cannot tell how badly. I believe that it is in its proper position. I will wrap it with wet leather. We certainly have no shortage of that," he said with a smile. "Father Bob, can you find me something to use as splints?"

"I'll certainly try."

When he got back he saw that Father Pete had applied the willow bark that he had simmered for tea and was wrapping it with a strip he had cut from a wet hide.

"This will shrink so I have to be careful not to make it too tight. It will get hard and support the break." He handed her a cup of the tea and continued to work on the leg by adding the split branch that Father Bob had brought. He wrapped it again to keep them in place.

"Now let me take a look at this ankle. Moonflower, I know that it is hurting, but can you move your foot up and down?" She did. "Can you move it around like this?" He showed her with his own foot. She was able to do it but grimaced.

"That hurts a lot," she said.

"Yes, you poor dear, I know it does." He packed it with the last of the willow bark and then wrapped it loosely with wet leather and tied it in place with a cord he had found near her tent. Tears slid silently down her face as she looked around at the wet mess that had once been her orderly and well cared for home.

Father Bob had hurried to the church to get something to make a comfortable pallet for them to lie on. He stopped long enough to pull the cross out of the mud and put it into the church. Quickly he brought a fur from each of their beds and he was also trying to keep a huge bundle of dry grass, from dropping in the mud as he returned.

"Here, Father Pete, if you can put this down for her to lie on, we can prop her leg up with the grass and cover her with this one."

"That is good, but we need more. Bring all we have and have the children bring many bundles of grass."

"Father, the children are gone. They have all left the camp with the women. I don't know where they have gone."

"Then we will have to bring them ourselves."

They packed the tent with several layers of dry grass, hoping that it would create a barrier against the wet ground. Then with the furs down they took Sweet Grass in and asked her to lie close to the far side. Chief Dark Wolf and Growling Bear carried Moonflower in and placed her on the dry fur that the priests had provided. They put her leg up on a bundle they had ready and then covered her and Sweet Grass with soft furs.

"You ladies should rest now and we will see if we can help anyone else," said Father Peter.

"Father Bob, where do you think the women all went. It feels so strange with them gone."

"Yes, and I am thinking that God has shown us this for a reason, although I am not sure what it is yet. There are no women, no fires and no one is cooking food. We need to go make food. We can easily collect several big cooking pots, and make the biggest batch of stew that we can. Once it is cooking, we can come back and help put up another tent or two, before dark."

The ground on the hill of the church is dry and the area beyond it. We can lug some of the hides and furs there each time we go. Then we can work them as time allows. It is wonderful that as far as we know, no one was killed."

"Thank you, Lord, for protecting the people, in this camp today and for guarding their lives. We know that they probably don't feel like they are very blessed right now, but they will see it later on. Please help us to be your servants as we serve the people. Amen"

After starting four big kettles of deer stew and starting another one with willow bark, simmering, the two priests worked as a team pulling cups and bowls and spoons from the mud. They made a pile near their fire and returned to put up two tents and carry the water logged contents to the dry grass of the hill.

"It's hard to believe it but we need to go get some water to clean things. The lake is only half full and we can't go into that lake bottom mud or we will get stuck."

"I have an idea. I'll collect all the water bags that I can find and take them into the woods to that little stream where I shot the bear. Do you remember?"

"Yes, Bob, but that is quite a ways and it is getting dark. Let's collect the bags and maybe they will hold enough clean water to get us all through until first light and you can go then."

"Let's go check the ladies and take them some stew and tea and see if they have any idea where there are any water bags," said Father Bob.

They searched until it was impossible to see, and then they returned to the church with just four mud caked water bags.

The men came and appreciated the stew and a dry place to sit. Most of them stayed right there on the hill all night. Chief Dark Wolf went to his tent and stayed with Moonflower and Sweet Grass.

In the morning light Flying Eagle and Snow Star worked to put their tent back up. They pulled all the wet and muddy objects from inside and spread them on the grass by the church like everyone else. Night Hawk had not found Spotted Fawn but he was doing the same thing they were. He was struggling to do it alone. Growling Bear had his up, but he too had done it alone. Big Flower was not in camp. Very few tents were up. The men were getting worried. They had called and searched the edge of the woods, but the women were hiding, cowering in fear.

With a few more water bags located, Father Bob left for the little stream, with eight bags in all. His mules and Father Peter's horses had been near their shelter and they were all fine. He and Rudy knew the way. They took one other mule to help carry the full water bags on the way back.

Flying Eagle said that he would take a couple men and go hunting.

"I will not come back until I have food for the people," he said. "Perhaps we will find more of our horses on the way. Mine has returned and a few others. Some of the big work horses are in the edge of the far woods. We will need them to put the big tent back up."

"That is good, Flying Eagle. I hope you will find a good fat deer and more of our horses," said Chief Dark Wolf.

Flying Eagle approached the big work horses slowly and was able to catch them with the help of Snapping Turtle and Sleeping Bear. They led the team back to coyote, the young man that was watching the herd when the quake hit. They suggested that he take one of the riding horses that had returned and use it to find some more of the absent ones.

"Take time to fasten these to a tree before you go. We don't want to lose them again."

"Yes, I will, thank you, Flying Eagle."

Flying Eagle loved the deference in the young man's voice. He turned his horse quickly, so the other two hunters would have to follow him as he entered the big rocks. He stopped abruptly.

"Our path is blocked ahead. We will have to find a new path through. This may be why some of the horses have not returned.

They tried different passageways, each time having to turn around until finally they discovered a way through that brought them out on the prairie, near the wagon trail.

"We should go back and mark the new trail now so it will not be difficult when we return," said Sleeping Bear.

"I don't want to take the time. We have already spent longer than we should have getting through there. You go back and see if you can mark the path and return with a couple of pack horses."

Sleeping Bear had already intended to do just that, but he didn't like being told to do it by someone twenty years his junior.

"Where will you head so that I can easily follow?"

"I am hoping that we can find game along the path that the people take to the summer council. That area gets more rain and so there is good grass. Good grass brings the animals."

"That is a good plan. I will return and hope that we will be successful." Before entering the rocks again, Sleeping Bear thought about what he should do to mark the way. If I put something on the rocks and have to turn around it will be difficult to correct the marks. This time I will drag a stick, close to the rocks and if I make a mistake I can easily correct the mark in the dirt. When I am sure of the new path through, I will bring grease and mark the rocks with it. It will stay on long enough for us to learn the route.

Being a sharp minded tracker, Sleeping Bear didn't take very long to return to the young man doing his best to keep the herd settled and add to their numbers. Coyote had found three more horses and had been able to bring them out of the woods.

"You serve the people well, Coyote. I have need of two pack horses. Which do you recommend?"

"They are all still skittish, but I will be glad to help you choose two of them" Coyote was proud that this seasoned hunter had asked him.

Soon Sleeping Bear was on his way again, using a pouch of grease he had obtained from Father Bob and a leafy pine bow to paint a splotch on the rocks as he followed his trail and led the pack horses through the big rock area.

Flying Eagle and Snapping Turtle had headed left as soon as they rode out of the big rocks. They knew that the edge of the tall grass region was a likely place to see game. They preferred not to enter the tall grass, and if they had no success there, they would follow along the edge of the trees traveling west along the Hickory River. Sleeping Bear was pleased when he saw his fellow hunters ahead on the prairie. They had stopped to rest their horses and were waiting for him to catch up.

"We need to find fat deer so the grease will drip and sizzle and smell delicious. Our women are hungry by now. They have to overcome their fear and return to us."

"Yes, I miss Dancing Willow and Blue Stone and Happy Song. That baby is a joy. I don't like that they have gone out of camp. What could they be thinking?"

"Who knows what a woman thinks?" said Snapping Turtle, "but I know that I wouldn't mind eating a chunk from that deer you just described." They laughed together easily as they started out again, moving slowly across the prairie.

"Our horses are scattered all over the prairie. Look over there in the trees. That stallion has some of ours. I recognize that black and white paint and that one with two white feet. I've ridden her before," said Snapping Turtle.

"I know we are here to get meat, but I wish we could take our horses back before he leads them farther away from camp."

"It isn't possible to do both, but at least we know they are safe and look well. It is amazing to me that they are this far from camp. They must have bolted through the big rocks before the old path was blocked."

"They could have come through the woods and followed along the bluff," said Sleeping Bear.

"I see movement over there in the edge of the tall grass," said Flying Eagle. "It is too far to tell yet what it is. I don't want to shoot one of our horses. Let's move closer.

Go slow and be quiet," he instructed as if teaching a pair of novices. It irked the experienced hunters.

CHAPTER ELEVEN
IS IT THE SICKNESS?

After Mathew Morgan the blacksmith from the settlement had come to the ranch, with the report that many people were ill in Silverville; the crew of men that had come with Tom from the lumber mill, left the "S. and J. Ranch," abruptly and hurried back to town, filled with concern for their families.

It didn't take Sarah and David very long to gather the medicinal supplies that she thought might be needed. They followed the empty wagons back to town and found they were needed badly.

Even the men at Fort Connors were ill. With the help of Mathew Morgan, they went house to house caring for the sick, both young and old. Gentle Fawn and a soldier named John, were able to help at the fort.

When Sarah and David returned three days later, to the ranch, they were relieved that the people there were well. They had not gotten the sickness. She feared that the men that brought the lumber to the ranch could have also brought the sickness.

However, Sarah continued to sense a feeling of distress. She felt that something was very wrong at the camp of the Blue Stone People.

When they arrived, Sarah's worst fears were confirmed.

"David, it is not the sickness, but something terrible has happened here."

The orderly camp was not recognizable. The communal tent was down. Many family tents lay on their sides. The lake was brown and roiled as the new springs stirred the mud from the bottom constantly. The only thing that was the same was the small church. The cross was gone, only the pile of stones marked where it had stood.

They stopped but the priests were not there. She noticed that the cross lay on the floor of the church and had been cleaned. She thought that it would have been muddy. Everything she saw was wet and covered with mud.

"David, what has happened here?"

"Look, I see Chief Dark Wolf. We should talk to him first," he suggested.

"Where, is he?"

"Over there, with the men. They are trying to decide what they can do for the big tent so they can raise it again."

"It looks like everything has been violently pushed back, away from the lake."

"Chief Dark Wolf, Greetings," said David.

"Hello, Father," said Sarah.

He stood looking at them as if he didn't comprehend that they were there. The shock of what had happened to him, his family, and the people, was written on his face and frozen in his eyes.

He turned as if he was about to walk away.

"Father, what has happened here?" He stopped and finally acknowledged them, by answering.

"Your God has taken his anger out on the people! He shook the ground and tipped the lake into the tents of all of us. Some are injured. More are hiding in the woods. They fear that He may do it again, and your mother and Sweet Grass are badly injured. They were under the heavy wet leather of the big tent. We had to cut the seams to pull them out."

"Where are they?"

He walked away then without saying anything more and slumped down on the small knoll that still remained a place of consolation and meditation for him. It has been three days, he thought. Why aren't they coming back to camp to help?

They inquired of the men and found out that Falling Stones and Running Deer had ridden to the summer council, hoping to bring back a healer and to tell them what had happened.

"They left here three days ago, I think," said one of the men. "Maybe it was two days ago, I'm not sure."

"Can you tell me how Moonflower and Sweet Grass were injured?"

"They were in here," said Night Hawk. "I am sorry Sarah. One of the big poles fell on them. We are trying to get the ropes back in place so we can pull it away with the big horses. We have got to fix the base and repair the leather seams before we can stand it up again."

"Thank you Night Hawk. Can you tell me where they are?"

"We took them over there. The priests have been doing their best to care for them and everyone else."

"Why is no one cooking? Where are the women?"

"They ran into the trees and are gone. I am sure that they fear that the ground will shake again, or the lake water rise and dump on their tents. Only two came back. They are there in that tent. One is sick and the other is Big Flower. She just sits and won't talk. Her son, Cub, is with Growling Bear, over there."

"The priests have been making food and delivering it. They stood on the hill there in front of the church when it happened. I saw what happened. The whole hill lifted up, church and all and that's when the lake looked like it tipped and it dumped water over the whole camp. Fish were in my tent! I was lucky. I was able to put my tent back up quickly. None of the poles were broken. I pulled the wet furs out of it so they can dry. They should be worked, but there is no one to do it. I don't know where my wife, Spotted Fawn is. Nightingale was with her, so I guess they are together somewhere."

"Night Hawk, you have all been through a terrible ordeal. I think what we all need is a big fire. If the women see it, perhaps they will come back. Will you help me?"

"Yes, but we will have to go far to get dry wood."

"We will do what we must, to get things back livable."

David helped and soon they had a modest sized fire blazing.

"Night Hawk, has anyone gone to round up the horse herd?"

"No they scattered and they are not back. Coyote has found a few. Gray Cloud has been helping to get some of the tents back up."

"Ask him to come here please," she said. I hope he has his flute, she thought.

"Hello Gray Cloud. How are you?"

"I am alright. But so much is wrong that I don't know how we will get it all back the way it was."

"You can't. It will be new and different. It will be better. You will see."

"Do you have your flute?"

"Yes, I keep it here." He pulled it from a leather case that hung on his chest.

"Good, please go to the usual place that you sit, and play as if the herd was there. I think some of the horses will return when they hear the familiar sound. I noticed

Coyote sitting on the rock of the herd watcher. Does he have a flute?"

"No I haven't sensed that he wanted one. I will talk to Singing Wind and perhaps he will make him one."

"Has his burns completely healed? Can he play the flute again?"

"No, he still has pain but it will be better with time."

"That is good, Gray Cloud, but for now, let Coyote ride among the rocks and the far woods and to the north, to see if he can find any horses and bring them back. The poor things are frightened, too. Please play Gray Cloud. It will give comfort to all who hear it." He smiled as he walked toward Coyote.

Sarah ducked into the Chief's tent that Night Hawk had indicated. It was larger than most family tents but crowded. The priests had provided dry furs for them to lie on and she could see a kettle of stew near the door, with bowls and spoons that someone had collected.

"Mother and Sweet Grass, hello, how are you doing?"

"Sarah! Oh Sarah, I am so happy that you have come," said Moonflower, with tears in her eyes. "It is good that you have come. We have never needed you in the camp, more than we do now."

"Night Hawk told me that you were both injured when the poles of the big tent tipped over. Where are you hurt?"

"Your mother has been teaching me to sew. We were sitting together when the ground began to shake. The pole came down and hit my shoulder and arm. Your mother has a bad leg. The pole was on her leg for a long time until the men cut open the seams on the tent. Then they helped me out and were able to lift the pole up. They were holding it on a big rock but the rock tipped and the pole rolled off the rock and hurt her ankle and foot." She was talking fast and excitedly.

"I heard that the priests have been helping. Did they make willow bark tea? What have they done for your injuries?"

"The older one made us willow bark tea and he put some grease on my arm and the scrapes on her leg, but that's all. He and Father Bob have brought us food. They brought that stew a little while ago."

"Sweet Grass, are your legs hurt?"

"No, I told you, it is this arm and shoulder."

"Sarah was frowning.

"Step out here where there is room for me to check your injuries."

Sweet Grass did as she was told, but preferred to stay inside. She felt safer being cared for. Outside the tent something more might be required of her and she sensed it.

Sarah examined the shoulder and arm and decided that it was comforting that Sweet Grass really needed.

"I think that the Great Spirit loves you very much. That heavy pole could have hit your head and killed you. Instead all you have is a bruise and scrape marks. Here, is a piece of cloth, it is dirty, but it will make a good sling. You will only need to use it for a day or two," she said as she tied it in place. "There, now you can take this fur in your good hand and sit on one of the logs near the fire." Sarah stuck her head back in long enough to tell Moonflower that she was taking the stew near the fire and that she would be right back.

Sweet Grass is acting too young and too upset. I find it hard to believe that she is the sensible girl that I trained to be the healer for the people, she thought as she settled both the stew and Sweet Grass near the fire.

With Sweet Grass out of the tent, there was more room. Sarah was able to check her mother's more serious injuries.

"The priest did a good job of wrapping your leg. The bone is broken, but it feels like it is back in place. She examined it and replaced the bindings and support. Your ankle and foot are badly bruised and scraped too from the weight of the pole and rough bark. Can you move your ankle?"

"Yes, but it hurts a lot when I do. He packed it with willow bark."

"I will make a poultice. I brought many of my medicinal herbs with me. As soon as I get it made, I will put it on for you but in the meantime I will have a couple men help you out of here so you can sit by the fire, too."

"Sarah, do you think I should?"

David and Night Hawk carefully took her to sit near Sweet Grass. Someone had found a willow back rest and they put her where she could use it and be comfortable. Sarah returned to the fire with several pans, pots and cooking spoons. She found a brightly colored blanket that had once been beautiful, now in the mud being trod on. She pulled it up and scrubbed it as clean as she could at the edge of the muddy looking lake and tossed it over a thorn bush to dry.

"The sun and breeze is drying the camp. We need the women back to work the hides and furs or they will be ruined. David, see if you can find a drum and someone to play it. Also get someone to start bringing wood for the fire."

Sarah tied Moon Boy, Thunder and Pretty Mother near the center of camp where they could easily be seen. She knew that everyone would recognize her white horses. She started the plants simmering in a big pan, near the fire and then when she spotted the priests, she hailed them and asked them to bring their guitar and tambourine.

"We need the sound of a celebration. Please do your best to get something going that will bring the women back. They sang and played and once Moonflower felt relief from the poultice she clapped and sang as loud as she could.

Sarah carried several big kettles to the edge of the lake and filled them with the brown water and placed them within easy reach of the fire. Next she wandered the camp collecting drying racks until she had so many in a row that it was reaching nearly all the way around the fire.

Morning Dove came back and sat down next to Moonflower. They began to talk.

"I am sorry Moonflower, I felt like a coward, hiding, but I couldn't make myself walk back across the open grass where the tents and everything lay in the mud. I knew you were in the big tent and needed help. I should have come to you. Please forgive me." Tears slid down her cheeks.

"Morning Dove, there is nothing to forgive. You could not have helped me. It took many men. Thank you for coming back now, and soon things will be back to normal. You will see."

Next Dancing Willow and Blue Stone came out of the trees. She held Happy Song in her arms. Sarah hugged her and asked them please to sing as loud as they could. Snow Star came with Watching Owl. He was wrapped in the white rabbit fur blanket that Sarah had made so many years earlier. Somehow, Snow Star had kept it clean and dry. Dancing Willow and Blue Stone clapped and sang. People were talking, laughing, and singing.

Slowly Big Flower walked across the camp and took Cub from Growling Bear.

"We are going to be alright," He boomed. "We are going to be alright!" Big Flower laid her head against his chest and finally she was able to release the tears and fear, knotted up inside her. She sobbed and held tight to him. Chief Dark Wolf walked back from his little hill wondering if all this had happened so that he could be shown the wonders that he saw for a moment before the fissure closed. He sat down on a log near Moonflower. The woman that had been in the tent with Big Flower came out. She had been sick with fear. Other families were slowly reunited after days of panic and the added hardship of separation.

Sarah stood up in front of the small group gathered at the fire and simply said that her heart was rejoicing.

"You look puzzled. I am joyous, because the Great Spirit has protected the Blue Stone People. You have all sat at communal fires where your shaman has danced and chanted for the many spirits that he knew. You now know that the Great Spirit is the strongest, the fiercest, the mightiest, the most loving and caring of all. This terrifying event could have killed many. Not one person was killed. We have two women with healing injuries." More people slowly joined the group, coming out of the trees from every direction, wanting to hear what was being said by Sarah.

"I have gathered some drying racks but I am sure that we can find or make many more. All the meat and dried foods in the caches, must be brought out, rinsed in clean water and dried or it will rot. No one will have food to eat. The furs need to be greased and worked or they will be hard. The water in the lake is good and fresh. Dip in a pan and wait a little while. The brown that we see is sand being stirred from the bottom of the lake. I filled these pans just a few minutes ago. All we need to do is pour it into a different container. It is clean and clear. The sand is on the bottom of the pan. We can rinse the meat and hang it on the racks and it will be good. Let's all get busy before the meat spoils."

Many families strained to remove the wet fallen tents and wet furs and hides so they could open their caches. Some brought pans and kettles filled with lake water. The activity and voices brought still more people from the trees and surrounding area.

Chief Dark Wolf approached and wrapped his arms around Sarah.

"You have done what I couldn't. They will recover now. Look, I can see people at every tent. Soon things will be livable here again. Thank you, Sarah. Can you stay a few days? I need to talk to you about something important."

Of course Father, but first, I want to tell you and Mother something. It is a good thing." She motioned for David to join her. She took his hand and looked at him with a big smile. "David and I are going to be married. It will be here, by the little church and Mother you will be able to see my wedding. We will have a celebration feast and the people will be happy again."

Moonflower hugged her and then she reached for David and pulled him down where she could hug him, too. Snow Star was so happy at the news that she was bouncing.

"The camp is a muddy mess. How can we prepare a wedding and a feast?" she asked.

"Well I think we will all have to work hard to clean things up," said Chief Dark Wolf laughing out loud.

When the priests heard what she had said, they were concerned.

"She is not a Catholic. We don't know if she is even baptized," said the older priest as he headed back to the church.

"We must pray about this and get the cross put back up right away. It can't lie in the middle of the floor any longer."

The people worked hard the next few days to restore their camp. They were excited to hear that there was to be a wedding. Blue Stone worked harder than most. She had managed to keep her wedding dress and Running Deer's wedding shirt, clean and dry.

Their tent's location far from the side of the lake and the fact that she had wrapped them in old hides greased on the outside, just in case it rained when they moved back from the Omati all had been fortunate circumstances. She had hung the bundle with them in, high in the tent out of the way, all aided in preserving them from being ruined. Sarah and Blue Stone spent many hours adding leather to the bottom of Blue Stone's dress so that it would be long enough for Sarah.

"It is a darker yellow than his shirt, but it looks like it is a long red top with a yellow skirt," said Dancing Willow when she saw what they had done.

"We have done wonders considering that most of the dyed leather in camp is stained with mud. Try it on, with the head piece, Sarah," said Blue Stone. "You will look beautiful. This is so wonderful. I never dreamed that my special friend would wear the dress that I made and wore," said Blue Stone. She looked like she was about to cry.

"Don't you dare cry? This is a very happy time," said Sarah. "Now I need to do something about footwear and I need to ask Mother a question. I will be back later," she said as she slipped the dress and head piece off and carefully placed them in Blue Stone's arms.

"I can't believe it. Our Brave Sparrow is getting married," said Dancing Willow. She placed the dress safely inside her tent and hung it up with the shirt.

"Mother, how are you feeling today?"

"I think my ankle is much better, and I can't tell about the leg. It aches, but I am satisfied that it is healing. Sweet Grass is much better. She has taken the sling off her arm and I saw her scrapping a hide over in the shade earlier."

"That is good news. Mother do you know where the gray wolf fur is, that hung in the communal tent?"

"I think that the furs and all the meat have been removed. You should ask Sweet Grass. She has had women working, but I can't say who has done which ones or where they have taken them. The men made a lot of new racks for us and the meat was salvaged. That is the meat from the big tent over there. Sweet Grass found bags of wet salt and used it to rub every piece. She has been working very hard."

"Thank you, Mother." She spotted Sweet Grass helping to clean out a tent on the far side of the camp. I think that tent belongs to her brother, Sees Far and his wife, Slow Foot. All the other tents are up and opened to dry out. Theirs is the last one.

"Sweet Grass, How are you?"

"I am well. My shoulder aches a bit but mostly I am fine."

"That is good news. I have a question for you. Do you know where the big wolf fur is that hung in the big tent, the fur from the wolf that killed Red Fox?"

"Sarah, I don't know. The men brought armloads of heavy wet hides and furs to us over near the church. Many of us were working them. The ground there was never covered with lake water so it was a dry place to lay them all out. The priests said they didn't mind. Did you notice that they put the cross back up?"

"Yes, I noticed. Should I go over there and look? Are they all still there?"

"I don't know. I think so."

Sarah checked every hide, but the big gray wolf fur was not among them. She asked the priests.

"Hello Sarah. Tomorrow is your big day. David was here earlier. We have talked a lot with him. He is a nice young man," said Father Peter.

Sarah laughed at that remark.

"Of course I agree with you. I have a question. Did either of you see a big gray wolf fur here, when the women were salvaging the furs and hides. Many remain, but the one from the wolf that killed Red Fox is not here."

"Yes, Sarah, it is here. One of the women took special care to scrape and oil it until the leather was soft again. Come in the church and see. I hung it on the back wall for all to see each time they come. I didn't damage it. I sewed loops on the back so it can be easily taken down and put back up. I have been brushing it. I must also confess that I rubbed a little yellow ochre on the two sides, so it would look the same as it did. I hope that is alright."

154

"That is perfect. At the end of our wedding promises, I want to wrap it around our shoulders as we leave the cross. Is that going to be a problem?"

"No not at all. Are you sure Sarah that you don't want a Catholic Mass first and a longer service?"

"I'm sure, Father Bob, I just want to do what we discussed."

The camp was clean, and all the tents stood farther back from the lake, but in their proper positions according to status. Many had raised the ground in their place, to help keep rain and mud out. The flaps still stood open to allow moisture to leave. The grass in the linings was pulled out to allow air to circulate. The main area around the communal fire was dry now and the meat had been placed on huge woven mats waiting for the last bit of dampness to leave the ground. Most families were planning on digging new caches, in the back of their tents. The locations of most of them now would leave the old holes exposed to rain or snow.

Everyone had made an extra effort to dress in their very best clothes. Much of their clothing had been ruined or badly damaged, but each had located, polished and now donned their heavy stone necklaces.

No song to the sun god would echo over the lake this morning or any other morning from now on. The old woman was the last of her belief in the camp and she had given up the ritual that was frowned upon. She didn't think the lake was sacred anymore. She was still afraid of it.

Moonflower giggled nervously as Chief Dark Wolf and Flying Eagle carried her to a place of honor on the grass where she would be able to see the entire ceremony. Flying Eagle, Sleeping Bear and Snapping Turtle had left before Sarah and David arrived and they had promised

Chief Dark Wolf that they would not return until they had enough fresh meat to feed all the people.

They had returned just before dark with two deer. Snow Star had proudly prepared them both for the large fire that burned in the center of camp. Small fires burned in front of many tents, as good scents filled the air. The women had also salvaged some of the dried foods they had gathered and now they were doing their very best to make a wedding feast for a couple that was held in high esteem by everyone.

The lake had continued to fill until it was necessary to make a new path to walk around it. Its size now remained stable and the edges were clearing. They hoped that in time all of it would be clear again.

Sarah was not displaying her usual, in charge, manner on this special morning. She had been so busy during her time in camp, that she had not had time to acknowledge the serious step that she was about to make. It wasn't that she was questioning her decision. She wasn't sure why she was so nervous. She could feel herself tremble as she slipped the beautifully beaded wedding dress, over her head. Moonflower's tent was the second largest, and the only one large enough for Sarah, Blue Stone and Snow Star to all stand up in it, at the same time. The big community tent had not yet been resurrected. Chief Dark Wolf was determined to wait until the ground was totally dry before standing the big poles up again.

The messengers had returned from the summer council but after delivering their report to the council Chiefs, were unable to convince any of the healers there, to come back to the camp of the Blue Stone People with them. They had held a meeting and asked, but none of the healers could come. Their people were fearful to have their healers make the journey. The council gave their sympathy and the suggestion that the Blue Stone People plan on being the game hosts for next year.

It was just as well, now. Sweet Grass was nearly healed and Moonflower's injuries had been dealt with and she too would be well by the end of summer.

Dancing Willow was pleased that her husband and son-in-law were both back in time to attend the wedding. Running Deer was proud that David would be wearing his wedding shirt.

Sarah's hair had been washed and braided in many small braids. Now that it was dry, the braids were carefully removed, leaving a full head of wavy blond hair to compliment it, the head dress was placed on carefully and fastened.

"You are almost ready. I want you to wear this. I will get it back from you when you change out of the dress."

Blue Stone slipped the single Blue Stone, on a cord of yellow yarn and blond hair over her head very gently. She kissed Sarah on her cheek.

"There, my sister, you are ready and you look very beautiful."

Snow Star wrapped the white rabbit fur blanket around Sarah's shoulders.

"Wear this. You are shivering. Wear it just until you stand beside David. It is so special to me. This will add another memory that I can tell Watching Owl and his wife someday."

"Thank you Snow Star. I am blessed to have two sisters. I love both of you."

The priests were thrilled to be officiating at their first Christian wedding in the camp of the people. They had drawn lines with powdered chalk stone, on the grass, and had asked the people to seat themselves on the grass, on the outside of the lines. This left a four foot isle for the bridal party to use.

Everyone was there, seated and excited. What a difference Sarah has made in the people in less than a week, thought Chief Dark Wolf as he sat down beside Moonflower.

Both Gray Cloud and Running Deer had practiced with Father Peter, and now with the guitar and a soft drum beat the music most loved by the people began.

David whispered into the tent.

"Sarah, are you ready?"

"Yes, David, I am ready," she said as she stepped out to see a very princely looking man, wearing a yellow leather shirt and dark brown leather trousers. His hair was freshly oiled and braided with beads that matched the ones on the shirt he had borrowed. "You look very handsome," she said as she slipped the white fur around her shoulders and took his hand.

"There are no words to say how lovely you look Sarah. How is it that someone so special would choose to marry someone like me?"

"Silly, I love you. Let's do this," she said with a big smile.

The beautiful music, played softly and sung sweetly, greeted the amazing couple with praise to God. Alleluia, Holy Holy, Alleluia, Alleluia.

They walked slowly, past the sparkling lake, across the grass between the people and stood, in front of the cross, where Sarah had led the people to the Lord. She handed the white fur blanket to Snow Star and kissed her cheek as Father Bob, started the ceremony with a prayer of blessing, first for the couple and then for all the people gathered there. The promises were said first by David and then by Sarah, each made a special effort to say them loud enough to be heard by everyone. Finally the ring that David had made with love was placed on her finger. David kissed her and held her a bit longer than Father Bob would have suggested, but the people loved it. The flutes, guitar and drum changed from the soft sound to one of joy and celebration as the couple stepped over to her father. He held the authority and accepted the honor, to stand and to hand David the huge gray wolf fur.

"Sarah, come under my protection," said David loudly. The people applauded and laughed as David kissed her again and he wrapped the fur around both of their shoulders, and pulled her to him.

They led the people to the feast and Sarah took one final circle of the fire in front of all the people, wearing the beautiful dress that she and Blue Stone had transformed. She touched, smiled, greeted and laughed with each one before she stepped into Moonflower's tent and changed into the clothes she had worn when she arrived. Blue Stone stepped in and received the dress on her arms and then Sarah returned her single blue stone necklace. Sarah hugged her friend before she stepped out to find David outside, holding the yellow beaded shirt. He handed it carefully to Blue Stone, thanking her again for allowing him to wear it.

"This Blue Stone binds us together. You will always be my sister and friend," said Blue Stone as she tried to hug them both with her arms full. We will leave early in the morning. I may not see you then, but perhaps next time I do I will see you wearing this, too." Sarah slipped a large gold nugget into Blue Stone's hand. "Don't ask where I got it. I can't tell you right now."

Blue Stone looked at the large gold nugget in her palm, knowing that Sarah had another story to tell. Sarah turned to Snow Star and handed her a nugget of equal size and beauty.

"I love you, Snow Star." She hugged her tightly and then stepped out of the tent.

"David, the people are nearly back to normal, and you my sweet, funny, and wonderful man will always be my only love. We are forever together, but tonight you should enjoy the fun of the celebration and your friends, because we must leave at first light tomorrow to go home and plan another wedding."

"That's the Sarah that I know and love, practical and matter of fact. Sarah there is no one here that I want to be with, more than you."

They walked, hand in hand, until it sunk in what she had said about another wedding.

"Sarah, are you serious?"

"Come on, let's go to the feast,' she laughed. Sarah gave Moonflower a nugget, a bit larger than the other two. She thanked her for loving her and taking good care of her as she grew to be a woman.

When it came time for the little ones to go to bed, Sarah stood for just a moment and pulled David up beside her.

"We want to thank all of you for the love that you have shown us tonight and through the years as we were growing up with you in this camp. If you desire to give us a wedding gift, which some of you have indicated, I would ask this? Instead of gifts to us, give your hearts to Jesus. Love Him and Thank Him that you all are alive and the camp of the people is back in order. Thank Him and Praise

Him each and every day. Be glad that you are here and that you are The Blue Stone People.

Sarah and David left the camp before most of the people were awake. She glanced at the small herd and smiled at Singing Wind. He sat on a brown mare, riding slowly around the periphery of the area; occasionally he made a short side trip to bring another horse back to the herd.

"It was a good thing, coming when we did," said David. "I can't wait to tell Ben that we are married."

"David, you mustn't. That would spoil it for them. We can have Reverend Brown come and have a wedding in Ben's new house."

"Sarah, we are already married. I don't understand why you don't want to tell your family."

"We will, just a little later." She laughed and rode swiftly away on Moon Boy with Pretty Mother close to her side. Thunder instantly took the challenge and they raced across the Prairie toward home.

When they slowed their horses, suddenly Sarah remembered, Chief Dark Wolf said he had something important to tell me. I wonder what it was. I wonder if I should go back.

CHAPTER TWELVE
WE MISSED THE SUMMER GAMES

Growling Bear wandered around the camp, doing little things to help where he could, but he soon recognized why he was feeling at loose ends.

I worked so hard for many moons shooting arrows and rolling logs and throwing big rocks, and now we have missed the summer meeting and the games. If only that earth shaking had waited until we returned. Now I will have to keep working or I will not stay strong.

He stepped into his tent and put his arms around Big Flower's waist.

"Woman, you are the best wife and the best mother in this whole camp. I think you are beautiful and I like your cooking." He kissed her on the lips and then said, "Would you feel bad if I go for a walk in the woods once in a while?"

"No, I won't feel bad, now that I know you are not displeased with me." She smiled as he left her and walked into the trees behind their tent.

Snapping Turtle saw him go and he also entered the woods at a different location. He circled around knowing where Growling Bear was headed.

He smiled when he drew near and heard a large rock clunk as it hit its mark.

"Growling Bear, it is good that you still work to keep strong. I have something to tell you. Flying Eagle was planning on cheating at the summer games. He has a special new bow that shoots farther and more accurately than those made by hand by our men. He bought it at our trading spot and has it hidden. Even now after the shaking and water coming into our camp, I saw him ride to the far woods with a long, covered package across his legs. He still practices."

"So what if he practices? It does not assure him that he will hit the mark a year from now."

"There is something else you must know. Flying Eagle has a friend that prepared the logs for the log roll. He had him put color on them, so he could tell them apart. One of the logs had been soaking in water since early spring. It would be far heavier than all the others. It was to be colored red. He was going to make sure that you got the red one."

"Snapping Turtle you are a good friend. I must think on this."

"Maybe we will not have to wait an entire year," said Snapping Turtle. "Perhaps he will also grow impatient with waiting.

*****

The days of summer grew their hottest, and the women were glad to go to the woods on an adventure with Father Bob. He reassured them, that now that the children's shade area had been rebuilt farther from the lake and the story mothers were comfortable while caring for the little ones, that there was no reason that they could not go with him, with confidence that all was well.

"Bring your gathering baskets, and an empty sack or two. You never can tell what we will find. Bring a water bag and a lunch and wear your traveling shoes. I want you to be relaxed and comfortable. This has been a very hard year for all of you." He had been warned to stay away from the bluff, by Chief Dark Wolf, when he gave permission for them to use the woods behind the lake for the little adventure. The women work hard. It will do them good to go in the woods. It is cooler there, he thought.

Moonflower isn't ready to do things like that yet but her leg is getting better.

Growling Bear was upset when he heard that many of the women in camp would be walking in the woods. He did not want his practice area to be discovered. He and Snapping Turtle hurried to dissemble the target range and cover the rolling logs with brush.

"They are quite careless about observing their surroundings," said Snapping Turtle. "I think we needn't have bothered. If they had looked in our direction, they could have seen us, but they were all talking and looking down or up into the trees. Women are such strange creatures."

"Yes but it is hard to live without one," chuckled Growling Bear.

"It was a good thing, when you brought Big Flower back from the summer meeting two years ago, as your wife. Everyone knows that you truly love her and Little Cub. Now she is going to have another child. You should be very proud of her. I am glad for you."

"Yes, I may have another son before the coldest weather."

"They are lucky that we are not a wolf or a bear," said Snapping Turtle.

"They make so much noise that they would scare any animal away. We should return to camp. Let them have their little outing," said Growling Bear with a smile.

The women looked here and there to find good food to gather, but the weather had been hot and dry.

"The nuts are still in the trees. It is too early to gather them. Father Bob, why did you bring us here?"

"Soon you will have an answer," he said smiling broadly.

164

"I hear water," said Corn Silk.

"I smell water," said Dancing Willow.

"That is why we are here. Ladies you have worked so hard this summer. You can take one day to have a little relaxation and fun. Look over there behind those rocks and bushes."

"Oh, this is so beautiful. Look at the lovely little waterfall," said Dancing Willow.

"Thank you for bringing us here Father Bob," said Butterfly. She splashed the water over her face and hair and then fully clothed, she sat down under the falls and let it pour over her. He laughed, recalling that he had done the same thing when he first found it. They all gathered around, quickly dropping anything they were carrying. Footwear was pushed off and each carefully began walking in the shallow stream.

"You will find that it doesn't go very far. It disappears past those trees and flows under a big rock and is gone underground. I have never seen anything like it before. I knew you would enjoy it."

When she had finally cooled off, Butterfly followed the others cautiously walking in the water to see where it ended.

"Listen, to the delightful sound it makes, said Dancing Willow." She stood perfectly still with her finger to her lips to indicate that they should stop moving or talking."

"It sounds like music. How pleasant it is here. Father Bob, it is delightful. Let's get our things and sit here where we can listen to the water's music while we eat our lunch."

Butterfly wrung water from her skirt and long braid before picking up her things.

"I think you should all sit under the falls before we head home. It feels so good." She giggled and sat down on the grass near the others.

When we have finished eating we have a choice. We can nap, or we can walk a little ways in that direction, through the trees and we will be on the edge of the tall grass. We could pick a sack of grain before we head back. The only problem with that is that we will have to carry it back. We didn't bring pack horses.

When Big Flower returned late in the afternoon, to their tent, she found Growling Bear deep in thought. He did not sense her presence until she plopped down the heavy sack she was carrying and spoke to him.

"Growling Bear, we are back. I will go get Little Cub from the story mothers and then I will fix your meal."

"You don't have to hurry. I ate with Chief Dark Wolf just a little while ago. With Moonflower still staying off that leg, the people of the camp continue to take them more food than they can eat." He turned to ask her if she had enjoyed her walk in the woods but she had hurried away to get her son.

I wonder if she heard me say that I am not hungry. He stood in front of his tent for a moment and then paced off the distance to the edge of the new path around the lake. I think we have room enough. It could be done right here. He walked to the farthest tent and paced off the length of the camp, pretending that the large fire pit was not in the middle of everything. I think I want to talk to Night Hawk and Snapping Turtle as soon as I can get them away from camp.

"Chief Dark Wolf, good morning; Moonflower, how are you today?" asked Growling Bear.

"I am getting well. It is nice of you to ask. Are you alone and hungry again?" teased Moonflower.

"No, Big Flower takes good care of me. It is my eyes that are hungry to see more of our horses back. Sleeping Bear said that they saw many of our mares with a stallion on the prairie when they were hunting. I would like to take a couple men and ride out to locate them. Then we can make a plan to catch them and bring them back."

"Other things have been repaired or restored since the shaking of the ground, but not our horse herd. It remains scattered and leaves us vulnerable. I am glad that you are concerned and plan on doing something about it," said Chief Dark Wolf with a smile. "It bothers me, too."

"I plan on taking Snapping Turtle and Night Hawk. We will leave as soon as they are ready."

"Thank you Growling Bear, I can always count on you. Will two men be enough?"

"I don't plan on catching them, this trip, only to look and see where they are and what can be done to get them back."

Chief Dark Wolf nodded and stepped into the big tent to check the progress that the men had made. They had added many supports and the holes were deeper that held the biggest poles. He was pleased and felt that it would stand until the weather aged the leather so much that it had to be replaced. That will not be while I am Chief, he hoped.

Sleeping Bear had explained his markings on the boulders of the big rock area so well, that the three men rode through on the path with no hesitation. Coyote had taken the initiative to make sure that the big pots of water were still whole and filled with new water.

"Sarah was right about the lake water. It is clean and tastes fresh. The shallower edges of the lake are clear now and only the deep center shows the brown color where the springs bubble and stir it," said Night Hawk.

Growling Bear slid off the horse he was using and watered it. The others did the same.

"I didn't bring you here to talk about water. My friends we are here for two reasons. You must have figured that out, when I asked you and no others. The first is of course we must find more horses for our herd, but I want to get your opinion on something." They got on their horses and rode side by side as Snapping Turtle indicated the route they had taken when the horses were spotted.

They rode along quietly for some distance before Growling Bear spoke.

"One thing is for sure, Flying Eagle has not stopped practicing with his special new bow and I have continued to challenge my own strength. Do you think that we could hold the summer games in our own camp?"

"What are you thinking?" Night Hawk asked.

"I don't want to wait a whole year. He gets better and I get older. I need your help to make the center of camp as clear and level as the field at the summer council."

"We all felt bad that we missed the summer games. I think every man in camp will want to be involved in some way, but I don't see how that will resolve the problem. Flying Eagle had a heavy log made for you to roll. He cheated. He needs to be taught a lesson," said Snapping Turtle.

"Do you think we could make our own heavy log? No, I don't want to cheat, but we could make him think we did. We could make our own red colored log and make sure he gets it. It would be interesting to see his reaction. His guilt would convict him," said Growling Bear with a big grin. I think he will do anything that he can to avoid it." They laughed and offered ideas for other games, but the conversation always returned to the log roll.

"How can we color the logs? All the dye in camp was ruined when the lake spilled into the tents," said Snapping Turtle.

"That won't be hard. I see women in our camp wearing many skirts made of bright colors from the cloth they have received at the trading spot. We can get enough to tie strips of the cloth around each log, one blue, one yellow and one red."

"Yes we will make a point to put a red strip on both ends of the red log and if we wet the cloth in the lake and wrap it on just before the game begins, he will be sure the entire log is soaked," suggested Night Hawk laughing heartily. "This is going to be more fun than going to the summer meeting!"

They stopped for a few minutes, letting the horses enjoy the grass of the prairie while they ate some of the food their wives had packed.

"I think we should head into the tall grass and go all the way to the spring where the people camped when we hunted the buffalo. We are not in a hurry and if we get a chance to see the horses, we will be on the far side of them and maybe we can push them back toward the big rock area."

"That sounds like a good plan Growling Bear. That is where we saw them last time."

"They have no reason to move with water from the river, and shade from the trees and all the grass and grain they could ever want." Night Hawk knew that Growling Bear would have made a good Chief had the circumstances been different. He always thought things through completely.

"Night Hawk I need you to go back to camp and get Coyote and Gray Cloud to help you. I want you to string rope across the spaces in the big rocks so that the horses have to take the new path. I want them to be able to go right through if we can get them there. Put several hunters near the woods so they won't go that way. We don't want frightened horses running through the camp. People would get hurt. Tell Singing Wind we need him to play his flute for them when the time comes. We want them to slow down as they move through the big rocks. That area is familiar to the ones we had. Put some men in the far woods and some more on the north side of the horse field. If we get them back it will be a good thing for the people."

"I will do it but how can you two men get all those horses to go where you want?"

"Snapping Turtle and I are hoping that Sarah's God will make them want to go home." He laughed, but Night Hawk couldn't tell whether his friend was being sarcastic or if he meant what he said. He didn't claim him as his God, he said Sarah's God.

Growling Bear headed his horse into the tall grass and Snapping Turtle followed closely. Neither of the men liked riding in the grass that walled them in completely. Only the sun overhead gave them a sense of direction. They rode as quietly as possible. It always seemed like they were disturbing the natural balance of things, if they talked while in the tall grass.

When the people traveled to the summer meeting, they always hurried through this part of the journey.

Growling Bear spoke in a whisper as he slowed almost to a stop. He pointed up, showing Snapping Turtle the tops of the trees ahead. Like the good hunters they were, they knew not to talk out loud, just in case the herd was nearby.

"We will need to use our blankets to move them. I sense they are not far. I don't want to use our rifles at all. The calmer we keep them the easier it will be to keep them together. We have to manage to do that. If they scatter, we won't have a chance of taking them back."

"You are right, but I would like to put a rope on the two that we brought from the fort. I know I will recognize them right away."

"No that would stir them all into running, and we have only one chance at this. We just want to start them moving toward home at an easy pace."

"You are right, but when we get them back, I am claiming both of them. After this, the Chief won't deny me."

"I am sure he will let you claim them, if you can train them."

"Look they are right where we thought they would be. You were right. They had no reason to move."

"Well if you are ready, let's give them a reason!" With loud whoops and flourishing bright colored blankets the two hunters startled the quiet herd. They ran instinctively in the opposite direction that the men came from, with their stallion leading the way.

"As long as we can keep him heading the way we want, they will go with him." This was no slow walk through tall grass; it was a full out run across the clear prairie. The men slowed their mounts to an easy pace, not wanting to wear them out. If the herd grew tired, that was fine. It would make them easier to handle.

"All we need to do is just keep them in sight and moving in the right direction," said Growling Bear.

"It will be dark soon," observed Snapping Turtle.

"The full moon will give us light enough. They will stop if we don't push them. We will keep our distance but I want to keep them moving. Let's spread out and I want you to ride farther to the right. That should turn them slowly back toward the big rocks. I am going to drop back a little and then when the time comes I will circle around and leave them nowhere to go but into the rocks."

"It is a good plan, Growling Bear. You are a good leader." Snapping Turtle was worried that the horses that had carried them all day would be too tired to finish the job. Growling Bear had thought of everything else, but not being a person that invested time and love in animals, he didn't realize that his horse might not have a burst of speed just when he needed it.

"Growling Bear, we must rest our horses and give them water. They have carried us far. We need them to be strong."

"We can't stop now. The herd could get away from us."

"We have no choice. Look at them. Their heads hang down, and they will not go much farther. If we stop now, I think the herd will bed down. It is night and they are tired too."

"I don't want to stop. This will ruin my plan. If we lose them, it will be your fault!"

Growling Bear slid off and pulled out the waterproof pouch that Big Flower had put in his saddlebag. He was angry, but not at Snapping Turtle. He was thinking that even his wife had known that he would need to rest his horse and give it a drink. He was ashamed and feared that this flaw in his plan could cause it to fail. It was his fault and his alone.

"I am sorry Snapping Turtle. You are right."

Snapping Turtle was holding up a water pouch for his horse with both hands and softly talking to it. Growling Bear copied but his heart was not in it.

He sat down beside Snapping Turtle and waited impatiently.

"What do we do now?"

"Rest,' said Snapping Turtle, as he stretched out in the grass and yawned. With nothing to do, Growling Bear decided that he would lie down, too. He tied his horse to a nearby bush and began to snore as soon as he stretched out in the grass.

As the first light began to fade the stars of the late summer sky, Snapping Turtle nudged Growling Bear's foot.

"I think after another drink for all of us, that we should be on our way."

"The herd is still there, but the stallion has put himself between the mares and us. That is his job, to protect them. That is why they stay with him."

"Snapping Turtle, I am sorry. I am not wise about animals. There is much I can learn from you."

When the two men separated and Snapping Turtle began to ride a little to the right of the herd, the stallion took them away from his path and moved them to the left. Snapping Turtle looked over to the area that he thought Growling Bear would be riding, but he wasn't there. He was riding swiftly away to the left, preparing to get far enough ahead of them that he would be able to carefully turn them at the right time.

Snapping Turtle felt an exhilaration as the huge boulders finally came into view in the distance. Far to the left, stood Growling Bear, where he had dismounted and rested his horse. He got back up slowly, lifting the blanket and wrapping it around his shoulders. He walked his horse to the wagon trail and stopped with it facing the boulders like a sign pointing the way. Snapping Turtle slowed his horse to a walk, easy does it, he thought as the stallion stopped. His herd gathered close behind him and they too stopped. He is hesitant to enter the big rocks. I hope that Night Hawk and the others have done their job. If we can get him to start down the path, they will all go.

Snapping Turtle had to decide on his own what to do. It was too far to communicate and too late in the plan to change it now. He lifted his blanket above his head and spun it and gave a war whoop that prompted Growling Bear to do the same.

Snapping Turtle yelled and hollered as loud as he could, he was shaking the blanket and charging the back of the herd. The noise and strange sight startled the stallion and his instinct to fight was overcome by his preference for flight. He dashed toward the only opening that was visible between the big rocks. His herd followed! Snapping Turtle came closer, but softened the sounds he was making and lowered the blanket. Growling Bear did the same and approached slowly. The herd was crowding into the entrance of the path and the two hunters blocked the passage way so they could not retreat.

The beautiful stallion raced through the rocks and out onto the wide open space designated for the horse herd of the people. His herd followed breaking free of the path they pranced and immediately most of them seemed to relax. Numerous horses felt that they were home. The men in the far woods and on the north side cheered as they watched the drama unfold before them. Singing Wind played his flute with joy as he saw many of the horses that he had guarded in the past. A few strolled to the back side of the lake to drink as they had done before.

The women had been instructed to keep the children in the big tent until they were told that it was safe to bring them out.

The priests were amazed at the skill with which the hunters of the people had brought the horses back.

"Some of those horses are new. I have never seen that big stallion before," said Father Pete.

"I don't know how they did it, but I think this is his herd they have brought here."

"He is beautiful. Do you think he will stay?"

"No Pete, but it is just as well. He should run free.

CHAPTER THIRTEEN
IT IS DECIDED

The additional horses seemed to give the people back a feeling of confidence and protection. Falling Stones and Gray Cloud rode the periphery of the area. Coyote had asked Singing Wind to make him a flute and he had promised to do so. Singing Wind played softly and the horses watched as the stallion moved back and forth across the wide meadow. The opening to the path through the boulders was blocked by a many fingered branch, but that would only provide a feeling of security to the horses that felt this was home. He watched for his chance and the riders watched him.

Night Hawk caught the two foals with little effort and tied them to the back of his tent. He went to Chief Dark Wolf and was granted his wish to keep them as his own. In exchange he was told that he was to help with the herd until the new horses were all useful.

"Falling Stones, Chief Dark Wolf said that I may claim the twin foals, but I am to help you and Dark Cloud to tame the new ones and calm the others."

"Good, I am glad. They are a nice pair. I know you will give them good care. I have been trying to decide which ones have been used to hunt and which are new. We can certainly use your help."

"The one over there with white front legs, I know. She is still skittish, but has been ridden. Let me see if I can get her to come to me. I have crackers in my pocket. He talked to her and coaxed her but she backed up when he got near.

"This isn't going to be easy."

After getting his own horse, Night Hawk deliberately walked his horse through the herd, touching and talking to the horses he recognized. He stopped and leaned over, offering crackers or little apples, anything that Butterfly would part with from her stores of food. It wasn't long before he had several friends following him. He slipped a rope on them one at a time, taking time to go slow and making it comfortable for them. They were kept together tied to the trees at the back of the lake where they could reach the water and sweet new grass. The stallion had slipped away the second night, taking a couple of beautiful mares with him.

"We need a fence that we can put them in. We can't keep them with the woods on two sides, they can walk away anytime they want to," said Falling Stones. He had picked up many of the white man's ways while talking to Sharp Knife.

"I am going to talk to the Chief about it." He didn't know that Growling Bear had been talking to Snapping Turtle and had decided to talk to the Chief about holding the summer games in the camp before cold weather. Both men were about to propose projects that would require a lot of men and many days of labor. They arrived at the Chief's tent at the same time.

Chief Dark Wolf had been watching the work of his men in the meadow and was pleased. He greeted both of the men with a smile.

"You are making fine progress with the herd," he said to Falling Stones.

"Growling Bear, you look like you have something on your mind."

"Yes, I need to talk to you."

"Me too," said Falling Stones.

"Come lets go in the big tent and then Moonflower can rest."

As soon as the three men stepped in, Sweet Grass offered them tea or food.

"Thank you Sweet Grass, we are fine. You may go visit with Moonflower if you wish."

She left quickly, feeling glad that she had done her job, by offering.

"Now, let us talk. Growling Bear what is it that you wanted to talk about?"

"I prefer to wait. Let Falling Stones talk."

"Chief Dark Wolf, my request is simple, yet it will require much time and work. I would like to fence part of the meadow, so that we can keep the horses that are gentle together and keep the new ones from running away."

"Wouldn't that require two fences?"

"No, I am thinking one strong fenced area with a divider down the middle."

"How much of the field do you want to fence?" I'm not sure. It will have to be big enough so they don't eat all the grass up."

"Falling Stones, I think that is a good idea, but we need to give it some thought. We can have a meeting tonight and discuss it. Growling Bear, you did well bringing the horse herd back. We are all glad to see many horses in the field again."

"Many helped to bring them back, I will talk later." He rose and left the tent quickly knowing that the protection of the herd took precedence over games. He thought about it until his head ached. It all seemed so unfair. Evil plots against me, he thought.

Then in a flash, it came to him. We can make a game of building the fence. It will make fun of the work. It will go much faster.

"Who can cut the tree down the fastest? Who can dig a hole for the post the deepest? Who can throw the stones to hold the posts the most accurately?"

"What did you say? Little Cub was making noise, and I didn't hear you."

"I asked if you are feeling well."

"Yes, but I think this baby is going to be a big one."

"My poor Flower. You are tired. There will be a meeting in the big tent for the men tonight. You should go to bed when Little Cub does. Don't wait up for me."

"Thank you Growling Bear, I will do that."

Growling Bear was sure that his idea was a good one, until he saw Flying Eagle sitting with Chief Dark Wolf on the knoll overlooking the camp. He will talk the Chief out of it if he hears of it before the meeting. I need to talk to Night Hawk and Snapping Turtle. He wasn't sure if Singing Wind would think it was a good idea. That young man always seemed to think of things in terms of work. Growling Bear wanted to get several men in favor of his idea before the meeting.

Falling Stones had managed to get a rope on one of the new horses. She was pulling back and trying to free herself. Night Hawk rode up beside her and put his arm around her neck and scratched her ears. He talked softly and when she turned to bite at him, he put a piece of sugar candy in her mouth.

"How will you secure the herd during the building of the fence?" asked Growling Bear. "The men will make noise and frighten them."

"That is a good question. Have you any ideas?" Night Hawk said he thought that if they could just get them used to a rope, it would be possible to put them on hold lines on the far side of the lake, away from the work.

"I think the faster the fence is built, the easier it will be for you who work with the horses," said Growling Bear as he walked back to the main part of camp. He was still envisioning a set of targets at one end of camp with the men and their bows standing at the other.

The priest came up beside him and startled him when he spoke.

"What are you looking at Growling Bear?"

"Nothing in particular, I was just feeling glad that the tents are all up and dry and people are doing normal work. Night Hawk could use another batch of that sugar candy you make. They are trying to get the horses used to a rope so they can secure them before they start building the fence. There is a meeting about it tonight in the big tent. The faster the fence goes up the better for the men and the horses. I don't think they like a rope on their necks and it could be dangerous if something frightens the herd and they came running through here. Someone could get hurt."

"Yes, I agree. A fence would make it safer. I'll make the candy now and I'll see you at the meeting. You will come to the lesson in the morning won't you?" Growling Bear had moved away and didn't answer. He knew that the priests would talk and agree. The church stood near the herd. They would both come. That would be two more that would want it built quickly.

It was too hot in the big tent. The men gathered around the communal fire sitting on the logs, without lighting the fire.

All the men in camp had been notified and the men with families wanted a fence between the herd and their children. As soon as it was mentioned they were in favor of building it right away.

"It would be a good thing. It would protect the church and the camp," said Father Pete. "I would be willing to help and so will Father Bob."

"Growling Bear stood up to seize the moment. "If we make it a competition, it will be done very quickly. We can turn the work into games. We missed the summer games this year. This can be our own summer games."

Night Hawk quickly figured where this conversation was going and he stood and agreed, so did Snapping Turtle.

"The sooner the fence goes up the better. We are still losing horses. We can't stop them unless they are tied," said Falling Stones.

Growling Bear stood again and explained his ideas for games. The men liked them and added more. The Chief was pleased that he was not hearing dissension.

Flying Eagle didn't like the idea of games where he didn't have an advantage. He stood with a scowl on his face.

"How long will a fence stand that they rush through?"

"My men always do well no matter what they put their effort into. Cut wood is cut wood. Piled stones are a pile of stones and who can say a hole is bad?"

Chief Dark Wolf laughed and saw the smiles on the men's faces.

"It is decided. We will build the fences to hold the herd as soon as Gray Cloud and the other men can get ropes on the horses and get them all secured on a safe line."

"Growling Bear, would you like to plan the games and decide how the winner will be determined since it was your idea?"

"Yes, thank you my Chief, I will think on it and we will talk about it soon."

As he walked away, he already knew that he would suggest a stone toss. Hole-digging would test a man's strength, especially in the dry, late summer meadow. Chopping branches can be a challenge and then we can surprise them at the end when they think the games are over, by dragging and tagging a set of logs. I know Night Hawk and Snapping Turtle will help me with getting things ready. I will need to check with our craftsmen to make sure they have prizes ready.

*****

Growling Bear stood with his hands on his hips, looking first at the camp and then the horse herd from the vantage point of the Chief's knoll.

"Well, if you are really there, this will be a good time to show me. Sarah called you; "the Great Spirit" and nearly everyone in our village followed her to the cross by the church and said they believed in God's Son, Jesus. You know I am not moved by all the music and words that the priests read out of their special book. I don't like or understand them and I don't believe most of the stories they tell, but like I said, if you are real, I could sure use your help to keep me strong and make me even stronger. I am not young anymore and I will have another child to hunt for very soon. Oh yes, about that, they say that you control even the weather and are greater than all the other spirits. I would like another son. If you are there and are willing to do these things for me, then I promise I will go talk to the Priests and go to the lessons, oh, and thank you."

He strolled through the camp smiling but at the same time he was wondering if it was possible to make a deal with God.

Big Flower was not asleep when he returned. She was sitting up, sweating and moaning.

"The baby is kicking my ribs and hurting my back! Growling Bear, Please get Sweet Grass and Morning Dove. It is my time to have this baby. I am in great pain."

He ran through the camp shouting the news that Big Flower is having the baby! He stuck his head in the big tent, waking Sweet Grass with a shout and then rushed to tell Morning Dove.

"Big Flower needs you. The baby is coming," he said.

"All is well Growling Bear. Calm down. Please get Little Cub and take him to Dancing Willow. She will watch him." He ran back to their tent, scooping up the boy so abruptly that he frightened him and he began to cry loudly.

Sweet Grass gathered the things that she had been taught would be needed. Her hands were trembling as she pushed aside the flap on Big Flower's tent. Although she had the training, Sweet Grass was young enough that she doubted herself. Morning Dove was already there and calmed the young healer.

"Growling Bear, you cannot be here. Go to the big tent, or go hunting. This is women's work," instructed Morning Dove. Moonflower felt bad that she was not there to help Sweet Grass. Before the ground shaking, they had talked about it and Moonflower had promised her that she would be there. She sat in her tent feeling helpless.

"Dark Wolf, wake up. Help me to go to Big Flower's tent."

"No. Why are you waking me in the night to go visiting?"

"She needs me; I promised her that I would be there to help."

"Who needs you?"

"Sweet Grass needs help. She is still unsure of herself. I must go there. The baby is coming."

"Did you say that Sweet Grass is having a baby?"

"No Dark Wolf, Big Flower is having the baby and I must go there now!"

Growling Bear was pacing the middle of camp. He saw Chief Dark Wolf struggling to help Moonflower.

"Wait, I will tell the women. They should go to the big tent. Stay there Moonflower. My tent is too far and too small for all of you. I will ask them to come where there is room." He hurried back to his tent.

"Sweet Grass, and Morning Dove, can we move Big Flower to the big tent. Moonflower would like to be with you when the baby comes."

"Yes, Growling Bear, it is not too late to move her. We will help her. Start a big pan of water heating in the tent and then get out of there," said Sweet Grass. "From now on all babies should be born in the big tent." The women agreed that Big Flower needed room to breathe. They helped her to walk between contractions, and when they got there the tent flap was tied open and a small fire was heating a large cooking pot of water. Moonflower had instructed the men to start a second pan with willow bark tea and a third smaller one for Sweet Grass to use anyway she might need to. Old hides were piled high in the corner away from the door and one was spread out in front of them, ready for Big Flower to lie on.

When the three women entered, they were pleased and hugged Moonflower as they passed her and settled Big Flower on the area already prepared for her. Sweet Grass took over and handed Big Flower a branch that had been peeled.

"Bite this when you are ready to push." Morning Dove, closed the flap and tied it shut. "Moonflower is that Willow Bark tea?"

"Yes, I had them start a batch and they will bring more scrapings soon."

"That is good, but I want to add a few things to it, and we will have some tea also, but of a different kind."

From her corner in the back of the tent she brought two handfuls of medicinal herbs that she added to the willow bark and then in the smaller pan she poured crushed cherries and berries she had dried. Next she added mint to both pans and covered them.

"The big pan is hot enough," she said as she moved it away from the fire and placed a stack of soft white flannel cloths near Big Flower. "We have things now that we never had before. I am glad that we have the blue stones to trade and Snow Star to choose a few things that are very useful to women."

With a cup of tea in one hand and a fresh warm wet cloth in the other, she knelt beside Big Flower and asked her to drink all of it. She wiped her face and hands and took the cup back for a refill.

When the next contraction came, the women knew that it was time. Big Flower put the stick between her teeth and didn't make a sound. Morning Dove pressed her back forward and Moonflower held her hands tightly as she squatted over the old hide.

"One more push, one more and we will have a head. I see the baby's hair, lots of it! Push Big Flower, push your baby into this world."

She did push and after a lot more work, Big Flower found herself holding not one, but two baby boys. God had answered Growling Bear's prayer in a mighty way. They didn't know of his talk with God, but they were sure that something very special had just happened. There had been no signs that she would have twins. She had gone into labor, just at the time she had anticipated. These babies were big and healthy. They had not come early. It was no wonder that Big Flower had felt the pressure on her back and kicking on her ribs. The women laughed with joy and were delighted to gently clean and wrap the babies in the soft white diapers and blankets. The babies howled with loud and strong cries that amazed the camp. Growling Bear walked back and forth outside the tent flap until he could no longer stand the wait.

"I am coming in there now. Open this flap or I will cut the ties!"

"You may come in now Growling Bear," said Sweet Grass. Big Flower was sitting up smiling when he entered.

"I am glad that you are the best hunter in camp, because you now have three sons to raise and feed," she said. He knelt beside her with tears in his eyes. He picked up one and then the other placing a kiss on their cheek before returning them. Then he kissed her, and she saw his tears. "Growling Bear, I love you."

"Thank you Big Flower, they are my sons! I have three sons!" He bellowed. "Chief Dark Wolf, I have three sons!" He ran about the camp celebrating until there was not a person left that he had not told many times. Finally when he calmed down, he strolled out to the knoll that he had seen Chief Dark Wolf use many times when he was thinking and needing solitude.

"So, you are real," he said softly. "You have shown me that you create life. No one suspected that Big Flower would have two babies. You did this to make sure I knew it was your hand at work! You are the Great Spirit, just as Sarah said. Thank you for the gift of two sons. Now I know that you intend to make me strong enough to win the games and to sustain my position with the men. Fill me with the strength of youth, so I may see my children's children. Thank you, Jesus, Son of the Great Spirit."

At that moment he felt like he could do anything!

In the morning, he was disoriented at first when he opened his eyes in the big tent. He had fallen asleep beside Big Flower. Sweet Grass had a huge kettle of stew going outside, and another one of mint and lemon grass tea.

After again looking at the babies in wonderment, he dashed out saying he had a lot of work to do. He was cutting sticks to measure the depth of the holes for the posts but decided that the number of shovels available in camp would limit the number of men that could dig at one time. I need to talk to Gray Cloud and Falling Stones to find out where they intend to fasten the safe rope for the horses. We should start the fence on the opposite side. He spread the word that he needed every shovel in camp placed on the hill in front of the church by morning. They talked about how far apart the posts should be and how tall the fence should be. That determined the height of the posts. How they could fasten the railings to the posts became a problem until Falling Stones remembered that

Sharp Knife told how the man built a cabin by notching the logs so they fit tightly together.

"We can do the same with the fence. I think we should get the women involved in this job, too. They could make strong cord for us so we could tie the notched boards just to make it more stable," said Falling Stones.

Growling Bear saw the problem as another challenge for a game. This one was for the women. He sat down in the shade of the children's play area, and with a large handful of twigs, he constructed two fences. One was straight but not stable. The second miniature fence, he built by altering the path of the fence, first left and then right, back and forth. He blew on it and it stood, even without posts in the ground. This is how we must do it, he thought. It will be more work, but it will stand and be strong. The Chief watched from his knoll as Growling Bear paced off a pattern in the dust in the center of camp. He made lines and marks until he was satisfied then he motioned for his friend Night Hawk to come and take a look.

"We were watching you, drawing pictures in the dirt. What are you doing?"

After his explanation and his miniature demonstration, Night Hawk said he liked it and returned to the horses. He sent Gray Cloud and Falling Stones to hear his idea. Coyote had made headway with a young colt. He was now able to walk up to it and scratch it and pet it without it backing up. He slipped a rope over its head and let it hang loosely and then took it back off. He had worked with a young filly with the same exercise. They were watching him and listening to Growling Bear at the same time. He felt slighted that they didn't give him their full attention. Their comments were good but they hurried back to the herd.

Chief Dark Wolf had observed it all.

"What do you think of our new herdsman? He has a gift for the horses doesn't he?" he asked as he walked over.

"Yes I suppose so but that is not my concern. I have figured out a good plan for the fence. It will take more work, but we will have a strong fence that will last and we will have fun doing it."

"I heard about your request for the men to bring their shovels. I am glad that you are getting started with the planning. The sooner the herd is fenced the better I will feel. Maybe then we can all relax and feel as if we are back to normal. How are you going to turn hard labor into fun games of challenge?"

"I would like you to leave that up to me. I have already planned many games. There will be a need for the men to gather rocks to stabilize the posts and tree branches need to be marked to be used and measured. I would like to have a communal fire as soon as possible so that we can explain to everyone what we will need them to do to prepare for this year's games. Could we do it tonight?"

"I think tomorrow night would be better. Give the women time to prepare food and I will send the hunters out and hopefully they can bring back fresh meat." He walked away smiling and hailed Bending Grass to pass the word that he wanted to talk to all the hunters except those working with the horses and to tell the women to prepare for a communal feast tomorrow at sundown.

"Yes, my Chief, I will do it right away."

Growling Bear was pleased that the Chief gave his suggestion significance, and was turning it into a celebration of sorts. He watched Chief Dark Wolf sit down on one of the logs by the dark fire pit. That gives me an idea. We can use the young hunters to bring all the trimmings from the posts and rails to a big pile near here so that we can use them for kindling this winter. I will call it a fire race. The women each need to gather reeds and strong fibers to make the cord we will need. They should each gather their own supplies and be ready for the cord game. We can also have a fire starting contest for them. Then we can use the fires to char the bottom of the posts. They will last longer that way. We will need teams to help prepare the fire pits along the route of the fence and what should I do about prizes for the women. They usually don't participate at summer games. I will talk to Moonflower to see what she suggests.

Hunters began to gather around the Chief. Before long Growling Bear realized that if he stayed in camp, planning games, that Flying Eagle would automatically step in as lead hunter. He couldn't allow that now. He hurried to stand beside the Chief.

"Growling Bear, if you have too much work to do, you can stay here and the others can hunt," said the Chief.

"No that is fine. I can hunt and think at the same time," he joked. "I do it all the time." His hunters enjoyed his light hearted answer. He was not known for levity. They said they would all be ready in just a few minutes. Most of the men had located their favorite horses. The herd had new horses added, but some had yet to be found. The men would watch for their horses while they hunted.

Growling Bear had been using the same big brown mare since he had orchestrated the return of the herd. He had treated her with more kindness and respect since his moment in the field when she was badly in need of water and rest. She nudged his hand for attention and he slipped her a treat from his pocket. He had been tethering her separate from the herd and checking that she could reach water and grass several times during the day. Others had noticed the change in his behavior.

Big Flower was receiving help from many of the mothers in camp and they had a pouch of food and a full water bag ready for him when he rode up to their tent. Little Cub was with the story mothers and she and the new baby boys were asleep in their tent. The sides were rolled up just a bit and the flap was open to allow the air to stir through.

The many men that were ready had gathered at the entrance path to the big rocks. Father Bob was there, hoping that he would be welcome to bless the hunt and participate.

Growling Bear joined the group and listened as the priest asked God to make the hunt successful and to keep the hunters safe, and then he added, "Please keep our families and friends safe while we are gone."

"Father Bob, come ride with me," said Growling Bear. This put Flying Eagle again in a position to have to ride behind Growling Bear.

When the hunters reached the prairie, they hesitated, not launching out on their own until Growling Bear indicated the direction they should go. He directed some toward the Silver, while he led the others to the edge of the big grass area.

Back in camp the women worked and worried about their diminished supplies. Much of the food, prepared and dried, to be used for the feasts at the summer council had been destroyed. Something as simple as the feast for the next night placed a heavy weight of concern on the shoulders of the women. They worried if they would have enough food for the coming winter months.

Sweet Grass didn't have the status or influence of a prominent experienced healer yet, as Sarah had, but she felt that she should use the small persuasion that she had, to encourage the women to forage for food and hopefully the healing herbs and plants that would be needed. She wandered the woods and edge of the prairie beyond, ranging far in hopes that she could discover a new source of food for the people.

When she returned with her baskets less than full, she felt she was failing the people.

Moonflower sat in the shade beside Morning Dove.

"I heard that they are planning some summer games here. That is what the communal meeting is all about tonight. They are going to build a fence around the horse meadow and the women are going to be expected to make cord enough to help hold it all together," said Morning Dove.

"They should put pine pitch between the boards. That would help hold it. Once that gets on my hands, I have a terrible time getting it to let go," Moonflower rubbed her hands together, bothered by the thought.

"That is a good substance, but how would they get enough to do any good?"

"They will be cutting many pine trees down to make the fence. If we tell them they should tap them first and collect the sap, do you think they would listen?"

"Probably not; men are always in a hurry, but it is the right time of year to do it. The maple trees will soon start to give the sweet sap that is so good in the wintertime."

"I wish my leg was completely healed. I would go with you and we could tap a few to see if our idea would work. They would still need the cord but the sap would help to hold it, too."

"Moonflower, where are we going to get enough tough grass and fiber to make that much cord? It will be necessary to gather a lot."

At that point, Sweet Grass joined them and said that the dry summer was making it very difficult for her to restore her collection of healing plants.

"The men can only appreciate some of the consequences of this strange summer," she said. "If we could travel to the tall grass area with horses, we could gather the grain and use the stems to replace some of the woven things that were ruined. Many of my herbs grow there on the edge of the tall grass, because that area gets more rain than we do."

"That's it!" Morning Dove's exclamation startled her companions. "We need to go there; where there are supplies! We have to convince the Chief that they need to take us there! They can hunt while we work. If they want to have a women's game of cord making, they will have to hold it there!"

"We can have a contest on grain picking too. It can be fun. We should have prizes though. What can we offer as prizes that everyone will want?"

Sweet Grass creased her forehead as she thought hard.

"We have women that are experts in special skills. Morning Dove, you have made some of the most beautiful baskets in camp and Moonflower, your bead work is especially beautiful. I am glad that you are teaching me how to sew, and I saw one of the baskets that Corn Silk makes from the long pine needles. Perhaps she would part with one. Yes, if we could get them all to agree to pitch in, then we could have lovely prizes. Those of us with less crafting skills can help with chores while the women work on the projects for prizes," offered Sweet Grass.

"We will need to use pack horses to bring the grain and cord back. The stems of the harsh grass that grows there is strong and when mixed with the stems of the tall grain, it would work well for cords. Some of the baskets that we made in that area are still strong. They were dirty, but when we washed them, they were still useable." Moonflower was sure that the men would appreciate their contributions to the communal meeting.

CHAPTER FOURTEEN
WARRIORS FROM THE NORTH

Just then, Coyote rode into camp shouting.

"Chief Dark Wolf, Men have come through the north woods and Gray Cloud, Singing Wind and Night Hawk have stopped them there at the edge of the meadow. They told me to come and get you!"

"What men? Are they soldiers?"

He asked as he mounted the horse tied to the back of his tent. He always had one or more horses ready for his use.

"No, not soldiers, warriors from the north and they are hard to understand."

Chief Dark Wolf didn't hear the answer to his question. With reins in one hand and his rifle in the other, he rode swiftly through the field to the place where he could see his men and the strangers gathered. The intruders had slowly gotten off their horses, in an attempt to offer assurance that they intended no harm, yet Chief Dark Wolf and his men detected the remnants of war paint on their horses and an occasional little spot on their skin.

"Who are you? Where do you come from? How is it that you dare to enter the territory of The Blue Stone People?"

"We are all that remains of the Abalinah. Our Chief, Gray Fox, is badly wounded. He is there in the trees with our women. We are few. We are looking for help. We did not know of your camp. We were searching for anyone that could help us. We mean no harm to you or your people."

Chief Dark Wolf signaled that his men should stay on their horses. He slid down, carrying his rifle and followed

195

the man that had spoken, into the trees a short distance. On a well-padded travois, lay an old man with long, snow white hair. His highly adorned shirt was soaked with blood. Three women darted into the brush as he approached.

"How many of you, are there?

"We are few, my Chief, three men, three women, and our old and honored Chief. Do you have a medicine man that would be willing to help him?"

"First I must know what has happened. Where are the rest of your warriors? How was your Chief wounded?"

"People we do not know came into our camp as the sun god began to warm the grass. They rode into our camp from the sun. We did not see them until they were upon us. They swept through our camp and killed all they could find, men, women and children. They left our Chief in the dirt where he fell from their arrow. They burned our tents and took two of our women and a small boy. One of the women they took was mine. We mourn for the loss of our people and fear for the life of our Chief. He is my father."

The men, waiting on their horses could hear both sides of the conversation. Singing Wind glared with distrust at the three men standing in the edge of the trees. He felt that no good would come from extending kindness to this group. He could discern a definite evil intent.

When Chief Dark Wolf indicated that they should ride as far as the small building on the hill, and wait there, his men were very concerned. From that vantage point the strangers could view the entire village.

Chief Dark Wolf rode swiftly into the camp and stopped at the big tent.

"Sweet Grass, bring healing herbs and bandages, an old man has need of your help. They are taking him to the church."

"Why don't they bring him here where I have everything I need?"

"Woman, you have much to learn!" He stormed. "You must do as I say, and do it quickly!"

"Yes, Chief Dark Wolf, I will come as soon as I have everything gathered."

He stuck his head in the tent where Moonflower rested, and said that he felt that the people of the camp were in grave danger.

"Send the first person you see, to tell the women that they are to go to the woods and hide. They are to stay there until I say it is safe to come back. We all know they are good at hiding in the woods," he said with great displeasure.

Father Peter was preparing to say mass and was surprised when the strange men and women brought the very old and critically wounded man in the door and gently settled him on the soft grass on the floor.

His immediate fear was that the old man would die and they would seek retribution. His healing skills were very limited.

"Welcome, come in, would you like some tea?" He felt foolish asking but he hoped he could fill the time with something comfortable until someone he recognized came. He breathed a sigh of relief when Chief Dark Wolf entered.

"These people claim to be all that is left of the Abalinah. That is a people I do not know. They came through the north woods and they say this is their Chief and the biggest man's father. Can you help him? He took an arrow in the chest."

"Yes I can see that he is badly wounded. Why have they come to me? I am not a doctor."

"You must try to help him. It is not right to send him away. He will die."

"Chief, he will probably die anyway. Father Pete lifted the man's shirt off with the young woman's help and saw that the wound was badly infected. How long ago did this happen?"

No one answered until he looked directly at the young woman that hovered near.

"How long since he was shot?"

She answered but he didn't understand her. She held up five fingers and then added one from her other hand while shrugging her shoulders and looking puzzled.

Father Peter motioned for Chief Dark Wolf to step outside. The biggest man started to follow them, but Gray Cloud blocked the door.

"They are not telling you the truth. He has a gunshot wound. The bullet went all the way through. It looks at least three days old and it is infected. He has lost a lot of blood. Nothing has been done for him, not even the simplest wrapping to slow the bleeding. I will do my best but I don't trust them. We must stay alert."

From his vantage point, Gray Cloud could see the women in camp silently moving from the tents and disappearing into the woods behind the camp. Food had been quickly pulled away from their fires, covered and left to wait.

Sweet Grass felt her legs tremble as she walked the path to the little church. She was praying for the Great Spirit to come and help her, more now than ever before.

She was aware of the women exiting the camp. She was deeply wishing that it included her. She talked to herself as she walked slowly carrying two baskets and two kettles. You must be a take-charge woman! You must be like Sarah. Pretend you are Sarah and act like she would. You can't show fear. You must be strong. The priest is there to help you; hmm he intimidates me, too. Her inaudible pep talk was not as uplifting as it could have been, but she stepped in the church giving the impression that she was prepared to deal with the problem at hand.

Father Pete had a small pan of water steaming with willow bark scrapings and a larger one with mint, lemon grass and she wasn't sure what else until she stirred it and tasted the spoon. It was the root that put patients to sleep. Why was he making so much of it? Where did he get it? I wonder if he realizes what he has brewing!

"I am glad that his shirt is off and I want him off the grass and on a hide." The women seemed to understand well enough but didn't communicate clearly.

Sweet Grass prepared the crushed plant to fight infection and dumped the willow bark tea in with it and added a small amount of water. She had seen Spotted Feather's bullet wound and it was less than a day old. It was red and swollen, but not infected like this man's wounds. It appeared that they had not attempted to do anything for the old man, but drag him along with them. She stirred the big pan again, waiting to see what the priest was planning to do with it.

With the healing poultices in place she wrapped the bandage around and around his chest and back. "He is fevered. He needs to wake so I can get him to drink some of this," she said. The woman tried to wake him by speaking and patting his face, but was unsuccessful. Gray Cloud brought a pan of cold water in and placed it beside her. Sweet Grass timidly splashed a little on his face and he was awakened enough that the woman was able to hold the cup to his lips and he drank it down thirstily.

"Good, that will help him," she said smiling at the young woman. "I am Sweet Grass. What is your name?" She asked innocently. The big man stepped forward and pulled the woman back.

"She is Sheltah, Chief Gray Fox favored her. She is his last chosen."

While Sweet Grass had been busy treating the wounded Chief, Father Pete had made another batch of tea, with mint and lemon grass. He stirred sugar into the first batch and offered honey with it as well. The visitors sipped and then added generous amounts of the honey before downing the tea.

"Here have more," he said. Making sure the biggest man got plenty. Chief Dark Wolf took the cup of mint tea offered him and sipped it watching Father Pete as he added honey to his own cup. It was at that point that Chief Dark Wolf figured out what was happening. He watched as one by one the new comers sat down, leaning here or there. Before long they were all asleep.

"I didn't dare add a lot, Sarah gave it to me in case we might need it, to treat someone seriously injured. They won't stay asleep very long but maybe it will be long enough for a couple of our men to circle through the woods to make sure there aren't a lot more of them waiting to swoop into camp."

"Father Pete, you did the right thing. Thank you for being brave enough to do it. We will hurry. You better get a meal ready for them, so when they start waking up you can act like they were just resting after a difficult ride, and get rid of the rest of that tea."

"I will, and I think Sweet Grass should leave now and go somewhere safe."

"Yes, Go Sweet Grass, you did well. I am proud of you."

Sweet Grass was glad to leave and exhilarated by the praise of the Chief. She ran down the path, through the camp, passed the big tent and into the woods. She didn't stop until she saw Moonflower and Morning Dove hiding behind a bunch of bushes.

"What is happening? Why did he send word to us to leave camp and hide?"

"There are seven people in the church. They do not speak our language well. They talked very little. Three are warriors, one is an old man and he has been shot and there are three women. One woman is the old man's last chosen. I think that is like a wife. She stays close to him and seems fond of him although he is old enough to be her grandfather. Father Pete made a tea with Sarah's sleep medicine in it and they are all sleeping. Our men have gone to search the woods to see if they have others hiding in the trees. They will circle the camp, so pass the word that if any of the women hear a rider, just to continue to hide and be still."

Morning Dove, moved to her left and then to the right passing on what Sweet Grass had said.

"You were very brave to go to the church and help that man. I don't know if I could have."

"Yes, I think if Chief Dark Wolf told you to do it, you would. The old man is very weak and his breathing is not strong. I do not think that he will live until dark. I worry what the warriors will do then."

Chief Dark Wolf was at a serious disadvantage and he knew it. He spoke quietly to Gray Cloud and Singing Wind. Night Hawk had stayed with Coyote to continue to keep the herd together.

"If we find that they have hidden warriors in the trees, we are in grave danger. We must check the trees all the way around camp. Do it silently and cautiously, and quickly before they wake." Chief Dark Wolf rode over to Night Hawk. "You are a good tracker. I want you to go in the trees where they first came out and follow their tracks back. We need to know where they came from and why we have never heard of them. The only people I know of to the north are the Sentu and they live far, near the mountains. They have come to our summer council two times that I can remember. They come only to the seventh year gatherings, because they live so far. We need to know who these people really are. Go Night Hawk and be careful."

"I will go now and I will take two horses, so that I can switch and keep going." Night Hawk had to search the herd to find a second horse that he knew was a reliable mount. Many of the horses were gone with the hunters. They had taken a couple extra, being optimistic. They hoped they would use them to carry home the meat.

Chief Dark wolf sat on a blanket near the church. He hoped that his hunters would return soon. He had no one that he could send to bring them back. He was startled when Blue Stone came quietly near and whispered that she was going to go through the big stones and try to find the hunters.

"No, Blue Stone, it is too dangerous. They may be out there hiding and you could be captured."

"My Chief you know that I have hunted and I ride as well as many of the young hunters. This is something I feel I must do." He was amazed when he realized that she had boldly brought the second horse from behind his tent. It was all ready to go, with a saddle and water bag. "I have a rifle and I know how to use it. If I see more of the strange warriors I will shoot to warn you. Hopefully our men will hear and return swiftly."

"No! Do not shoot unless you are defending yourself. If you see more of them, immediately return and report to me. If you don't, continue on, and find our hunters. Thank you Blue Stone. God is with you," he said. He surprised himself by saying it. God be with all of us, he thought. Father Pete stepped out and watched her ride across the meadow to the start of the path through the big rocks and then he made the sign of the cross in the air in her direction. He was sending a blessing with her. He stepped back in the church quietly.

The Chief sat waiting, until he heard voices in the church. The priest was trying to communicate with them. The men came pouring out the door with the women following, and lastly Father Pete walked out.

"He is dead," he said softly to Chief Dark Wolf.

He stood as they filed out of the church.

"We must bury his ashes in sacred ground. We knew that he was weak, but we hoped that he would live a little longer," said the youngest of the men. We must build a fire on the highest visible ground and then bury his ashes there. I am Debon, the youngest. These are my brothers, Hondor, the oldest, and Kier. The women are Okallah, Hondor's second woman, Gamier, is Kier's woman and Sheltah is Chief Gray Fox's last chosen. It is our tradition that our dead be burned and then buried before the sunset the second day."

Hondor looked around and his eyes settled on the little knoll that Chief Dark Wolf favored.

"We will use that hill if it is acceptable to you and your people."

"You may use it. What will you need to send him to the spirit world?"

"He needs nothing. He is dead! He is gone," he said coldly, showing no emotion. Father Peter and Chief Dark Wolf watched as they pirated wood from the pile that had been gathered for the feast planned for the next night. The old man was placed on the travois that had brought him. Their men lifted it onto the pile of wood and stood watching as the women each brought a burning branch from a cooking fire and handed them to Hondor. He lit the pile in several places and stood watching as the fire blazed. Only Sheltah showed any emotion. She knelt nearby sobbing.

Hondor turned his back to the fire and asked their names.

"I am Chief Dark Wolf, and this is our holy man, Father Pete. He is a Jesuit Priest." Kier looked around and observed the absence of people in camp.

"Your people are like rabbits, they have hidden. Where are your warriors and women?"

Chief Dark Wolf instantly felt a pang of concern. Father Pete took it upon himself to answer.

"They are where they should be, doing what they should do. Why do you concern yourself with our customs? You appear to have few of your own." He wasn't trying to antagonize them, but he did have an idea that would buy them an hour. You should eat now, because soon we must hold Mass in the church. As visitors, you will attend of course."

"What is this mass you speak of?" Debon seemed more outgoing than the rest and spoke well.

"It is a ceremony that we hold in the church where your father died. It is to honor our God. Please sit here and

I will bring food. I have a stew and crackers, also greens that I picked just this morning. Would you like some more of the tea that I made?"

They sat on the grass and ate but refused his tea.

Kier went to their horses and pulled the blankets from them. He led them to the lake and then released them to roam where they pleased. They drank thirstily and finally wandered in the direction of the herd. It was then that Chief Dark Wolf noticed that the tails of their horses were braided and small branches of pine had been added. They looked like small brooms near the bottom. He had immediately noticed that the hair that should naturally fall forward between their ears had been neatly trimmed to a length of about two inches and something had been applied to make it stand up in stiff spikes. Their animals appeared well fed and well cared for.

Twice, Debon added wood to the fire on the knoll, making sure that it continued to burn brightly. Sheltah had not moved. She refused to be consoled. She did not eat with the others but continued her vigil. Chief Dark Wolf gathered the bowls asking if each person wanted more. Each one in turn declined. Father Pete headed to the edge of the lake to wash them and found that Okallah and Gamier were eager to perform the task. He was trying hard to do what he could to give Blue Stone time to find the hunters and for them to return.

Gray Cloud and Singing Wind had casually returned to the herd, indicating with a slight shake of the head that they had found no one concealed in the immediate area.

Father Pete was amused when the thought crossed his mind that finally, Chief Dark Wolf would be attending mass.

He made a big show of putting on his vestments, and placing the chalice and paten on the altar. The candlesticks were there and he lit the candles with great drama.

As he droned on, reading from the oversized book on the altar, he sensed that the people behind him were becoming restless. He turned facing the group, speaking in Latin. He opened a small golden bowl suspended on chains and lit the contents. As he swung it back and forth gently, it filled the small building with the pungent and unfamiliar odor of incense. He walked slowly to the back of the church, stepping out the door. He did it to see if any hunters had returned but he saw none. He swung the pendulum forward causing a great puff of the smoke to billow into the church as he stepped through it and proceeded very slowly to the altar. All heads had followed him as he went. He could feel their curious eyes upon him. He was thinking. What else can I do to drag this out? On his right, stood a small holy water font they had made by chipping a well in a natural rock. He dipped the chalice in it. Forgive me Lord, he said as he turned and walked to each person, slowly and deliberately sprinkling each one generously and then making the sign of the cross over them before stepping to the next.

When he saw Father Bob peek in the door from their sleeping quarters, he was so overjoyed that he nearly gave away that the hunters were back. Father Pete dried the chalice and poured the tiniest bit of wine in it. The rest of the high mass, the consecration and communion went quickly, with the usual prayers and blessings. His relief was not apparent to the strangers, but Chief Dark Wolf knew that something had happened when Father Pete lifted his hand in blessing and was smiling broadly.

206

Hondor was the first to step out of the church. He found that he was among many men on horseback. Sleeping Bear had shot a large deer and they were returning with it when they met Blue Stone on the wagon trail. Flying Eagle and several others were also back. They had circled around and were in the trees behind the tents where the women were hiding. Blue Stone had remained on the edge of the prairie to rest the horse she had ridden and waited to see the rest of the hunters returning. She wanted to give them the advantage of knowing about the people in camp.

Growling Bear spotted her from a great distance and knew instantly that something was wrong. He left six of his hunters to come behind him as he raced to her. She did her best to explain to him what was happening in camp. She saw the hunters coming with another big deer and told them, too.

Growling Bear entered camp casually with two of his hunters and joined the gathering at the church, while the other four escorted Blue Stone through the trees unobserved to wait with and guard the rest of the women. Camp was quiet and felt eerie.

When the hunters, protecting the women in the trees, saw the Chief standing in the center of camp, Flying Eagle rode slowly to him and dismounted.

"My Chief, what would you have us do?"

"As far as we can tell, our scouts say there are no others in the area. Let us stay on guard, but treat them as guests. Pass the word for the women to fill their arms with wood for the communal fire. Tell them to come back to camp, a few at a time. Our guests will all stay in the big tent tonight. I want a guard at the entrance to the woods behind the lake and another at the entrance to our path through the big rocks on both ends. Find Growling Bear and tell him that I wish to speak to him."

"Yes, my Chief."

CHAPTER FIFTEEN
NAMES AND GAMES

He turned to see two of his hunters helping Moonflower back to her tent. They settled her against a back rest just outside, and then got her cooking fire going. Morning Dove carried a large bundle of dry branches that she placed near the fire on the hill, before returning to her own cooking fire. She added a few branches to the glowing coals and soon had a small fire going. Sweet Grass walked slowly through the camp and like Morning Dove, she continued on until she stopped and added her arm load of wood to the pile that Morning Dove had started. She sat down beside Sheltah and put her arm around the young woman's shoulders.

He wasn't sure if it was miscommunication. He felt that it seemed deliberate. Each woman as she returned from the woods walked to the hill and added to the growing pile.

Soon the men and boys had an ample community fire burning. With Dancing Willow and Blue Stone preparing one deer and Corn Silk helping Morning Dove with the second. The camp took on the look and smell of something wonderful, happening. Good food and visitors, under other circumstances would be cause for a joyous celebration.

Growling Bear and a few others, continued to guard the area in the woods behind the tents until they were sure that it was safe for now. The hunters had escorted the people of the Abalinah, to places of honor at the fire. They were helped to stash all their belongings in the big tent and their bedrolls were spread on top of the many soft furs available.

Sweet Grass was finally able to coax Sheltah from her vigil on the hill. She placed her with the rest of her group and put a cup of chamomile tea with honey in her hands.

"You need this, please drink it and relax here. We will all eat soon."

Sweet Grass didn't want to be obvious about it but she quietly asked permission to spend the night in with Moonflower.

"Of course child, I don't blame you a bit for not wanting to stay in there with them. I will enjoy having you with us."

"Moonflower, do you want to move to the communal fire now? It will give you a chance to talk to their women. Maybe you can find out more about them."

"Yes, I will, if you can find someone to help me."

Snow Star came and sat near her as soon as she was settled. She had Watching Owl on her lap and he continually squirmed to get down. She held on to his hand and he toddled to Okallah and patted her knee smiling.

"He is usually not so outgoing," said Snow Star with a big smile.

"I had a son. He was nearly three," she said sadly. "May I hold him?"

"Yes, but he probably won't stay very long. He is very active."

Watching Owl reached over to the fringe on Gamier's shirt and pulled at the beads.

"Nah!" She said briskly and jerked away.

"I'm sorry, Gamier is tired and she has been through a lot," said Okallah.

"Yes, you all have," said Snow Star lifting Watching Owl and holding him in her arms. Sweet Grass came back and filled Sheltah's cup and then handed a cup to Gamier and Okallah. She offered the same brew to the men, but they declined. She knew what they were thinking, so she gave the next cup to Moonflower.

People continued to drift near and take their places, as dishes and pans were added to the feast.

Chief Dark Wolf stood and soon the people were quiet. The crackling of the fire and sizzling of the dripping fat of the two deer in the pits were all that could be heard.

"This night, is a night of celebration," he said, as he turned slowly, checking to be sure that the guards were in place before total dark fell. They were.

"We have many things to celebrate. First I greet our visitors from the north, the Abalinah. They are, Hondor, Kier, Debon, Okallah, Gamier and Sheltah." Each nodded slightly as he said their name. "Welcome to our community fire. We have prepared the big tent for your comfort tonight." The people applauded but with less enthusiasm than usual. The two priests arrived then and made a drama of placing a large kettle of cooked beans near the rest of the food.

"I am sorry. I made us late. I couldn't get the beans to turn soft, for the longest while. Please forgive us, Chief Dark Wolf. We meant no disrespect," said Father Pete. He spread a hide and covered it with a colorful blanket and sat down, behind and to the right of Moonflower.

"As I was saying, we have several things to celebrate tonight. Growling Bear and Big Flower please come forward and bring your three sons! This young man is Little Cub. He has two new brothers!" The people applauded loudly, cheering. Growling Bear had talked with Father Bob about his prayer and what he felt was an obvious answer. Then they had shared it with Chief Dark Wolf. He had thought long and hard about correct names for the baby boys. "Which boy was born first?" he asked.

"This one was born first. He wears a piece of yarn on his foot to mark him as the older."

"This child," said the Chief, taking him from his mother, is proof of the Great Spirit, Our Living God." Growling Bear asked the Great Spirit to give him a son. He said, "If you are out there, give me a son and I will believe." Suddenly Big Flower felt an increase of pressure on her back and added weight in her belly. The Living God, added another baby, another son, so we could not deny the mighty power of God. Yes, He is out there.

The priests told me about a pair of twin boys in a story in his Holy Book. This boy is of God, he will be called Esau. Big Flower smiled broadly as she took her baby back from the Chief and said his name.

"Esau, I love you, my son."

Chief Dark Wolf watched his people as he took the second baby in his big hands and held him out for all to see. He glanced at the Abalinah; they seemed to be holding their breath.

"The second boy in the story seized the heel of his brother as he was born."

"This boy is to be called Jacob." It was amazingly silent for a moment and then a burst of applause and cheers filled the air. Women gathered around Big Flower saying the baby's names and commenting about how much they looked alike, and how unusual the names were. The priests were very pleased that the Chief had accepted their advice and had given these boys, the first biblical names in the camp. Big Flower was escorted back to her tent and Little Cub was fed and tucked into bed for her. She would be cared for, helped and a platter of food brought to her tent, when the feast began. In the days to come, she would receive many gifts of fine leather and furs to help clothe the baby boys during the coming cold months.

The Chief had expected the women to gather around the newly named babies. He waited until they had calmed down and most had returned to their seats before continuing. He had noticed Debon walk to the little knoll and add an abundance of wood to the fire there. Debon returned and sat back down, but oddly the Chief detected that Debon appeared distraught. Until now, only Sheltah had shown any emotion.

Growling Bear had gone with Big Flower to their tent, and now he returned and sat down. The Chief asked him if he was prepared to present his ideas for the games.

"If you prefer to wait, I will certainly understand."

"I think this is a good time." He lowered his voice and spoke to the Chief.

"Maybe we will get a chance to see what these warriors are made of."

Growling Bear stood then and waited until the gathering was quiet again.

"We have been through a great deal of trouble and distress this summer. Things that could not be anticipated have happened to our camp and the camp of our visitors. We that are here have all survived."

"Nature was disturbed and she shook the very ground we sit on. She dumped the water of the lake into our tents and drove our panic-stricken herd of horses, faraway. Now we have recovered well. Our tents are dry and clean. Our food caches are filled and once again the people are able to rejoice."

"We have recognized that our herd would be easier to work with and could better be confined to the meadow if we built a fence around them. We missed the summer games at the summer meeting this year. It was unavoidable, but the building of the fence would provide us with many opportunities for fun, challenge and accomplishment. Some of us have talked about this and we have thought of many games that would provide fun while working toward the goal of completing a strong and lasting fence." Growling Bear had the attention of all the men, but the women were eager to hear about some fun for them.

When he had named the different games and described how they would aid in the building of the fence, each was met with enthusiasm.

Finally, Morning Dove stood and asked that everyone listen closely to Moonflower.

"She must still guard against putting weight on her leg, but her mind works well," she said laughing.

"I have heard the men say that strong cord will be needed to bind the sections of fence to the posts. We could move to the long grass area to hold the women's games first. There we could hold grain picking contests. The grain will be needed this winter, and we could follow those by gathering the strong grass and stems of the wild grains and have cord making contests. These games will also be an aid to the prosperity of our people. We cannot make cord here this year. The disturbance of the lake has pushed many of the cattails out where we cannot easily reach them. The grass has all been used as dry insulation in our tents. We need to travel to the long grass area. While the women hold their games, a few men can stay to guard us and the rest of the men could hunt," concluded Moonflower.

The women that had not heard the plan before were very excited and agreed. They had worried over food supplies. This would help their families greatly.

Chief Dark Wolf laughed and said that he had a feeling that the women had already decided to go and that the men had better go with them.

Sweet Grass said that they needed two days to prepare and that all the women were invited to take part.

It was at that moment that Hondor stood and asked to speak. Chief Dark Wolf nodded, giving permission.

"We are more than visitors. We are six lost people with no village. Our people are all dead. They have gone to the spirit world. Only one other of the Abalinah lives. He is somewhere out there. He is Standing Crane, our shaman. We searched for him, to tell him what had happened, but we could not find him. It was not uncommon for him to be gone for many days at a time. When he returned his power would always be increased. He is a strong and awesome shaman. He will find us one day soon. I am sure of it. I ask. We ask that we be allowed to stay and work, hunt and live with your people until we can decide what we should do."

He sat back down and the people were quiet. Chief Dark wolf stood and said that he would hold a meeting in the morning and it would be discussed then.

"Now, let the feast begin," he said. He walked over to Moonflower and leaned very close to her ear. "What is your impression of these people?"

"I have not had time to talk with all of them, but I see that their men are like all men, trying not to show how wounded their hearts are. The women are strong, but the one Gamier has been hurt many times. She has a wall up that does not even let children in. I fear how they will affect our people if they are allowed to stay. Have they no children? Were they all killed in the raid? Why were they not able to save one child? I am troubled by these people. You must ask questions of the men and find out more about them, and their customs, my husband."

"You are right, Moonflower. I will talk with them at the meeting in the morning."

"Sweet Grass made sure that all the Abalinah had plenty to eat, and tea to drink. She brought Moonflower a plate and they sat with the new women. Snow Star joined them and Morning Dove brought more tea for them all and then sat near them. She asked if they could weave and make cord. Okallah said that she could and would like to join in the games. Sheltah said she needed someone to show her how. Gamier sipped her tea and looked over at Kier often. She seemed to understand but was not willing to join in the conversation. Snow Star was starting to build a strong dislike for the woman.

Chief Dark Wolf held back until he was sure that the visitors were awake, before he stepped into the big tent and tied the flap open. Sweet Grass followed him with an armload of kindling and soon had a small fire started with a large pan of tea near it. She had gathered and washed all the cups from the night before and placed them on a tray along with honey and newly made crackers. The women slipped out as soon as some of the men began to enter. They realized that this was a meeting only for men.

In Moonflower's tent, the women could see Snow Star and Sweet Grass preparing to move her to the shade under a nearby tree. As they headed that direction, Gamier hurried ahead of them and spread a blanket and

Sheltah brought her back rest. Okallah came out of the trees behind the tents with a crutch she had made with a padded top. It was smooth and would work well so Moonflower could move short distances unaided. Gamier seemed friendlier than she had been the night before. She helped Snow Star bring out a tray with cups of tea and raisin cakes.

They had all settled there in the shade but little had been said. Moonflower wondered if the women had been instructed during their time in the tent together. Their behavior had changed, or at least it seemed like it.

"Kier will kill me and take a new woman," blurted Gamier. He thinks that I did not shield his son. They pulled him from me. I could not stop them. They took him away. He said I am no longer chosen!" She began to sob. Streams of tears ran down her face.

Moonflower looked from one woman to the other and she then realized that they had lost all their children. Okallah hugged Gamier and rocked back and forth.

"He will not harm you. No one will harm you. You could not stop them. He should not have said that, but he said it because he grieves. He lost his father and his son. His heart will heal. You will be chosen again."

Moonflower was concerned and puzzled.

"What is chosen?"

"It is when a man wants a woman, he chooses her. He can choose several if he is a good hunter and provides well. Hondor had Micalleg as his first chosen and then he chose Okallah. Micalleg was taken by the raiders. She is very beautiful. He is very angry."

The group of women observed Debon walk to the hill with a shovel. He dug a hole in the center of the ashes and continued to dig and scrape and dig and scrape until the little knoll looked clean. He walked here and there in the meadow, bringing back sod and replaced what had been burned and disturbed. He packed it solid and when he walked away, it would have been difficult to tell that anyone had been buried there. The women of The Blue Stone People were amazed at this ritual.

It was nearly noon when the men finally filed out of the big tent. Chief Dark Wolf walked over to Moonflower and asked if the women could be ready in the morning to go to the tall grass area.

"Yes, we can be ready." He walked around to the back of their tent and mounted one of the horses placed there for him by Singing Wind. It had been cared for and saddled this morning. He rode away alone, into the north woods looking troubled.

Sweet Grass and Morning Dove hurried to gather the prizes they had decided upon. Corn Silk was pleased that they liked her baskets of pine needles, but had a terrible time deciding which one she was willing to part with. They carried a large woven sack and it was placed inside. Morning Dove generously added two of her best baskets. Both had been made recently since the water had entered their tents.

"Morning Dove, we need more than these. What else can we add?

"Let's ask Snow Star if she has any new jewelry that Flying Eagle has made for the trading spot. We all like jewelry," said Morning Dove.

Moonflower felt helpless left in the shade while the others did the work. She inched herself to the trunk of the tree and with the help of the crutch she was able to stand. Snow star saw her and rushed to her side.

218

"Mother what are you doing? You know you can't put weight on that ankle or leg yet. Sarah said not until cold weather!"

"I was hoping that I could use it to get over to my tent and make a cooking fire. I want to make a big batch of crackers to take in the morning. I feel so useless, bothering people to help me move all day long. I want to help with getting things ready not be a hindrance."

Snow Star understood and hugged her mother as she helped her to the front of her tent.

"I just thought of something. Snow Star look in that basket back by the wall. I am not supposed to show anyone what is in there."

"Mother, it is full of the blue stones. All of them are very big!"

"Yes, your father has sorted them out of all the stones that the men bring, those are the largest. Choose one and it will be my offering as a prize."

"Will Father be angry with you?"

"Not if I don't tell him that I let you pick it out of the basket."

"They are all so beautiful. I would like to win any of them."

"Close the basket. Be quick about it!" Snow Star concealed the big piece of blue stone in her hand and slipped it in her pocket as Sheltah came over and asked what she could do to help. Moonflower put her to work starting the cooking fire and then sent her to gather a large bundle of grass, wherever she could find it. "I will give her a lesson in cord making after we make the crackers," she said to Snow Star. "Take your selection to Morning Dove and tell her to add it to the sack of prizes, but wrap it in cloth first at your tent."

Blue Stone came over and helped with making the crackers. They talked about Sarah and she said that she knew that if Sarah was there to take part, she would probably win all the games. Moonflower laughed and agreed.

Chief Dark Wolf rode back into camp just as the sun was setting. He stopped at the church and had a long talk with the priests. He seemed more relaxed when he walked through camp and sat down near Moonflower.

"You don't need to hurry in the morning. We will try to keep it fun. We will leave when everyone is ready. I will be leaving several men here as guards and the priests have promised to stay close and watch our tents. I plan to put the stone baskets in the meat caches and cover them with dried meat. They will store the extra meat that I will take them tonight." He felt that he had created a good plan.

"I need to tell you something," said Moonflower. "I gave a large piece of blue stone, to add to the women's prizes. I haven't been able to make anything nice enough since the flood. All the supplies have been used."

"Did any of the Abalinah, see it? Or where you got it?"

"No, we were careful."

"What do you mean, we? Who was with you?"

"Snow Star was here and I had her get one and wrap it and take it to Morning Dove."

"Moonflower, you should have asked me first. We are known for the blue stone. I don't want the new people to know that we have much of it here in camp!"

"I am going in our tent to do what I said. Please sit in front of the flap and see that no one comes near while I do it." Chief Dark Wolf was quick about it, but he had trouble lowering the baskets into the caches without damaging them. The stones were very heavy. He turned the baskets

220

on their sides and crammed the meat in all around and on top until they looked like a normal bountiful supply of meat. He replaced the lids on the cache and scuffed dirt in the seams and placed sleeping furs back over them, in their usual position. The meat that would not fit was in a thick linen sack that Flying Eagle had acquired at the trading spot. Dark Wolf had placed two heavy stones in the bottom. He knew that if the Abalinah were watching and they knew about the blue stones, they would think that he was taking them to be guarded at the church. He held the sack up tight under his arm and walked swiftly to the church.

CHAPTER SIXTEEN
TRYING TO TRUST

It was a beautiful morning as the women packed the satchels and tied them onto the pack horses. They were excited and it seemed to the men that all of them were talking at once. The new people seemed pleased that they would be involved in an activity that was new to everyone. The women made an effort to blend in by removing the pine branches from their horse's tails and washing the stiffening from the hair by their horse's eyes. Sheltah rode beside spotted Fawn and they seemed to be getting along well. The priests stood outside the church and blessed the ragged column of riders as it passed the church, heading for the path through the big rocks. Singing Wind, coyote and Gray Cloud were all staying to take care of the rest of the horses. Coyote sat on a rock, practicing on his new flute. It wasn't the best of sounds but the horses didn't seem to mind.

Night Hawk has not returned yet from his mission to follow the trail of the Abalinah back to their raided camp, thought Chief Dark Wolf. He was getting anxious, and feeling that he should have sent more than one and hoping that Night hawk had not become victim to anyone or anything. He thought of the missing shaman, Standing Crane that had been mentioned, and wondered if he was dangerous.

"Great Spirit," he prayed silently, "I am not a priest or a holy man. I do not feel worthy to talk to a God. The priests tell us that you are the greatest of all Gods and yet, you will allow me to make a request. Please watch over Night Hawk. Of all my hunters, he and Growling Bear are the ones that I trust the most and they are like brothers to me. Guard him while he is gone and please bring him back safely." He glanced at Growling Bear; as if he might have read his thoughts.

As always, Growling Bear rode next to him and Snapping Turtle had ridden at the end of the caravan. He turned back as soon as all the people had traveled through the path. He would guard the entrance to the big stone area. He studied the woods to his left and could see Sleeping Bear leaning on a tree just inside the tree line. Others were posted. The entire periphery of the camp had been secured.

The women stopped for lunch halfway there and surprised everyone with the nice treats they had prepared. It was late in the day when the tall grass stood at the edge of their temporary camp. They felt comfortable with a nice fire going in the center. The men had carefully prepared the area to avoid any accidents with the fire. Moonflower would not be able to pick the grain, but the other women had agreed that they would provide her with a mountain of supplies for weaving a grain sack and also for the cord making contest. Many of the men had stayed to watch and offer safety to the women.

In the morning, as the first challenge started, the grain stems were cut close to the ground. The women ran with them to their blankets where they shook off the grain heads and dumped the stems in a growing pile. The women of the Abalinah were keeping up and Okallah was doing better than most. Moonflower watched as Gamier and Sheltah worked as a team. Gamier cut the stems and ran them back to Sheltah. She shook them hard and piled them neatly, just in time to receive another bundle. I don't think that is quite fair. If they end up with the most they will somehow have to share the prize.

"This is such fun. It is a shame that Big Flower and the story mothers are missing it," said Moonflower.

Chief Dark Wolf sat beside her on the same blanket, knowing that she would love to be competing if her leg and ankle would allow it.

"Maybe we can do this again; another year and you will win the prize. You are good at all the things you do. Don't feel bad that you are not picking the grain. I have a feeling you will be the one that will make the most cord of anyone." She recognized that he was trying hard to encourage her. He didn't want her to feel bad. He was surprised when she insisted on coming. He and Growling Bear had carefully lifted her up on one of the gentlest old mares they had and she accepted that it was a good horse to use considering her condition. Sweet Grass had brought willow bark tea with her in a water bag and had given a cup to Moonflower with her lunch. She knew that Moonflowers leg would be aching after being on the horse. She is brave to do this. I wouldn't, if my leg was broken, Sweet Grass was thinking. She too was cutting the long stems and was surprising herself at the good, fast job she was doing.

"They all have so much. How will you decide the winner?" he asked.

"I have a large jar in one of my packs and after the sacks are made, Morning Dove and Sweet Grass will measure the grain into the sacks."

"Well I am impressed. You have thought of everything!" The participating women were all sweating and laughing, and hurrying to get as much grain on their blankets as they could; as they anticipated Moonflower hollering stop.

"Stop," she shouted. "You may shake out what is in your hands, but that is the last bit," she said.

As each woman finished her race, she reached for her water bag and took a long drink and then plopped down on the grass nearby. Chief Dark Wolf noticed that the women of the Abalinah were sitting on the corner of their blankets as if to guard their grain.

"It looks like they think the others will take grain from their piles," he said softly into Moonflowers ear so the others could not hear.

"Yes, I noticed that. It is as if they do not trust us," she replied in a whisper.

"Now you should all rest your hands and backs for a while." Snow Star was still breathing faster than normal, but she decided that a snack was in order and carried around a basket of shelled nuts, mixed with dried berries.

Growling Bear talked to some of the men and they came to the Chief with the suggestion that while the women were resting and then weaving the big sacks to take home the grain, they wanted to head to the trees along the river and see if they could find any game to take back.

"It is good to hunt, but leave five men here to guard. The rest should hunt."

As soon as the hunters had gone, the rest of the men were instructed to check the tall grass farther on and to stay alert. The Chief's caution caused the men to be edgy. They wondered just what it was that he feared.

"Does he know something that he hasn't told us?"

"I think he is just being protective," said Flying Eagle. "What do you think of the new people?" he asked.

"I am glad they went with Growling Bear. They make me uncomfortable," offered Bending Grass.

225

"You are too young for them to concern you, but let's spread out and check quietly. There is probably game in here, and our sounds will move them toward our hunters."

"Flying Eagle, the women were making so much noise that I think all the animals have fled."

"You are right, but we must do what our Chief has asked us to do.

As the women rested, Moonflower had closed her eyes, encouraging others to do the same. She had a suspicion. Those who do not trust are usually not trustworthy, she thought. She watched through her lowered lashes as Gamier slowly handed Okallah, handful after handful of grain to add to her pile. They are determined that one of them should win. Why is it so important to them? She wondered.

"Let's wake up." Moonflower clapped her hands. "We can't sleep the day away. Get a drink and flex your fingers, and get comfortable. Your sacks must be tightly woven so that the grain does not fall through. It must be the width of this stem." She took a hand full of stems tapping them on the ground until they were even and then cut them off at about two feet. Snow Star handed each woman a stem, to use as their pattern.

"Mother, please use my supplies to weave a sack for my grain. Watching Owl is awake now and he will never let me sit and weave without many interruptions. He is having fun and I am not the good weaver that you are."

Blue Stone came over with her bundle and sat a few feet away and so did Dancing Willow. Morning Dove had moved closer. Soon all the women, including the new ones had formed a ring, each sitting just far enough away that their supplies were not reachable by the next woman.

"Once we begin you will only have the supplies that you have gathered beforehand, so be sure you are satisfied with what you have. I am going to pass around a pouch. It is filled with bear fat, to help protect your hands. Some of the grass is very harsh, but that is why we are here. It will make strong cord. We will be making that tomorrow. Is everyone ready? Begin."

Suddenly, for the first time during their waking hours, the women were quiet. Each one struggled to start their first few rows. Sheltah made a little grown as hers fell apart and she had to start again. Morning Dove, picked up her bundle and moved over near her.

"Sheltah, I am Morning Dove. Weaving is something that I love to do. Watch and I will start over, so you can copy my movements." Sheltah carefully mirrored each slow motion until she had become comfortable with the simple action.

"Thank you Morning Dove. I will be slower than the rest, but I am learning a new skill. This is fun."

"Be sure you pull it tight as you go along, so the grain will stay inside. You are doing well." Gamier and Okallah were working hard, and Gamier was frowning as she concentrated.

"Now, remember," said Moonflower, "this is a game, and it is supposed to be fun, so now lift your weaving above your head, to do the rest of the row you are on."

"What? Oh Moonflower, you are being tricky," laughed Morning Dove. "I can't see what I am doing up there."

"That is the whole idea. Now when that row is done, hold it out in front of you." Sheltah was having a difficult time and when she held it in front of her, she had several tangled strands. Others were moaning too.

"Moonflower, you didn't tell us you were going to make it even harder!" Dancing Willow had a mess.

"You can fix it and continue, but expect more changes," said Moonflower. She waited until she could see that everyone was making smooth progress. "Now, everyone, pass the weaving to the right!"

"Oh, Moonflower, you are really having fun at our expense. Aren't you?" The women were laughing and even the Abalinah were grinning as they discovered that they were actually having fun.

"Work as fast as you can. No slowing down just because you are working on someone else's," she instructed. She watched as they worked and giggled.

"Don't be leaving holes in that," said Blue Stone to her mother, laughing loudly.

"Now give the weaving back. I want you to mark it as yours with a bead from your hair or a piece of yarn from your blanket. Do it anyway you want to but it should be different from the others in some way. Okallah pulled an olive piece of yarn from the fringe on her blanket and held it up to show the others.

"I will weave this in until it is used up. It will make a line across the weaving."

"That is a good idea Okallah. It will make a stripe." Blue Stone pulled a blue bead from her hair and slipped it over a piece of vine that she was using. Moonflower had added a bone bead and then when she saw how pretty it looked she added another and another until she had six in a row in the center of her weaving.

"That is pretty," said Gamier. "I would like to learn how to make the white beads that you use."

"Most of the bone beads are made by our men in the winter when other work is difficult to do in the cold. They cut and drill them, but we usually do the polishing."

Gamier smiled but continued to concentrate on her work. She had done nothing to mark her work. While others took time to add this or that, she continued to weave as fast and tightly as she could. Moonflower was puzzled until she realized that no mark was her mark. Clever, thought Moonflower.

"Stop," said Moonflower. "Everyone stand. This is to rest your back. I have a backrest but I know by now your beginning to feel it. Walk to the person across the circle and trade weaving. Now go back and sit. Now you may begin.

Lay all the way back on the grass and with the weaving in front of you, continue to work."

"If the men see this, they will think we are really lazy," said Morning Dove. "I have never tried to weave lying down. The grass is dropping on my face," she laughed.

"Now sit back up, stand up and take the weaving back and get your own. You may begin as soon as you are settled." The work progressed and conversations started about cooking, sewing, and then the summer council.

"We should suggest this game to the women at the summer meeting. It is fun and we are making something useful. I still use mine that I made when we met the buffalo and discovered the many uses for the tall grass," said Corn Silk.

"I think that we should do this game ourselves, every year," said Blue Stone. I like this game. We can always use the sacks that we make."

"The men will be returning soon. We need to stitch the sides of our work together and determine a winner before much longer. You have worked hard ladies. Be proud of what you have made."

"Stop! Everyone please stand up and hold your weaving up. Snow star has a piece of cord and she will measure for you." She went from one to the other and then asked Gamier and Morning Dove to lay their work on the grass and she measured again.

"Morning Dove, your work is beautiful as always, but Gamier's is tight and just a little bit longer! Gamier is the winner! Morning Dove hugged her and said she was proud to lose to such a worthy opponent. Most of the women had been reminded to bring their bone needles and they immediately began to stitch the sides of their sacks. Moonflower had sent Snow Star to the women that had remained in camp. She borrowed their needles and had made sure that they had enough so that everyone could quickly stitch their work into sacks.

Sweet Grass got the big pot and very carefully it was filled to the top with the grain and poured into each woman's sack. Morning Dove smiled a lot making sure that they knew that she was not unhappy about being second.

"Okallah has more than anyone else, by nearly half a pot! She is the winner of the grain picking contest!" Sweet Grass announced it loudly. The women all clapped and cheered for the two winners.

"Tomorrow is the cord making contest and the most important reason we are here. Prizes will be given after that contest, before we head back to camp," said Moonflower. She smiled when she thought of the big bundle of soft rabbit furs bundled in the sack. They had gathered one each from many women. Any woman could enjoy them and the winner of that prize will have fun making something cozy.

The hunters and all the men that had stayed near drifted back to the temporary camp. Those that had been near the trees thoughtfully brought back bundles of dry wood for the fire. The women had packed more food than needed and it was all shared until they were satisfied. No cooking was done. The women were making fun of it, but the men understood how hard they had worked. Sweet Grass made a large kettle of tea for everyone to enjoy, but as soon as the sky turned dark the fire was allowed to die down to a soft glow. The people snuggled down feeling secure, with two men on guard. Others would take the watch in the middle of the night. Chief Dark Wolf continued to be cautious.

Growling Bear woke before the rest of the camp. One of the guards had shushed him as he stood up and stretched. A large black bear lumbered across the prairie, heading for the river. Silently Hondor asked Growling Bear if he would allow him to use his bow to bring down the animal. Our women need his fur for winter. With a nod, he lowered his rifle and the guard stepped back. Hondor's arrow was swift and true. By then, most of the eyes in camp had been watching. Applause and praise filled the air. The huge bear was cleaned, but not skinned. He was wrapped in blankets and placed in the shade.

"You will need to get him back to camp quickly. Flying Eagle, go with Hondor, and have the story mothers preserve the meat and skin. Stay alert."

"Yes my Chief."

"You are a good shot with that bow, did you make it?"

"Yes, all the men of the Abalinah make their own weapons. It is required to become a man. I have made several."

"That is a good thing. Come let us see what we can find to make a travois to take that heavy bear back to camp." The two men rode toward the far trees together.

"As soon as we get our bedrolls back together, and have a cup of tea, I think we can start gathering supplies for the cord making contest," announced Moonflower.

Knives were already flashing in the bright morning sun as the women created huge piles of mixed growing weeds, vines, wild grains and anything they thought would hold up. Sheltah had never made cord. She closely examined the tough cord that had been used to tie the grain sacks shut and she saw that it was just simple braiding with a fourth strand added. I better sit near Morning Dove again, she thought. I have no idea how to braid with four strands instead of three. She watched the other women and cut the same type of materials. Morning Dove walked over to her and asked her if she wanted to sit close and watch her start. Sheltah grinned and gave her a quick hug. She hurried to cut more supplies. Her pile was not as high as the others. Snow Star had left Watching Owl with his grandmother and she was cutting and piling supplies for Moonflower.

"This is good for growing hunters. You are a hungry boy this morning." Moonflower spooned the cooked grain into his mouth between his bites of sweet crackers that she had made in a special batch just for him, the day before they left the village. He sipped from the cup of water she offered him and opened his mouth for more.

"Keep cutting," she encouraged. "They will need a lot of cord." The pile next to her was growing ever larger as women ranged farther to find the right supplies for their own piles. "That is good Snow Star. Get as much as you can. It challenges the others to gather more."

Watching Owl was full and he took one last sip of water before trying to leave Moonflower's lap. He was hard to hold when he didn't want to stay.

"Snow Star I don't think I can keep him here any longer," she called loudly. Gamier, dropped her supplies against her pile and returned her knife to a leather sleeve on her waist. She scooped the boy up from Moonflower and carried him facing his mother.

"He wants to toddle around. Is it all right if I put him down? I will watch him for you."

"Thank you Gamier, I appreciate it. He always wants to explore. He is hard for my mother right now. When he starts squirming, it hurts her."

"Kier is sad and we miss our son, but he said that I am still chosen. We will have another child when the spirits bring it."

*****

Chief Dark Wolf and the hunters all wandered ranging far, hoping to have game to take back to camp. They were bored with watching the women making cord. Huge coils covered the ground beside each woman.

When he saw how red and sore, Moonflower's fingers and palms had become. He put a halt to the game.

"Please stop! That is enough cord. Your hands tell how hard you have worked ever since we arrived. It is time to measure and give the prizes."

Moonflower asked Okallah, to help Sweet Grass with the measuring. Each woman watched in anticipation.

"Look, said Okallah, they were awed by the length of Moonflower's cord. It was nearly five steps longer than all the rest. Moonflower is the winner," she said. The women and men applauded and cheered. "It is time for the prizes."

"Chief Dark Wolf, The prizes for our winners are all in this large sack. Would you do us the honor of pulling one out and awarding it to Okallah? She is the best grain picker here!" said Morning Dove. Everyone applauded.

He felt around in the sack, realizing that there were five prizes and there had been only three competitions. He decided to do something a little different than the women were expecting.

"First I want to give an award for team spirit. I watched as the grain picking progressed. Gamier cut the grain and brought it to Sheltah. She shook the grain off and piled the stems, and they worked hard together. This award is for them." He pulled out the two beautiful baskets, made by Morning Dove and gave them each one. Sheltah's basket was a bit smaller, and had a lid.

"These are very lovely. Who made these? Oh thank you so much."

"I made them, and I will be glad to show you how, if you want to learn," said Morning Dove. Both women nodded grinning. They were not expecting praise or a prize.

"Now, Okallah, You did have the most grain on your blanket, but some of it was there because Gamier handed it to you while the rest of the women rested. I saw it.

At our camp, we require all people that live with us to be honest and trustworthy. Your husband, Hondor, has asked me to allow the six of you from the Abalinah, to stay with us and your actions have made it necessary for me to continue to think on it, and you must promise to be honest in all you do from now on."

"I will, I promise. I am sorry," she said to him and to the women surrounding them. "I thought if we didn't win and show that we are hard workers, that you might turn us away." Sincere appearing tears, slid down her cheeks as she started to walk away.

"Wait," he said, I have a prize for you. You did have the most grain." He handed her the heavy piece of blue stone. "Polish this and make a necklace. Each time you look at it, it will remind you, to always live by the standards of The Great Spirit and The Blue Stone People."

"The spirits have rewarded me. This is beautiful!" she said

"No, Okallah. The Great Spirit has forgiven you. You said you are sorry. He heard you and moved my heart to give you that prize. There is only one God. He is the God of The Blue Stone People."

Sweet Grass hugged Okallah, and smiled. Each woman showed her in some way that they had forgiven her for cheating.

"Now; Moonflower has won the cord making contest."

"No, do mine last. Gamier won the weaving contest! Give her the prize for that," said Moonflower.

"Well Gamier, it looks like you will have two prizes to take back." He reached in the big sack and deliberately fumbled around a bit. "I think this bundle of furs is yours." She squealed with delight and rubbed her cheek against them.

"Thank you, all of you. We are learning so much and having so much fun. It is nice to be here with you."

These contests were very important for the people. Thank you Moonflower," he said as he handed her the last prize, the pine needle basket. Inside it he had cleverly slipped an added prize that no one there knew about. "That knife was made and decorated by Falling Stones. He gave it to me to add to the prize for the woman that made the most cord. It is certainly the most beautiful knife in camp."

"It is wonderful, and so useful, I will treasure it always," said Moonflower. "You are always full of surprises," she said laughing.

"I think if we pack up quickly, we can be back in camp just as the sun sets or a little after, or do you want to stay here and leave in the morning?" He didn't hear an answer but saw them all hustling to gather the few personal things they had brought.

Sweet Grass pounded clover and added it to the bear grease in the pouch. It was passed to each woman as they prepared to leave. It would take several days before handling anything would be comfortable again.

As they entered camp, those left behind, gave a cheer of greeting.

CHAPTER SEVENTEEN
THE CHALLENGE

Flying Eagle rode up beside Chief Dark Wolf.

"Night Hawk has returned. He is asleep in his tent. He has had little rest and less to eat or drink. He is wounded but doesn't want anyone to come help him. His wife is caring for him.

Also, Standing Crane is here. He also is asleep. He is in the big tent."

As the horses were unloaded and released into the herd, Chief Dark Wolf noticed that three pale tan horses stood at the edge of the lake together. They had the spiked hair near their ears and eyes, of the Abalinah tradition, but their tails were clean, long and beautiful. They are nice animals, he thought, as he stood wondering what he should do first.

That question was answered very quickly by Growling Bear. "The priests come. They return your package and they say they have news."

"Thank you," he said as he looked up to see Father Pete coming down the path, with a wide smile. Father Bob's face betrayed that he was less than pleased about something.

"Here is your sack, safe and sound. If you would like to put it away, we will wait and then we would like you to follow us back to the church."

The way he said it left no room for discussion. The sack of extra dried meat was quickly dispatched to the rear of the Chief's tent and he walked along with them wondering why they were being so mysterious.

As soon as they entered the church and sat comfortably on the bundles of grass, Father Bob began to explain.

"In your big tent, is the most evil man we have ever been near! We felt we should warn you."

"You must mean Standing Crane. Why do you say that, what has he done?"

"He has done nothing that we know of yet, but we can discern his evil spirit from here."

"You must be very careful. He is in direct commune with the most evil of all dark spirits. His powers are strong and he will not allow your people to worship God. He will interfere. We are certain of it. He has brought demons into your camp," said Father Pete. We fear for the people.

"When he rode into camp and tied his horses by the lake, we hoped that he was like the others that have joined you, but he is not. They have dark spirits but he is the evil source. Be wary. We had to warn you. Please do not let him stay." When the priests had finished delivering their message, Chief Dark Wolf noticed that they were sweating and Father Pete's hands were shaking.

"Are you ill? You are too upset. Calm down. It can't be as bad as you say!"

"It is worse than we can convey," said Father Pete.

*****

Snapping Turtle was so relieved to have the rest of the men return that he hugged Growling Bear and slapped him on the back.

"I am so glad that you are back. I did not want to be here alone with that thing in the big tent!"

"What thing, what are you talking about?"

"I am talking about their shaman. He rode in here passed two guards, rode through the horse herd and the men watching the horses couldn't see him, until he tied his horses near the lake! He walked through the camp, and went in the big tent and went to sleep as if it was his home! I am the only one that saw him. They thought I was crazy until they finally saw the horses there. They swear that they did not see him ride in!"

"Growling Bear, something is very wrong here and I am so happy that our people are back. I know whatever is going on that it will take more than me to deal with it."

"Snapping Turtle, I think you are tired and our women will be happy to see us. I want to see my sons and you need to go see Butterfly and rest. We are all back. I am sure it is not necessary that you stay on guard now. If it will make you feel better, I will ask the Chief."

"Yes, I don't want to leave my post until he says it is alright.

With Moonflower settled in their tent for the night, Chief Dark Wolf strolled to the knoll out of habit, but recent events seemed to stop him from sitting down on the newly replaced sod.

Instead he deliberately turned his thoughts to the fissure that had opened and the blue stones it had revealed. He walked out to the herd, waving to Singing Wind and Gray Cloud with a smile. He noticed that Coyote was again playing his flute. He has improved, thought Chief Dark Wolf.

As he slowly walked the path around the lake, heading back to camp and his tent, things seemed quiet. The women are tired. It will be a few days before it feels normal again, he thought.

"It will never, ever be the same, not the same that you call normal." Bowing low before him was a very tall, thin man with tangled long gray hair that swung down momentarily covering his countenance. His presence startled Chief Dark Wolf. He hadn't seen him there, but instantly knew who he was.

"You are Standing Crane. I was told that you had arrived and The second boy in the story seized the heel of his brother as he was born. were sleeping."

"Yes, once in a while I sleep, but it really isn't necessary. I do it when I can find nothing else to do. Your people are so quiet. We need to wake them and have a celebration. We can dance and sing and have a ceremony and a feast. Yes, let's get them up and have a feast. We can roast some of the deer that are there with your herd."

In amazement, Chief Dark Wolf watched as a large number of deer walked among the horses. As he continued to look, one by one they disappeared, seeming to blink away into the darkness.

"It is getting so dark; I can't even see the horses. How could I see deer? You are good at conjuring. Go from me!" Chief Dark Wolf spoke with such authority that Standing Crane bowed again and disappeared. The priests are right. We must get rid of him. Even the air around him is putrid.

Sleep was troubled for most of the people in camp that night. No one was working at normal activities the next day.

The second morning Growling Bear scratched near the flap of Night Hawk's tent and asked to talk to him. Spotted Fawn held her daughter's hand tightly and looked all around before stepping out of the tent and walking away swiftly.

"I need to get water. We will be right back," she said.

When he stepped in near Night Hawk, he could see that something was terribly wrong. Night Hawk's face and hands were blistered. He appeared to have been badly burned.

"How did this happen to you?"

"I saw the shaman coming at me and I tried to stop him. He did it, with just the wave of his hand. He was there in the north woods, just watching our herd and when I approached him he did this to me."

"Night Hawk, I am so sorry to see you in such pain. Have you had Sweet Grass try to help you?"

"No, I didn't send for her. Keep her away. He may harm her, too."

Growling Bear went straight to the Chief.

"Have you seen Night Hawk? I just saw what that thing did to him! We must do something fast!"

"I agree. I want you to start getting ready for the games as fast as you can. I think I know what to do. We need the fence and we must get rid of him!" The Chief headed for Night Hawk's tent with a stern look on his face.

All the men were happy to do anything that was suggested by Growling Bear. He set teams in the woods stripping small branches from the trees so that posts and rails could be cut easily. By the next morning some additional men had helped to catch all the horses and they were securely tied to lines behind the lake where they would be comfortable and safely out of the way. The meadow was clear for the games to begin. Huge piles of rocks were gathered at regular intervals down the center of the field. The fence line was marked and the spot for each post was indicated. Sections of six posts and the rails between them were assigned to teams.

Hondor, Kier, and Debon were each assigned to different teams. They had all tried hard to prove themselves worthy to be accepted by The Blue Stone

People. Like their women, Chief Dark Wolf worried that they might do something that was not in the game plan.

When it was time for the games to begin, He gathered all the men around him. The women were there, too, eager to watch the spectacle and see their men excel.

"We are all here to do a task for the people." Chief Dark Wolf spoke clearly and slowly. "You must follow the rules you have heard spoken by Growling Bear and Gray Cloud. If you try to do anything to give your team an advantage, you will be eliminated. If anyone is injured, the game stops until the injury is examined and treated. If possible then the game will begin again. Growling Bear, do you need to add anything?"

"No. Are all of you ready?" The men scattered down the marked line on the field. They were watching Growling Bear. Each team had just one shovel. They had to dig six holes as deep as the stick they had been given. It had to be wide enough to stand with one foot flat in it.

He held his hand high in the air, with a piece of yellow cloth in it. The breeze was strong and the cloth whipped back and forth.

"Begin digging," he shouted, bringing his arm down to his side. The women had gathered on the grass, sitting in friendly groups, on the hill just outside the church. The priests stood outside for a moment and then went in their sleeping room returning with arms loaded, carrying their furs. They distributed them to each cluster of women, offering protection against the strange cold wind that grew stronger.

Father Bob and Father Pete were ready to work on the next set of holes. Their shovel was already in use by one of the teams.

As they watched, and cheered the progress, Father Pete felt a fierce pain in his left arm. It grew unbearable and he collapsed. Father Bob shouted to Sweet Grass. She hadn't noticed his distress; both priests had been standing behind the women. She hurried to him, not sure of what she could do. She listened, laying her head on his chest. There was no heartbeat.

"Quickly, take him in the church. Take off his shirt and sit him up straight. I will be right back." She ran down the path to the big tent and grabbed a small pan and the only herb that Sarah had taught her to use, to make the heart stronger. She never told me what to do if the heart stops beating! I have to make it start again, she thought. Frantically she scooped the pan full of the cold lake water and dashed into the church. He sat propped up and bared to the waist. His chin rested on his chest.

"Father, I am sorry, I know it is cold but I must do this!" She threw the water at his face and chest in one icy blast, and just as suddenly he took a loud gasp of air and began breathing. She listened again to his chest. "His heart is beating again. Thank you God, Thank you Great Spirit," she said almost crying. "Father Bob, please dry him and make him warm again, I must make medicine." With her small pan half full of water, she added the herb conservatively. She couldn't quite remember how much she was supposed to use.

"We have some things there in the back hanging on the wall if you want to use any of them. We have willow bark and there is a tin with some honey." She added them willing the older priest to open his eyes and live. Father Bob had covered him and now was on his knees near him, praying the rosary. To Sweet Grass, his prayers sounded similar to the repeated chant of a shaman.

As she moved to get the pan and a cup, she was startled by Standing Crane. He stood just outside the wide open door of the little church. He spoke in a harsh whisper.

"Is there anything else I can do for you? You did say you wished they would go away, didn't you?"

"That was a long time ago when I was young. They frightened me, but not anymore. Please leave us."

"Please, hmmm, do I frighten you?"

"No. Go Away."

"Isn't it a sin to lie? Your God will not answer your prayers. You are a sinner. See how your hands shake. You cannot even pour that pitiful brew into a cup." He ridiculed her.

When she looked up from the cup, he was gone. Father Bob continued his prayers uninterrupted. He had neither seen nor heard Standing Crane.

She carefully spooned small sips from the cup. He opened his eyes wider than normal, tightly grasped the blanket over his chest twisting it in agony and slumped down.

They instantly realized that Father Pete was dead. Father Bob changed his prayers to the prayers of the last rites, of the Catholic faith, making the sign of the cross on Father Pete's forehead and on the palms of his hands with Holy oil. He prayed.

As soon as the last rites ritual was complete, he lit the beeswax candles on the altar and began the mass for the dead, wearing his black vestments.

Sweet Grass and Father Bob had been totally unaware of the activities taking place on the field. She was silent, numbed by the first loss of a patient, until he finished. She knelt near the altar and silently wept.

"I failed him and I failed Jesus," she cried. "Standing Crane was right. I am no healer. The Great Spirit will not heal when I am near. I am a sinner, I lied when I said I wasn't afraid of him."

"Who are you afraid of?"

"I lied, I said I wasn't afraid of Standing Crane, but I am. He killed Father Pete because of me! He said so."

"Sweet Grass, you are not making any sense. When did you talk to him?"

"He was here before Father Pete died. I was pouring the medicine and you were right over there praying with your beads and he said he was making him go away, because I said I wanted both of you to go away, when Father Pete first got here. I was frightened of you both but I'm not now!"

"Sweet Grass, you are a good healer. God sees your heart. He knows everything you think and feel. Standing Crane is evil. He is a deceiver. He has come here to work an evil plan. We must stop him. He knew that Father Pete would oppose him with all of his spiritual strength. If he killed him, that is why, not because you said something a long time ago. We need to tell the people what has happened."

*****

Outside, the men and women were standing in small clusters. The competition had been halted. Growling Bear and Flying Eagle were arguing loudly. Chief Dark Wolf was trying to stop them and ended up knocked to the ground. Flying Eagle had raised his fist to shake it at Growling Bear and had accidentally hit the Chief. The people were stunned.

Standing Crane stood for all to see laughing loudly.

"So this is what you call a fun competition and team work! It is sad that you do not know how to work or play together," he said before starting to laugh again. "I must say, this is fun to watch!"

"Cease that! You disrespect the Chief of The Blue Stone People! You are here as a guest. How is it that you dare to mock the people?" said Father Bob.

"Your own silence diminishes the dead priest's position here. Why do you not speak of him?" An audible gasp came from the people. "He won't tell you, but I will. He died of fright. His heart does not beat. He is in there cold and ready to meet his God. If his God is so powerful, why was the priest afraid of me?" Everyone except Father Bob backed away from him.

"I am not afraid of you Standing Crane. Why do you want people to fear you? You strut and use your evil power to fool people, creating images in their minds. Chief Dark Wolf tells me that you tried to convince him that deer were among our horse herd last night. You have convinced Night Hawk that he is burned. His mind has manifested the blisters, but he is not burned and you are nothing more than an insignificant magician!" Standing Crane stepped away from Father Bob and moved closer to the Chief and his men. Once again they backed away from him.

"Is there anyone here that thinks he is stronger than me, or smarter? Is there one person here that wants to challenge me in a game? Any game will do. Flying Eagle, you argue with Growling Bear about spilling water where you are digging a hole. Do you think yourself wiser and so crafty that the rest wouldn't know that water on the ground will make the dirt easier to dig?" He paused enjoying the fact that he had the attention of all the people. "Hondor, do you wish to defend the men of the

Blue Stone People or is your new found loyalty superficial? Maybe Growling Bear, head of the warriors and hunters wants to challenge me. Is there no one?" He spread his arms wide, grinning broadly and turning from left to right, including everyone. The people were silent.

"I challenge you, Standing Crane, to fight me with knives, here on the hill in front of the church; tomorrow at noon. Today I must bury my friend," said Father Bob softly.

"I accept your challenge little priest. Tomorrow we will fight to the death. Once you are gone there won't be such a disgusting odor in this camp," he declared. "We will burn this church and that awful cross and I will dance on its ashes!" He turned and strutted back to the communal tent, laughing loudly as he went.

"Father Bob, he is cunning. You must not fight him. You are not a warrior!"

"Chief Dark Wolf, I know that you are worried that if I am killed, the people will have to live under the dominating power of Standing Crane. Hear me now, all of you. Our God is an awesome and mighty God. You came to Him at this cross. You chose Him. He lives inside of each one of you. You must believe that He will be here to fight with me and for us all tomorrow. You must believe He will overcome and crush the evil that is in Standing Crane!" The people murmured softly and nodded.

Father Bob walked back to the field, picking up one shovel and then another. He returned with one in each hand.

"Here, take these and show the people that although you disagree, you can work together. Please dig the grave for Father Pete. We must bury him."

"Father Bob, where should we dig?" Flying Eagle asked.

"If you would, put it here on the side of the church, and while you do that, I must build a box that is big enough to hold his body." He took a stick and drew a rectangle on the ground. "It must be this big, and make it very deep." He said it looking at the two men that still held the shovels, but had not moved.

"Dig!" Said the Chief fiercely, quelling any chance for an objection.

The rough casket was made of split logs with the bark on the outside. Snow Star brought her most beautiful blanket and gave it to Father Bob, to use as a liner. Others came and as the men carefully lowered his body into the box the people stood waiting. Each one placed a small token of respect in the box. A rabbit fur from one, a wooden bowl filled with dried fruit from another, the people continued to place objects in, until Father Bob was concerned that the lid might not fasten on. The thing that touched his heart the most was a small boy leaning in and placing a piece of sugar candy in Father Pete's hand.

"He made candy for us. I know he liked it a lot. He should have a piece with him, for his journey," he said. "I saved that for a long time, but that's alright. He should have it." Father Bob wrapped Father Pete's hands around the rosary that he had used daily while leaving the lump of candy in his palm.

The ropes strained as they lowered the coffin with the hefty priest into the ground, and many people helped to replace the dirt. Bending or kneeling on one knee, they pushed the dirt over his grave with their hands.

"He fixed my broken arm," said Quick Snake. "It is strong again. He did well."

"He played music and made our children sing and laugh," said another.

"I liked the stories he told."

"He was a good man," said the Chief.

"I will miss him," said Father Bob.

"We will all miss him," said Growling Bear. The people spoke in agreement and were surprised that he had offered his feelings, openly before them. He walked to the first large pile of stones, which had been gathered for the support of the posts in the fence. He picked up one and returned with it, placing it on the grave and then slid his arm around Big Flower, taking one of the new babies from her. Little Cub trailed behind as they walked as a family, down the path to the camp and entered their tent.

Flying Eagle followed his example and brought a stone from the field and placed it beside the one from Growling Bear. He took Watching Owl and walked with Snow Star, back to their tent. Chief Dark Wolf walked to the pile and brought back two stones, he handed one to Night Hawk, who stood there, clear of blisters and looking healthy.

"Please help me take Moonflower back to our tent," said Chief Dark Wolf. "I will be back in a few minutes," he said to Father Bob. Each man made the walk to the pile in the field and placed a rock, some large, some small, on the grave before taking his family to their tent.

The village was silent. Chief Dark Wolf walked slowly returning to the church and entered. Father Bob had been waiting for him.

"I am sorry that you have lost your friend. We all feel the loss."

"Chief Dark Wolf, what have I done to you? I feel overwhelmed! What if God chooses to let me die? I have placed you and the people in a terrible situation."

"You did not create this. Have you ever fought with knives?"

"No, not really; but once I did when I was a kid, that was before I went into the seminary. In a battle, man against man, with knives, I know he has an advantage. His arms are longer and he is taller than I am."

"You must not let him defeat you with such thinking before you begin," said Chief Dark Wolf. "Remember the story Father Pete read to us from the bible? It said that God allows us to be tested by the evil one. In the story, God said he could test Job, but he could not kill him. You must remember that. You are definitely being tested, but I feel in my heart that God will give you the power to destroy him. You were urged in your heart to accept the challenge. Now be brave and our God will help you overcome!" He slipped his arm around Father Bob's shoulders showing support. "Come now to my tent. People have brought more food to our tent. You must eat well and then get good rest tonight, and in the morning, talk to God until it is time to fight."

"Your advice is good, but when I go back, I must make my weapon before I can rest."

"You must do what you must do."

It was very late by the time Father Bob discovered that his bed and Father Pete's were in total disarray. The women had returned the furs they had been wrapped in during the start of the men's games, but not knowing which furs belonged to either priest they had simply put them all in the church. He crawled into the pile and the exhaustion caused by the stress and work of the day finally brought him a deep sleep.

It was the voices of the gathering people outside that woke him. As quick as opening his eyes he realized that he would soon be battling for his life and the souls of all the people in the camp. With great resolve, he opened the door of the church and without ceremony or greetings he ran to the edge of the lake with his clothes on and dove in. He stroked with his tight muscles, swimming until he felt strong and invigorated. Dripping, he dashed in the open door of the church and closed it.

He dried himself with the same towel he had used to wipe Father Peter's face and chest. His heart felt wounded but his spirit was strong. He had prepared his armor before sleeping. It was simply a clean dry cassock which he pulled over his head and buttoned all the way up. A stiff white collar snapped into place. He put on the shoes and socks he had worn when he had arrived. He noticed that his black shoes were scuffed and the soles worn thin, as he quickly tied them. Over his head he placed the chain that supported the heavy silver cross he had worn since it was placed there by the Jesuits when he had taken his final vows as a priest.

"This is my fighting armor," he said, "my shield and my helmet is your word and your grace; your presence is all I need to protect me. Heavenly Father, Your Holy Son died on the cross to save these people. Today I will use the golden cross from the altar as my weapon to keep them." He took it in his right hand and held it high.

He could feel the sun's heat beating on the roof. He opened the door and stepped out slowly into the glare of the sun. The people had gathered in front of the church, leaving a small passage way for him to walk between them. Many touched or patted his back, as he moved out to the center of the grass. Standing Crane was nowhere in sight. Father Bob looked around puzzled.

Then he saw him walking on the path; approaching slowly. He held in his hand a long bladed silver knife. It flashed in the bright sunlight. He too, wore black. What appeared to be a cloak covered his body in a film so sheer and light that it drifted around him like smoke with his every movement.

"We have been waiting for you. We are ready," said the shaman's voice.

"God is always ready. He is everywhere and He is here with me and in me."

"We too are always ready."

"You are but one lowly creature that has stepped through the doors of hell!" Father Bob shouted the words. He suddenly felt furious!

"You are wrong little priest. We are legion and you are about to die!" The sword in his hand flashed as he struck out. It captured the sun and became a blinding glare.

Father Bob knew that it was now, or never. He brought his right hand up exposing for the first time, the cross that he had ground into a sharp, tapering, pointed blade at the bottom.

"In the name of Jesus, I command you to leave us and return to hell from whence you came!" He rushed recklessly at the demon possessed shaman holding his weapon straight out in front of him with both hands gripping tightly around the arms of Jesus on the cross. He tripped, propelling himself forward even faster, falling against his enemy, and knocking him backwards to the sod!

There was stillness for a long moment, as the spectators gasped. The silence was followed by a loud roaring, screaming sound as the filmy, dark cloak that covered Standing Crane spiraled down into the ground and disintegrated, disappearing.

Father Bob struggled to quickly stand, pushing himself up off his opponent; not realizing that the battle was over until he saw that his cross-blade stood erect in Standing Crane's heart. It was shining in the sun, declaring victory, as the blood drained from the body of a gray-haired, scarecrow of a man.

Father Bob looked down at his feet, remembering that he had tripped. His left shoe was untied and its lace trailed out creating the hazard that had caused him to lunge forward, out of control. I never was in control, was I Lord? He thought.

He fell on his knees and prayed a loud prayer of thanksgiving and then the people, his people, God's Blue Stone People, began to sing the Alleluia, Holy Holy. He could see the communal fire being lit as Hondor, Kier and Debon carried Standing Crane's body and tossed it disrespectfully onto the back part of the growing flames.

Chief Dark Wolf smiled and placed his arm around Father Bob's shoulders again and walked with him into the church.

"Today we will celebrate God's victory." Debon handed the cross-blade to Father Bob. He had washed it clean in the lake.

"What will you do with that now?" asked the Chief.

"I think I will make a block of wood and stick it in it. It will still stand on the altar again as a sign of Christ's victory over evil."

They both looked for the long knife that Standing Crane had held. Many people helped them search, but it was not to be found.

The atmosphere in camp was light and giddy.

"I think this is the first time I have heard anyone laugh since He came to this camp. Look at the women. They are cooking for a feast. We certainly will celebrate and dance and sing. I feel good!" said Chief Dark Wolf as he kissed

Moonflower in front of everyone. "I think I need to do that more often!" He was being silly but the people loved it.

The men were piling extra wood on the part of the fire where the flames were consuming Standing Crane's body. Women had gone into their tents and put on their finest clothes and jewelry.

The Abalinah looked on with puzzlement.

"These people seem strange to me," said Hondor. "They had grave faces when they buried their priest but they put him in a box in the ground without using fire to purify him. Now Standing Crane is there on the same fire they use to have celebrations and they laugh and prepare. Well I for one do not care that he lost the fight. We must remember this day and why we were sent here. If we do what we were ordered to do by Chief Gray Fox, they will have days of mourning soon enough. I just wish there was a way to move things along."

Debon walked slowly away from the group.

AN INVITATION

If you do not know Jesus, as your Savior but you would like Him to be, please pray the following prayer. Invite Him into your heart. Commit your "New Life" to Him. He will be your constant companion, counselor, comforter, and protector, The Holy Bible tells us that He will never leave you or forsake you.

"Dear Jesus, please forgive my sins. Give me grace and strength Lord, so that I will not commit them again. Come into my heart so that I can start a "New Life" with you as my companion. I want to live according to your will and commandments. Bless me Lord and lead me in a life that is pleasing to you. In Jesus' Holy name I pray. Amen"

If you prayed that prayer, you are saved. You are born again. Your soul is whiter than the snow that caps the highest mountains. The angels in heaven are singing with joy as they write your name in The Lamb's Book of Life.

Get a Holy Bible and begin to read it. Find a good Bible believing church and start attending, so that you can learn more about Your Heavenly Father. What a wonderful God we have.

If you wish, you can sign and date your Bible as an outward sign of your salvation and that you have committed your life to Christ. Tell someone.

I will pray for you. God bless you. Louise Bouck

BOOK TITLES IN THE NEW LIFE SERIES

1   MORE THAN SURVIVAL
2   LIFE'S MANY JOURNEYS
3   THE LAND'S HERITAGE
4   THE STORY OF SARAH
5   TOGETHER
6   THE BLUE STONE PEOPLE
7   TEEWAHPANEE THE BOY, TWO
     FEATHERS THE MAN
8   THE PEOPLE OF THE LION
9   THE LION'S DEN
10 JUST THE BEGINNING

Watch for the prologue,

LITTLE MAN OF MY DREAMS, a love story.
The story of **KOZA**

†

About the author

Louise Bouck is a follower of Jesus Christ. She has been married to her husband, Dale Bouck for more than fifty years.

Until an early retirement from her fulltime job in 2000, not much time was available to allocate to writing or art. One of the many interests that Louise enjoys is painting on location. The lush greenery of Michigan, her home state and the abundant flowers in her grandmother's greenhouses and flower shop all encouraged her eye to appreciate the colors and beauty of nature.

Later after moving to Arizona, the rugged landscape of the mountains and desert stole her heart and took her artistic soul in a new direction.

Paintings in many media cover the walls of her studio, as she has deliberately turned her creative side more to the written word. Hesitantly she withdrew from the art gallery where her work was sold and left the position of resident artist at the local Historical Society Museum.

Louise has written ten books filled with exciting adventure, in a series of Christian; Bible based stories that she is now starting to release for the first time as she works on still another story and another painting.